# FOUL PLAY IN THE FOLIAGE

## A CALLIOPE INN COZY MYSTERY

## RUTHIE EAST

Cover design by Mariah Sinclair

Published by Gate Wind Press

ISBN (ebook): 979-8-9995221-0-8

ISBN (paperback): 979-8-9995221-1-5

# CHAPTER 1

E sther hadn't planned to be on surveillance duty before breakfast service, but here she was, on the lookout for the mischief-maker. He'd make an appearance if she waited long enough.

She killed the engine and gave herself a final once-over in the rearview mirror. Lipstick-free teeth? Check. Curls miraculously intact after a commute in the convertible? Check.

The gold nametag fixed to her blouse flashed in the early morning sunlight.

*Calliope Inn*
*Esther Bennett*
*General Manager*
It still gave her a small thrill.

The dashboard showed seven-thirty, right below a long string of numbers betraying the odometer's age. Esther didn't officially start until eight, but she liked to arrive early to check in with the breakfast crew and make sure the guests had gotten a good night's sleep.

Today, though, she'd sacrifice her clean punctuality record if it meant nabbing this guy.

*Come on, I know you're here.*

Esther had sandwiched her car between a hatchback and an SUV, hoping to keep a low profile, but was starting to regret not parking in a sunnier space.

The crisp October air sent a chill along her arms, which were no doubt dotted with goosebumps under her cardigan. But Esther was determined to savor every moment with the top down until the weather turned frigid.

She wrapped both hands around her coffee, the paper cup still warm even though she'd picked it up from Penny's Breakfast over twenty minutes ago. *And that's why I love you, Penny.*

No sign of him yet.

Guests had started mentioning the damage he'd done to their cars a few days ago. With a month until the annual Makers and Merchants Festival, Esther needed to get a handle on the situation. Business owners, residents, and tourists from all over New York would travel to Oak's Rest in search of local treasures and heartfelt services.

She wasn't sure what she'd say once she spotted him. Maybe she could lure him away from the property by dropping food at farther distances until he found somewhere else to take up residence.

She'd give him a stern talking to, at the very least.

Esther was glad to have the parking lot to herself. If he did show up, it'd be easy enough to hear him chatting, given how quiet the property was. Serene, even.

Oak trees, saturated in burnt oranges and reds, rustled their leaves like instruments playing to their own tune. Their own symphony nestled at the end of a quiet lane.

If she closed her eyes, Esther could almost hear the sounds of the lake, which was less than a five-minute drive away. The thrum of boat engines, the splash of tossed buoys. Living and working near water had an effect on Esther she couldn't quite name. The lake was simply always with her, wherever she was.

From the outside, Calliope Inn appeared perfectly still. The first time she'd ever seen the place, her only thought was, *Doll house.*

The fifteen-room Victorian home, its creamy ivory color a stark contrast to the green blanket of lawn that hugged it, stood on the property like a three-tiered cake fit for a princess.

A few of the guests had opened their windows, curtains billowing softly into their rooms. Soon, they'd start venturing downstairs, drawn toward the smell of coffee and whatever delight Bunny was whipping up for breakfast.

Esther knew the moment she walked through the front doors, it would be go-time. She'd hear her name repeated on a loop all day. Not that she didn't love it. She'd been manager for less than six months, and could still hardly believe it. Each aspect of the job was more exciting than the last. The responsibility, the way every day brought a new challenge only she could solve, it was everything she'd worked for.

Every once in a while, she'd let images of a future version of herself flit through her mind. Hanging the sign outside her own inn. Managing an even bigger team, one that could serve hoards of guests. Becoming such a titan of the hospitality industry that she'd be able to mentor other professionals. The article headline announcing Esther Bennett as the newest president of the Northeast Hospitality and Lodging Association.

For now though, NEHLA dreams aside, she was focused on being the best manager she could be. Which meant the Makers and Merchants Festival had to go off without a hitch. It was both the inn's first time hosting the festival and Esther's first major event as manager. Too many firsts hung in the balance for anything less than perfection.

Esther rolled her head, trying to ease the tension in her shoulders. She took a deep breath. Just her, the inn, and—the wind shifted, a gust of chilly air attempting to steal the knitted daisies hanging from her mirror.

On second thought, moving the car into the sun didn't seem like a bad idea. She'd do it quickly and quietly.

Esther whispered an affirmation to her car. "Easy, now. I avoided that pothole back near the stop sign, like I promised. You can return the favor by not scaring my target away."

As old and asthmatic as her 2005 ride was, she couldn't imagine trading it in for something newer. It was the first car she'd gotten at sixteen years old. She'd learned to be an adult with this car. Was still learning.

Plus, she liked the way the almost-black paint coat shone midnight blue in the sun. She wasn't above a little vanity.

She scrunched her nose as she slid the key into the ignition. As she was about to turn it, she heard a man's voice. She looked around. The first thing Esther saw was the clipboard, followed a heartbeat later by Faris Holliday, coming from the side of the wrap-around porch.

*No. No no no.* The inspection couldn't be today. Faris's inspections were the stuff of nightmares, and today was supposed to be a good day. She scanned the parking lot for the government vehicle. There it was, parked at the far side closest to the inn. She'd missed it in all her focus on catching the perpetrator.

Behind Faris, a second man appeared from around the corner. They approached the front door of the inn. Okay, good. They'd probably gotten there just a few minutes before Esther. Maybe they hadn't gone inside yet.

Could she intercept them and say the inn was closed for construction? Did she have time to call the health department and report that she'd seen one of their cars make an illegal U-turn? No. It was too late to get out of the inspection. She'd have to stay and get through it the best she could.

Esther jumped out of the car and took a few hop-steps before remembering her coffee and purse. She reached in, grabbed the purse, and slung it over her shoulder. Coffee in hand, she jogged across the parking lot and up the gravel path to meet the men on the porch.

Thankfully, they didn't notice her until she was right behind them. She gave her skirt a quick smooth and readied herself to feign nonchalance. "Faris, so nice to see you." She stuck her hand out, but Faris was busy scribbling on his paper.

He mumbled a disapproving, "Did you just get here?"

Esther tried to read the page he was writing on through the reflection of his glasses. "I was waiting for someone. Something," she said, shaking her head. "There's a cardinal that's been terrorizing our guests' windshields, if you know what I mean." She tried to sound casual, like she was inviting them in on a joke.

Faris looked up, unamused. "I don't."

"Nevermind." Esther turned her attention to the second man, who must have been new to the health department. Odd. Faris usually preferred to work alone when he was ruining people's days, but it looked like he wanted to share the fun this time around. "I'm Esther. I'm the manager."

The man smiled. "Ingram Ellis. I'm shadowing Faris for the month." He glanced at Faris, who was still writing, and gave Esther a *sorry about him* shrug.

"Well, welcome to our neck of the woods, Ingram." Esther walked ahead of them and touched the front door handle, still clutching her coffee for dear life.

Her phone started ringing, the sound harsher in the morning stillness. She fumbled to turn it off, but was struggling to maneuver with one hand. "Sorry, one sec," Esther said. Why did her hands choose that moment to lose all dexterity?

Faris sighed impatiently. "And they call those things *smart*phones."

Esther gritted her teeth. She decided to let the phone finish ringing, full volume. "Faris, I think you'll be happy to see we fixed those holes in the porch railing. I actually filled them all by myself, no contractor needed. Carpenter-*bee*-darned."

Faris disregarded her. He was looking around again, his head on a swivel, almost certainly making mental notes of all the issues he'd bring up later.

Esther pressed her lips together. She knew better than to attempt pleasant small talk with Faris. "A little carpenter bee humor. Anyway, should we head inside?"

Before she could turn the handle, Faris harrumphed behind her. "Is that your sign squeaking in the wind? You're going to need to oil that or replace it. The heightened moisture content in lake town air makes metals rust faster."

With her back to the inspectors, Esther allowed herself one dramatic eye roll. That should last her at least ten minutes before the urge came up again. The only rusty things on the property were Faris's people skills.

She looked down at her coffee. *Please get me through this day.*

# CHAPTER 2

J ust inside the front door, Esther jumped back as two little boys raced past her up the stairs. She lost the grip on her cup. The lid shot off when it hit the floor, spilling the last dregs of her sanity on the hardwood.

By the time their mother called out, "Incoming!" from the living room, the boys were halfway upstairs.

Esther managed a nervous laugh and glanced at Faris and Ingram. "Not a problem!" she called back. "We'll get...someone... to clean this up."

Esther turned to face the inspectors. "Faris, I know this isn't your first time here, but I'd love to give your colleague a tour."

Faris grunted as he scanned every inch of the entryway. Did he ever smile?

Ingram looked around too, but wore a curious expression that indicated genuine interest in getting to see the rest of the space. Esther knew the inn had an undeniable warmth, and she wore it quietly like a badge of honor. Even Faris couldn't take that from her.

Esther turned on her heel, not waiting for his disapproval. Warm, dark wood spilled down the staircase and wrapped its way back up to trim every door and window like a mahogany candy coating.

Esther could hear the crackling of the fireplace in the living room. Mort, their groundskeeper and head maintenance guy, must have come in early to light it. Maybe he'd sensed people would need extra comfort today.

In the living room, a large, floral area rug anchored the couch and reading chairs, on which several guests were reading newspapers or eReader devices. Large windows and a door to the side porch let in a blanket of sunshine to settle over the room.

Esther put on her tour-giving voice. "As you can see, our living room is a popular hub where guests start and end their days. Straight ahead is our lobby and reception area, where I spend a lot of my time when I'm not running around." She hoped the lobby wouldn't be buzzing with guests yet. Check-ins weren't until one o'clock, so with any luck, Faris would be off the premises before he could scare off any first-time visitors.

A few steps later, the lobby was in full view. The grand effect of ultra-tall ceilings was balanced by calming artwork, warmly lit sconces, and couches at either side of the room. A circular marble table at the center of the lobby featured an oversized vase showcasing a jewel-toned flower arrangement, courtesy of Busy Bees Floral.

Behind the lobby, separated by a glass wall, the dining room sat waiting for guests to seat themselves around its dark wood tables. The dining room also opened up with a wall of windows, so the backyard was visible all the way from the entrance of the inn.

At first glance, everything looked immaculate. That was, until Esther's gaze landed on the reception desk, tucked in the back corner of the lobby. Stationed behind it, in all her drooling glory, was a sleeping concierge.

Esther panicked. She turned around to Faris and Ingram. "What am I thinking? I didn't even ask you for your jackets." She extended her arms and tried to guide them back toward the entryway without revealing that something was amiss.

Luckily, Ingram didn't seem to notice, and Faris was so busy writing things down he wasn't aware they were being herded like sheep.

Esther took their jackets and hung them on the coat hooks fixed to the wall at the bottom of the staircase. The hooks ended at the door leading down to the basement, where Esther's personal office was. A sign that read *Employees* in pretty, hand-drawn calligraphy hung from the basement door.

"Sorry if I seem a little scatterbrained. We're hosting an upcoming town festival that's using up more than a little of my—"

"I don't care about your party," Faris interjected. "I care that your establishment meets the rules and regulations of the Ezra County Health Department."

Esther inhaled sharply, stifling what she truly wanted to say. She'd bet Faris couldn't get people to show up to a *party* if he was handing out thousand-dollar checks. "I'll be right back. I need to grab...some maps."

"Oh, don't worry about it," Ingram said. "We should get started—"

Esther cut him off. "Trust me. This place is a maze. Having a map will make all the difference. Wait here a minute."

She turned to walk away before either of them could protest. *A maze? Almost every room is visible from the front door.* She dashed to reception, hung her purse under the desk, and tapped Justice on the shoulder. No movement.

"Justice." Esther nudged her a little harder.

Justice snorted as she blinked awake. She moved a piece of blonde hair from her mouth and reached for the mouse pad, bringing the computer screen to life. "Seven forty-three. I was starting to think you weren't coming in today."

"I was trying to track down that bird the guests have been

complaining about," Esther retorted. She checked the time for herself. "And I'm still seventeen minutes early."

"I know, but for you, that's pretty much late."

"*You* started at seven and I just found you fast asleep."

"I was planning today's activities for the guests." Justice pointed to the desktop, where the Calliope Inn screensaver was still up.

Esther waved the lie away, remembering they had unwelcome visitors hovering in the entryway. "Listen, the health and safety inspector is here today. Could you try to be more..." She made circles with her hands. "Alert? You look like you've been kidnapped and don't remember how you got here."

Justice straightened in her seat. "No way. Faris the Ferret is back already? It feels like yesterday he scolded me about how I was asking for osteoarthritis if I didn't do something about my posture. Who says that?"

Esther nodded. "I know. I thought we'd have at least another month before inspections. Be on your best behavior, okay?"

Justice didn't respond. Her eyes slid past Esther. "Who's the hunk?"

"What?" Esther looked behind her to see that Faris and Ingram were making their way into the lobby. She whipped her head back toward Justice. "Best. Behavior. Please?"

Justice put on a fake innocent smile. "What? I'm nothing if not a shining pillar of professionalism. You worry too much."

Esther took a deep breath before starting back across the lobby. A few panicked paces later, she nearly collided with a wall of green linen.

Mort grabbed her arms to steady her. "Woah there. Sorry, boss. Do you have a second? I need you to take a gander at—"

Esther held up a finger and talked quietly. "I'm so sorry, Mort, I need ten minutes. The health inspector is here and he brought company. I'm trying to give his partner a fighting chance at not hating us as much as Faris does."

Mort widened his eyes. "You better not let him out of your sight. You remember what that boy did to my floors." His raspy voice made the comment sound even more ominous.

Faris and Ingram were closing in on them. Esther needed to speed this along. "I know, Mort. But maybe you can cut him a little slack. It was a rainy day and I'm sure he didn't mean to track all that mud inside. And it was four years ago." She patted his arm.

Mort's nostrils flared. "I had to scrub that mess from between the floorboards on my hands and knees. Even Sveta couldn't get it. Those floors took such a beating they needed a new coat of polish by the time I was done." He looked lost in a painful memory. "Sometimes I still wake up at night in a cold sweat with my arm scrubbing on its own. But there's nothing there, Esther. There's nothing there."

"We're going to need to see a guest suite. Show us upstairs," Faris demanded, appearing behind Mort.

Before Esther could respond, Mort turned to face Faris, all bravado as they stood toe to toe. He looked him up and down. "Chocolate is the name, clean floors are the game."

Esther stepped in quickly. "Since fall is one of our busier seasons, all the rooms are occupied right now. But I can connect you with our head housekeeper, Sveta. She'll be able to answer any questions you have."

Faris seemed only marginally interested. "Fine. We don't have time for a tour. We can show ourselves around." He looked pointedly at Esther. "On our own." With that, he started walking away.

Ingram mouthed *sorry* before hurrying after his coworker. Supervisor? Manager? She still wasn't clear on what the hierarchy was.

Esther stuck her tongue out at Faris's back. Grouch. She turned back to Mort. "I dropped my coffee at the front door when we walked in. Do you mind...?"

Mort gave a slow shake of his head. "It's starting already. He creates chaos."

Esther clasped her hands together. "You're the best."

"Anything for you, boss."

Esther let out a breath. Less than fifteen minutes ago, finding a digestively overactive bird in the parking lot would have been her biggest challenge of the day. What a luxury that would have been.

Esther felt something soft brush up against her leg. She looked down to meet an unblinking appraisal. The chubby, black cat looked up at her expectantly. She reached down to give Sesame a scratch on the head with her pointer finger. Sesame leaned in for more. "Good morning. I'm so worked up I didn't even see you coming."

Sesame had started hanging around the inn two years ago. Esther would put water out for her, then eventually, food. One day, when Esther showed up for work, Sesame ran right through the front door alongside her.

Esther left the front door open that day, assuming the cat would go back outside. Two years later, the only trips Sesame had taken back to the great outdoors were to vet visits.

Sesame was technically Calliope Inn's pet, not Esther's. But Esther took pride in making sure the automatic feeder and water fountains were always stocked and clean. She tried to make sure Sesame got exercise and play time every day, albeit in the privacy of the basement. It would probably look unprofessional for the manager to be running around in heels waving a mouse wand toy behind her.

Even on her days off, Esther made sure scheduled staff had detailed instructions to check on Sesame. Not that she was very high maintenance. She spent most of her days napping in a sun-soaked window or basking in the attention of guests.

Esther looked down at her furry friend. "You-know-who is here today. I bet he'd *love* if you were extra cuddly with him." She took small delight in imagining the look of horror Faris would pull if he found a cat rubbing up against his pant leg.

Sesame meowed back as if to say, *Not going to happen.*

"Well aren't you vocal today?"

"The feline is still under eight pounds, correct?" Faris was nowhere to be seen, yet his voice carried like a slammed car door.

There was no chance Sesame was under even ten pounds. "Yep!" she called out before bending down to warn the cat. "Keep a low profile, Ses. I'm gonna go see what's cooking for breakfast. If you see a scary man with glasses and the air of mass destruction, try to suck your tummy in."

With one final rub against Esther's leg, Sesame sauntered off.

Esther wondered if Faris would accept a delicious meal in exchange for mercy.

# CHAPTER 3

"Incoming?" Esther muttered, stumbling back from the gangly man who'd charged through the kitchen door. "Getting a head start on your marathon training? Why the rush?"

Clint looked scorned. "Bunny says if she keeps catching me snooping around her kitchen for scraps, she'll make sure I never eat from a restaurant in Oak's Rest again. Can she do that?"

Esther patted his shoulder. She knew she should have given the poor guy some assurance, but he was too easy to mess with. "Bunny can do anything."

Clint cast his eyes downward and shuffled through the dining room toward the lobby.

"Wait!" Esther called after him. "Can you still get us that supplier discount on the cutlery?"

Clint poked his head back in so only his eyes were visible. Sesame had a similar habit, peeking out from behind a plant or a package like a tiny, furry sentinel. "Yeah, but I'll have to drop them off next Saturday instead of Thursday."

"I thought you worked for Eatery Depot on Thursdays."

"Switched my hours so I could pick up a shift for Lacy's dog grooming service on Thursdays."

"You are the hardest working man in Oak's Rest. Maybe in all of Ezra County. Possibly, New York." Esther couldn't fathom how Clint juggled all his jobs, but she was grateful to have a free agent who could often help out at the inn on short notice.

"My mom wants me to save up so I can move out. She needs the basement to host her crochet club." Had he shrunken a few inches at the mention of his mother? Clint crossed his arms like he'd found out he'd have to share a birthday party with a sibling.

"You're on the right path," Esther said, trying to sound encouraging. "That's what your early twenties are for, right? Figuring it all out."

"I'm thirty," Clint said defensively. "I'm only ten years younger than you."

Well, that stung. "*Two* years younger," Esther corrected. She knew she needed to be more diligent about wearing sunscreen, but had thought all the freckled sunspots on her cheeks were hardly noticeable against her brown skin. "Anyway, I'm off to check on breakfast. See you around," she said, ducking into the kitchen before Clint could prod her self-esteem again.

"Do not let that risotto sit longer than forty-five seconds! Stir, stir, stir," Bunny's voice sang out from somewhere deep in her lair. Leave it to Bunny to have already moved on to lunch preparation before breakfast had even been served.

The kitchen was in its standard state of organized chaos, white-coated staff reaching over each other to grab utensils from the walls, tending to steaming pots, a low chorus of chopping and rolling filling the space between Bunny's orders.

Esther inhaled deeply. Heaven. The aroma of fresh baking and cinnamon mixed with strong coffee and a hint of something more savory was an instant comfort.

"Bunny?" She waited for a response, but nothing came.

Esther walked past the refrigerator, brushed her hand along the cookbook shelf, and dodged green stalks and bushels sticking out from the produce rack.

The long, stainless steel table at the center of the kitchen was barely visible under a sea of dishes. Tiered food trays showcased fruit assortments arranged by color, from bright mango and melon at the bottom, to juicy, dark blueberries at the top. Above the table, the overshelf displayed dozens of small plates of croissants and crusty quiches with specks of green and red.

As she turned the corner around the table, Esther zeroed in on the culprit behind her growling stomach. She stepped closer for a better look. The steam was still rolling off the sheet of golden-brown muffins with crumbling streusel and flecks of cinnamon. She fanned the aroma toward her face. Chai spiced apple streusel muffins. One of her favorite of Bunny's fall recipes. Dangerous.

"Oh good, you're here!" Bunny said, appearing from around a corner.

Esther straightened as if she'd been caught doing something naughty.

Bunny wore a black chef coat with magenta cuff accents and a hand-embroidered calliope hummingbird on each shoulder. It had been Esther's gift for Bunny's five-year anniversary as head chef at the inn.

Esther loved seeing her best friend wear the coat, which matched the magenta wall color of the kitchen and the black-and-white checkered tiling of the floor. To her, it represented Bunny being in her element.

She didn't have time to compliment the outfit, though, since Bunny was reaching toward her mouth with a spoonful of some-thing smooth and golden. "Try this." She was a good four inches shorter than Esther, but there was no stopping a chef in need of a taste tester.

Esther opened her mouth right on time. She tasted creamy risotto with tangy goat cheese, a small burst of sweetness from dried fruit, and a few crunchy seeds. The risotto had a subtle herbal flavor that tied the entire bite together. "That's amazing. Is that some type of cheese sauce?"

"Butternut squash," Bunny said absently, obviously eager for more information. "How's the crunch? Does it need more pepitas?" Before Esther could respond, Bunny turned her head to call out, "Luis, can I get some more pepitas?"

Esther put a hand on her shoulder. "Perfect amount of crunch. The flavor is just right. There's a little kick that I can't quite put my finger on. It's masterful. Truly."

Bunny cautiously accepted the affirmations. "I added a little white wine." It was clear her mind was already whirring with a new idea, not fully satisfied with the rave review. She valued constructive feedback over flattery. In her words, "No one grows if they don't stretch." Her pursuit of culinary greatness was almost certainly one reason Calliope Inn had begun to appear in travel magazines over the past few years, ensuring a steady flow of bookings.

"The wine is a nice touch," Esther said. "But I like to save my imbibing for after eight in the morning, so maybe you could spare one of those streusel muffins and a quiche? I'm running on fumes here."

Bunny smiled. "Benita de la Mora, at your service." She put the risotto spoon in the dish sink and wiped her hands on her waist apron, the mannerism she always did when she was excited to plate. "There's fresh coffee in the pot if you want some."

"Thanks. I spilled the last sips of my Penny's by the front door." Esther walked over to the coffee station, grabbed a mug from the wall, and poured herself another full cup. It smelled nutty and sweet.

Bunny snorted. "I still don't get why you insist on getting Penny's when you could drink coffee here for free."

"Things taste better when they're not from home." Esther blew on her mug, then set it down as Bunny approached with her breakfast.

As requested, Bunny handed off a plate with a quiche, a muffin topped by a pad of already melting butter, and a handful of fresh fruit. "So, the inn is your home in this scenario? You're great at customer service, but that's taking your manager title to a whole new level, don't you think?"

Esther had to choose between responding and trying the muffin. The glimmering pile of sugar was calling her. She took a bite and closed her eyes. "You are a genius, Bunny. Are you thinking of adding these to the Makers and Merchants menu?"

"Thank you. And I'm not sure yet. We're expecting lots of out-of-towners, right? I want to strike the perfect combination of familiar, comforting treats and 'our town's food could eat your town's food for lunch.' You know?"

Esther nodded, pretending to understand. "I trust your vision. Those visitors better bring their appetites."

Bunny had already moved on to examining a quiche. "I might try incorporating tomatoes into my next batch. I need to figure out the right moisture content so they don't turn out too dense."

Esther didn't know much about baking techniques. She preferred eating delicious foods to preparing them. "I can't believe it's already Makers and Merchants season. I haven't even gotten to wear the necklace Clint sold me last year when he was working for that independent jeweler. Remember the one he made from lake beach sand?"

Bunny shuddered. "Very...exfoliating."

"There was a lot of glue involved."

Bunny laughed. "I think Oak's Rest just has so many traditions it feels like we're always busy with something."

Esther smiled. "I love our little town, but we're a quirky bunch." She'd lived in Oak's Rest for eleven years, but she was still learning about all the history and traditions.

"I am kind of excited to see what drama unfolds leading up to the festival," Bunny said. "It's not an Oak's Rest tradition without a few mishaps."

"Except this one," Esther asserted. *Mishap* was not a word she wanted to hear in relation to her event planning. "Makers and Merchants is going to be a hit. Because we're hosting it."

Bunny twirled the end of one of her French braids. "Okay, that's fair. But what shade of red do you think Mayor Early's face will turn at town hall when someone asks if they can use fire?"

Esther and Bunny mimicked Mayor Bethany Early in harmony: "It's about safety!" They threw their heads back with laughter.

Esther took a sip of coffee as she caught her breath.

Metal clanged to the floor. A male voice called out, "I got it!"

Esther could see the reprimand written on Bunny's face. She'd spare the staff member from being scolded. "Luis, please tell your mom thank you again for letting us try some peppers from her garden!"

Bunny narrowed her eyes, probably knowing Esther had given the employee an easy out. But Bunny couldn't argue with free donations to her kitchen.

Bunny's scrutinizing look jolted Esther back to the memory of her unpleasant morning with the health inspector. She set her mug down next to her plate. "Oh my goodness. I got distracted by the muffins. Bunny, Faris is here."

Bunny froze. "Where?" She looked side to side, moving only her eyes.

"At the inn. Right now." Esther pointed to the door. "Walking around with his little clipboard like he owns the place. And he brought a friend."

Bunny crossed her arms. "Faris doesn't have friends."

"A coworker. Whatever."

"There's *two* of them?" Bunny asked in disbelief. "One Faris is one too many."

"I know. The new guy seems pretty nice. But still. Faris is extra...*Faris* today. He's on a warpath."

Bunny positioned herself at the worktable and began rear-

19

ranging plates. "I'm sure he's all bark and no bite. We'll pass, don't you think?"

Esther hoped so. She didn't know if it was the inspection or festival planning, but she was on edge. "I'm hoping to pass on the first try. I'm still trying to establish a good relationship with our staff in my new role. I don't want to make everyone's jobs harder by failing and having Faris come back for a reinspection."

Bunny looked at her like she was speaking an unfamiliar language. "What are you talking about? Everyone loves you. You're kicking butt as manager. I don't know how you handle petty guest issues with such grace, but you do. And the inn is more profitable than ever, right?"

Esther wanted to accept the praise, but had the nagging feeling she had more to prove. She hoped she could sustain the profitability long enough to give her staff raises. "Thanks, that's reassuring. I'm just...I don't know. I guess I'm nervous that if I can't be an excellent manager, it means I won't have what it takes to do my own thing one day."

Esther had always known she wanted to run a business, even when she hadn't known what kind. The ability to create an entire career out of thin air, waking up every day with no one to answer to but herself, seemed like a dream come true. Esther had taken her first job at Calliope Inn out of desperation, but a few years in, she knew her future was in hospitality.

Bunny paused fiddling with the plates. "Honey, if there's one thing I know, it's that you're going to be successful. I'd stay at any inn you're a part of. And there is no challenge I've ever seen you shy away from." She tilted her head in thought. "Except trying one of my recipes at home."

Esther grabbed her coffee mug. "I'm not the award-winning chef."

Bunny held her hands up in surrender. "I'm just saying. I gave you the same granola recipe I gave my fourth-grade niece, and she could do it."

Esther pretended to plug one ear as she walked toward the kitchen door. "Can't hear you from all the way over here, sorry."

"I'll call you if Faris says we need to tear the kitchen down."

"If you need to keep him busy, just ask him to follow your granola recipe!" Esther made a silly face over her shoulder and walked out of the kitchen, but let the expression fall as soon as the door closed.

Why was there a pit at the bottom of her stomach?

# CHAPTER 4

"That MISERABLE little—"

Esther paused, mid-stride, listening by the closed door of the Calliope Room. That didn't sound good.

Sniffling. Was someone crying?

Esther knocked twice and eased the door open. Kai Etana, the inn's wellness specialist, was wiping away tears. Her nephew, Lani, patted her back.

The Calliope Room was an all-purpose space that was easy enough to convert into a spa, craft workshop, or storage unit in a pinch. At the moment, it featured two massage tables, and several lit candles. They cast a warm glow and gave off a fresh, herbaceous scent, like a garden after rain.

Esther crossed the room and traded places with Lani, perching beside Kai on the table. "Kai, what's going on? What happened?"

Kai raked her fingers through her hair, the signature purple streak contrasting against her yellow cotton overalls. She sniffled again, but said nothing. Esther looked to Lani for insight.

He sat on the table facing them and hesitated. "Aunt Kai failed—"

Kai cut him off, zipping from sadness to rage. "He failed my spa. *Failed.* Not even a warning. That rude, power-hungry egomaniac."

"She's talking about the health inspector," Lani explained.

Esther took her time responding, sensing the volatility in the atmosphere. "I gathered that. Kai, sweetie, what do you mean, 'failed'? How could Faris fail you? Your spa is impeccable."

Esther realized she was overdue for a visit to Etana's Essence. Kai owned a spa in the town square where she performed miracles. The last time Esther visited, she'd been so relaxed after her facial and deep tissue massage she felt like she was walking on air the entire way home.

People had expressed some hesitation when Kai opened up shop and started offering cosmetic packages, claiming those types of treatments were something only celebrities did. Any worries quickly faded as people saw their friends and family members erase fine lines like movie stars themselves.

Kai was a self-made woman, through and through. She'd started her career as a nurse, but took on the beauty world after realizing the intensity of the medical field wasn't for her.

She'd moved to Oak's Rest from Hawaii, learning both her new trade and how to run a business at the same time. While her wellness services were a major selling point for the inn, Esther knew how physically grueling Kai's line of work could be. She had nothing but respect for the woman.

Kai cleared her throat, still thick with emotion. "I haven't read the full report. Faris saw me in the lobby, said he had my results in his car, and left to get them. When he came back, he handed me the papers and walked away. He didn't even say anything. The first thing I saw was the word 'FAIL' stamped in red. All caps. Has he never heard of bedside manner?"

"It's so messed up," Lani agreed.

Kai wiped her eyes. "I guess I should have known. Halley Jeffries strode right into the spa with her poodle during the inspection. I managed to shoo them back out the door before the dog could get too far inside. But Faris was even more ice-cold than usual after that. And the worst part? The sad look on the pup's face when he realized he couldn't come in for his daily treat."

The thought of shutting Sesame out of the inn made Esther's heart heavy. Luckily for them, the inn wasn't considered a medical facility. Frankly, she was shocked Faris hadn't reacted more strongly to an unauthorized animal at the spa. But that wasn't what Kai needed to hear. "I'm so, so sorry. In all the years of Faris trying everyone's nerves, I've never known him to flat out fail a business. What can we do?" She ran a quick mental assessment. Appeal? Request a new inspector?

"Want me to kill him?" Lani asked.

Kai broke into laughter and swatted at his chest. "Stop it."

Esther forced a small laugh when she realized Lani was kidding. She was sure he was a good kid. He *was* related to Kai, after all. But she didn't know him very well.

Lani continued, his tone playful. "I'll take the guy out for you, Auntie Kai. Say the word."

Kai sniffed, still smiling. "You're only here for six weeks. If I send you back to Hawaii with felony charges, my sister will kill *me*."

"By the way," Esther said, looking at Lani, "Thank you for offering to help your aunt out while you're here. She won't admit it, but she secretly loves having an apprentice." Lani was all Kai had talked about the few weeks before his arrival. Hunting down the taro chips he liked. Making sure she had all the streaming services with his favorite shows.

Lani smiled and looked at his aunt. "Is that right? Are you gonna show me how to stick needles in people's faces?"

"More than needles," Esther said, looking at Kai. "Science-based substances that will turn your frown into a look of unreadable mysteriousness."

"Someone save me," Kai said, covering her face with her hands. "Let's leave the injections to the woman who's licensed for that sort of thing." She pointed to herself.

"Just practicing my marketing speak," Esther said. "So, what happens with the spa now? Do you have to close until you can get it reinspected?"

"Thankfully not. I can stay open so long as I pass on the second inspection. If I fail twice, I'm toast."

Esther could tell how shaken Kai was. She tried to imagine how she would have felt receiving a failing grade. Worse, how she would have felt if the inn failed twice and had to close, even temporarily. She didn't even want to think about it. "I'm sure you'll pass on the next try. And if you ever need to pick up any extra work here, you're always welcome."

Kai reached out for a hug. "Thanks, Esther. I knew you'd be a great boss. We might need to push our wellness services on social media for the next few months, though. You know, in case my entire business crumbles before my eyes."

Esther tipped her head in a single, decisive motion. "Consider it done. And if you run out of work to do, I'm sure Bunny would be happy to have a personal taste tester help out in the kitchen."

Kai stood and gestured for Lani to do the same. She pointed toward the hallway and Lani turned to walk to the door. "Remember when I made the mistake of snacking on her chocolate ganache mini Bundt cakes?"

Esther remembered it very well. "She said if you could eat three in a row, the cocoa wasn't rich enough. Sent her into a frenzy."

"She was tampering with that recipe for a month," Kai said flatly.

"That was one of the most delicious months ever," Esther admitted. "To be fair, though, I wasn't the one Bunny was chasing around with a bowl of molten ganache."

Lani came back in, wheeling the spa cart ahead of him, full with product refills, spray bottles, and towels.

Kai retrieved a spray bottle and dark towel from the bottom of the cart. "She timed how long her batches of ganache took to run from the top of the cake to hitting the plate. The woman is a genius, but I think I'll steer clear of being her tester from now on."

"That doesn't sound like a bad job at all," Lani said. "Maybe I should split my time between you and the chef. Get a well-rounded experience." He took the cleaning supplies from his aunt and waved her away as she protested.

"I had to hide in the supply closet once," Kai said.

Esther stood as Lani approached the tables, realizing they likely needed to get ready for their next client. "Lani, I'm sure you'll get to take plenty of samples home with you during your time here," she assured him. "How are you liking Oak's Rest? Have you spent much time at the lake?"

Lani nodded as he began spraying down the tables. "It's awesome. I'm a little nervous about how cold it'll get as the weather cools down, but the lake is beautiful. It's not too different from home. Lots of good hiking trails, kayaking, tourists stopping traffic to take photos. Fewer volcanoes, though."

Esther wouldn't have guessed that upstate New York shared many similarities to Hawaii, but quietly basked in the comparison. "Oak's Rest has become a pretty popular destination, especially in recent years. It seems like people aren't only looking for luxurious, high-profile getaways these days. They're on the search for small-town charm, too."

In the decade she'd been with Calliope, the inn had gone from a little-known hidden gem to a destination even affluent guests sought. They were in an interesting phase where longtime guests were having to get used to making reservations in advance. The booking calendar had become more crowded with clientele who had assistants and managers who booked their travel plans up to a year in advance.

Kai stretched an arm across her chest. "City-dwellers are my best clients. It takes more than a five-hour drive from Manhattan to unravel all the stress they bring with them."

Esther sensed Kai was feeling a little better. She started toward the door. "Well, Lani, if you need anything while you're here in Oak's Rest, give me a shout. I know your aunt must be keeping you busy, but if you need some time to yourself, I know all the best quiet spots in town."

"Thanks. I convinced her to make me a copy of her house key." Lani raised a hand to his mouth and joke-whispered, "I think she wanted me to have to rely on her to come and go."

"That's not true," Kai objected. "I don't like too many copies of my house key floating around out there. It's a security thing."

Lani reached into his pocket and produced a rainbow gradient key with a palm tree design on it. "And does your security manual say your house key should have the world's most identifiable design?"

Kai shrugged. "It was on sale."

Esther laughed. "Sounds like you've got it all sorted out. I'd better get back to my station. I'm here for you, Kai."

Kai smiled. "Thank you."

Esther stopped at the reception desk and opened her purse. She tapped her phone screen.

*(1) Missed Call: Cameron Bennett*

Butterflies fluttered in her stomach. Maybe it was an accidental dial? Her sister rarely called her. Had someone died? When had they last talked?

She debated how to proceed. Send a text asking what was up? Call back at lunch time?

This was how the Bennetts operated. Everything needed to happen on their time, without exception. Anything less was a disappointment. She'd shed the role of being the family disappointment years ago.

She eased her grip on the phone, aware she was holding it a little too tightly, and stuffed it back in her bag. Esther turned, tilted her chin up, and headed toward the dining room to oversee breakfast.

Cameron could wait. One major interruption to her day was plenty.

# CHAPTER 5

That evening, Esther tiptoed into the town hall meeting from the side of the community center basketball court, hoping the mayor wouldn't notice her tardiness. She scanned the rows of faces.

There, at the center of the fifth row, sat Bunny, Kai, and Lani. A few stepped-on toes and several apologies later, Esther made it to her saved seat between Bunny and Kai. "What did I miss?" she asked, setting her bag down and placing her jacket over the back of the chair.

"Not much," Bunny said. "Whispered threats over aisle seats, high stakes musical chairs, the usual."

Town hall seating was a delicate dance. Sitting at the back, near the windows, meant straining to hear over the Canada geese squabbling on their way back from the lake. Even worse, a seat at the front meant giving up the crucial ability to smuggle in snacks.

The best seats in the house were right in the middle, where the sound quality was high and snacking could be done discreetly. If nothing else, town hall meetings were always entertaining.

"Bethany, my love, I beg you to consider getting us some new chairs," LouLou, the town seamstress, pleaded from the front row. "These little wooden folding things are child-sized. I'm a woman, darling. Plus, they aggravate my sciatica." LouLou flared out her shawl, the fabric hitting the person next to her as she shifted in her seat.

"At least you have a real chair," Clint called out from the end of the front row. "Mine is missing the seat. I've been squatting over an empty frame this whole time."

"Should have gotten here earlier," someone remarked.

Clint stood, running a hand over the thin patch of facial hair he called a mustache. "I had to cut my mom's pills! You promised you'd save me a seat, by the way."

"Sit down, Clint," Mayor Bethany Early commanded from behind the podium at the front. "You're blocking the view of the people behind you." She was wearing a light pink blazer with an American flag brooch fixed prominently to the lapel.

A chorus of agreement came from a nearby section of the audience. Clint huffed and squatted back down.

Bunny passed a tin of salted caramel popcorn. Esther grabbed a handful and handed it to Kai, who continued the chain to Lani.

Esther leaned toward Bunny so her voice wouldn't carry. "Everything went okay in the kitchen?" Faris had given the inn a passing inspection grade before lunch, which Esther was thrilled about, but she hadn't had a chance to debrief with the chef.

Bunny gave a thumbs up. "Piece of cake. Faris is always kind, respectful, and encouraging," she whispered.

Sarcasm was a good sign. If she could still joke about Faris's presence, he must not have been too much of a burden. "So, he was a pain, but at least he didn't tell us we needed to tear the place down and start over?"

"Exactly. I think Sesame tried to put him in his place. Faris couldn't stop moaning about how she was swiping at him and Ingram when they were trying to confirm she was microchipped." Bunny shook her head. "How they planned to do that is beyond me."

Esther fought a laugh. "That's our girl. Kind of glad I held off on clipping her claws."

The sound of Mayor Early shuffling papers got picked up by the microphone and reverberated off the walls. "Once again, I'll maintain that purchasing new chairs would eat into our Movie Night budget. Do we want to give up Movie Night?"

The projector screen, still lowered behind the podium from the viewing several nights ago, loomed threateningly blank. Esther hadn't attended, but heard there was a spirited debate over whether the lead actor had hair plugs.

Grumbles rolled through the crowd. Looking satisfied, Mayor Early cleared her throat and moved on. "Now, as many of you know, the latest round of health and safety inspections is under-way. To head off any FAQs, I'd like to remind everyone that no, we cannot fire or replace any specific employee of the Ezra County Health Department simply because we don't like him." A beat later, she added, "Or her."

That was diplomatic.

Someone in the back called out, "What if *him or her* finds joy in putting our businesses at risk of being shut down?"

Mumbled approval from the crowd.

Marcus Hall, who owned Hall Winery & Orchard with his wife, Aggie, stood in the second row. "Who does this guy think he is, waving his clipboard around, threatening the businesses we've poured our hearts into?"

The crowd's energy seemed to pick up momentum. Things were about to get good.

Aggie reached up to place a hand on Marcus's forearm from her seat, as if signaling for him to keep his cool.

He glanced down and gave the slightest dip of his chin before continuing at a more relaxed pace. "I mean, he had the audacity to fail Etana's Essence. He's out of control."

Esther took Kai's hand in hers, ready to offer support. Kai looked at her, clearly surprised at the mention of her business. Esther gave her a weak smile. It was a small town. Word traveled fast.

As if reading her thoughts, Kai blinked in understanding and turned her attention back to the front.

LouLou held up a finger like she was bidding at an auction. "Bethany, Faris slips farther off his rocker every year. Would it be unfair to assume he's targeting us? Unless, of course, he's equally talented at spreading misery through the rest of the county?"

A few people clapped.

Dev Singh, the owner of Used Books & More, stood from the row in front of Esther. "Give the young man a break, you all. He might not be the most warm and fuzzy fellow in the world, but I believe he is just trying to do his job."

Someone called out, "Easy for you to say, Dev. You're the only person in this town Faris even shows one shred of humanity toward."

Dev lifted a hand. "Fine. I will admit...his intensity can be a bit much. I'm all for safety standards, but there comes a point..." he gestured, appearing to be searching for the right words. "I cannot clean the dust off every book. People come to my shop for old things. My customers like dust. Nay, expect it."

"Let Dev put down the duster!" someone called out like they were trying to start a chant.

More clapping.

Mayor Early hunched at the podium, pinching the bridge of her nose as the crowd's comments picked up in volume. She placed both hands on the podium. "Thank you, Dev. You all know that in addition to my mayoral role, I, too, am an Oak's Rest business owner. So, while I understand your concerns, all we can do is try to remain in compliance and carry on." She sounded like a school teacher disappointed in her students for collectively failing a test. "With that, let's shift gears to upcoming town events."

Dev sat. The crowd settled after a few moments. The only matter that held the attention of Oak's Rest residents more than a heated discussion was a town event.

Mayor Early had regained some composure and stood straighter. "Our annual Oak's Rest Makers and Merchants Festival is right around the corner, and we have heavy preparation work ahead of us."

Esther's stomach somersaulted.

Lani leaned in. "What's a Makers and Merchants Festival?"

Kai patted his knee. "You'll find out, nephew. You'll find out."

Bunny started counting down. "And three, two, one..."

Unsurprisingly, LouLou was the first to raise a hand.

Mayor Early was reluctant to acknowledge it. "Yes, LouLou?"

LouLou projected her voice. "I think you should reconsider the no-fire rule. How am I supposed to showcase my flame-resistant fabric without a flame? Photos? There's no show business in photos."

Esther made eye contact with Bunny as she reached for some more caramel popcorn.

Mayor Early closed her eyes, her face taking on a pink hue. "For the final time, I will not be making exceptions to the no-fire policy. It's a matter of safety."

LouLou crossed her arms. "How long are we all going to be penalized for Clint's circus act? It was two years ago now."

Clint stood. Whatever his thigh workout routine was, Esther needed to find out. "I would have nailed that fire juggling act if it wasn't for the wind."

"Clint, sweetie, your little stunt cost you more than your eyebrows. It cost us our creative freedom!" LouLou said, gesturing toward the mayor.

Murmurs filled the court.

Mayor Early banged her gavel against the podium. "Clint, sit.

LouLou, enough, please. I think we're losing sight of what's important here."

Kai snapped twice. "Here's your answer, Lani. Listen up."

"The Makers and Merchants Festival is more than an opportunity to show off your latest party tricks. It's a valuable asset to our local economy. An opportunity to take pride in our slice of Ezra County."

Her eyes looked misty, as if she didn't recount this very speech every year. "Many of you are running businesses that have been in your families for generations. Your business, your trade, your work. It means something. This festival affords us a chance to show people what you do and why they should care."

Dev Singh stood to insert, "And eat good food."

Mayor Early looked tired. "Yes. And that."

Esther patted Bunny's knee, proud that the festival menu wouldn't go unappreciated.

"Business owners," Mayor Early began, "do post your entrepreneurial talents to your social media accounts over the coming weeks. Advertise any promotions you're planning on running. Spread our event by word of mouth. If you have any questions pertaining to the venue, your booth, or special requests, direct them to Esther Bennett."

All eyes turned toward Esther. A few hands shot up.

"Will there be somewhere to park my canoe?"

"Are you offering complimentary sunscreen? I need a lot of sunscreen."

"Is the inn's basement waterproofed?"

Esther stood and smiled to soften the clarification. "Via email, please." If she had any chance of keeping her communications straight, it would need to be done in an organized, searchable format.

Mayor Early nodded in approval.

After the meeting, residents spilled out of the community center into the thick evening air. The sun was low in the sky.

Esther couldn't see Lake Ezra, but the freshwater and soft mineral scent was close, like it was calling her home.

Bunny explained she needed to head straight home for some shut-eye before her six o'clock call time.

LouLou walked past and placed a hand on Kai's back. "I'm gonna need a little something for my forehead soon."

Kai winked. "I got you covered, LouLou."

"Never a dull moment around here, huh?" Esther asked.

"Never," Kai said. "Wanna grab a bite to eat with us before you hit the hay? I could hear Lani's stomach rumbling the whole time."

Esther laughed. "I'm gonna head home too. I want to see if I can get Sesame in for her yearly checkup at the vet early in the morning. Arriving before the staff is the only way to get a walk-in." There was no telling what her schedule would be like over the coming weeks, so she wanted to get Sesame squared away sooner rather than later.

Kai crossed her arms, amused. "Why don't you have someone else take her? Surely there has to be a member of your staff who could chauffeur Sesame to the vet. Maybe someone a little less vital to the operation?"

Esther wouldn't hear it. "She gets anxious. I'll need to swaddle her at least fifteen minutes before she goes back to calm her nerves. It's a whole thing." It was true, but Esther also took pride in being her caretaker.

"Alrighty," Kai said. "Tell Miss Sesame to be a brave girl. We'll see you tomorrow." She and Lani waved before peeling off.

Esther opened her phone to double check she'd toggled on the alarm for the following morning. She felt herself grimace when she saw the time it was set for. She had a feeling tomorrow would be another long day.

# CHAPTER 6

Sesame was not a morning cat.

She pawed at the inside of her carrier, vexed as always to be confined to her box-shaped jail.

Esther fought the urge to drive straight back to the inn and let Sesame free. "Hang tight, Ses." She reached a finger through the bars to rub Sesame's forehead. "Twenty minutes of being uncomfortable is worth a year of being healthy, isn't it? You wait. We'll be done in no time."

Sesame didn't look convinced. With what sounded like a sigh, the cat stood, turned, and plopped down, backside to the carrier door.

"Oh, come on, Sessy Pie. We're not even on speaking terms anymore?"

The parking lot of Pawsitively Supreme Vet Care, better known as "Paws," was deserted so early in the morning. The cerulean blue wood-paneled building sported light blue window shutters. Stout planter pots lined the entrance, from the foot of the staircase to the end of the accessibility ramp.

Parallel to Paws stood What's the Scoop? Creamery. The butterscotch color of the petite building mirrored the sun's glow, which was just starting to break through the treetops in the distance.

Last year, Esther and Bunny had the chance to harvest the sap from a small grove of sugar maples with a nature conservancy group. Bunny still had a bottle or two of the pure syrup stashed somewhere in the kitchen. Moments like those made Esther feel small in the best way. Like she was one small thread in a web of life cycles and ecosystems, constantly humming under surfaces she couldn't see.

Out front of the creamery stood a beach directional sign. Its posts were painted with the names of the most popular flavors. There was Triple Berry Pie, Maple Bonfire Crunch, and Esther's guiltiest pleasure, Nutty by Nature.

She wished the creamery was open year round, but the owners only opened for spring and summer, and spent the rest of the year in Pennsylvania, living with aging parents.

Esther reached into her purse for Sesame's treat bag. Distraction by food was one of the most reliable tactics for getting through a vet visit without drama. Sesame would tolerate a surprising amount of fussing and handling for a crunchy outside and meaty center.

Esther had planned on saving the treats for inside the appointment, but who was she kidding? She couldn't resist spoiling the little loaf. "Here, Sesame. For being such a good girl." Esther shook the baggie, which earned her a glance over the shoulder, followed by a full body turnaround.

Esther aimed a treat through the carrier door, but when Sesame pawed at it, the snack tumbled to the car floor. Esther made eye contact with Sesame as she reached down for it.

The cat looked at her as if to say, *Don't even think about it. I've seen your floors.*

Esther inspected the previously light gray carpet. It had seen better days. In fact, the treat had landed on a small patch of dirt with a twig sticking out.

She held her hands up. "Okay, okay. Let's get you a fresh one. But be honest. Was that to get even with me for bringing you here in the first place?" Esther deposited a clean treat into the carrier. She held the dirty treat in the other hand, and dug around in the glove compartment, hoping to find a napkin. No such luck. Should she leave it in the cup holder?

She looked around the parking lot and spotted a dumpster behind the creamery. "I'll be right back, Sesame. Stay here. I'll crack the window for you."

The cat stared at her.

"What? You're the one who judged my floors. No time like the present to start keeping the car clean, right?" She opened her door and swung her leg over. "Not like we have anything better to do."

Despite the wake up time, Esther had to admit she enjoyed the stillness that hung in the air, a calm only early risers got to experience. The veterinary office was a few blocks from the town square, tucked away in a pocket of town with low foot traffic, especially now that the creamery was closed. If not for the rustling leaves and the birds having their morning conversations, it would have been deathly silent.

Esther jogged up the walkway, wishing she had a tissue or glove to open the dumpster lid with. She wasn't a total germaphobe, but touching trash cans had always freaked her out. She tried not to think about the diversity of garbage-loving creatures, four-legged or otherwise, that had been there before her.

The dumpster bore a sign that read, *FOR TENANT USE ONLY. VIOLATORS WILL BE FINED*. The threat made Esther chuckle. She imagined a scoundrel wearing a beanie and black eye mask sneaking up to the dumpster, throwing away their burger wrapper, and letting out their best villain laugh, knowing they'd gotten away with it. Oak's Rest wasn't exactly an epicenter of petty crime.

She gingerly lifted the lid and tossed in the disgraced treat.

Relieved not to hear any alarm sirens, she closed the lid and turned to walk back to the car.

Outside the Paws entrance, Esther jumped as something scurried past her foot. She looked down in time to follow the end of a squirrel's tail as it ran toward a clearing in the trees behind the dumpster area she'd come from.

Esther placed a hand over her thumping heart and started again toward the car, but as her gaze shifted, something about the clearing caught her eye.

The ground was hidden under a patch of tangled branches and dense early autumn foliage, piled high, and growing taller, still, as leaves lazily departed from the trees above.

Something pale and flat stuck out from a mess of leaf litter. Maybe a takeout container?

Esther debated ignoring it, but decided cleaning up the environment cancelled out using private property for her own trash-disposing convenience.

She stepped to the edge of the brush. Up close, it didn't look like styrofoam at all. A scuffed white sole stood out against the browns, yellows, and oranges of fallen leaves.

Why would someone throw out shoes in decent condition? And why in the woods, when the dumpster was right there?

Esther sighed. From then on, she'd keep her car stocked with gloves at all times.

She nudged the leaves with her foot, hoping to find the laces and grab the smallest surface area possible. The leaves clung like wet newspaper. "Really?"

She groaned as she bent down, aiming for the shoelace. She gave it a tug. It didn't budge. Was the shoe filled with concrete? Why was it so heavy?

Esther decided on a new method. She picked up a broken branch and used the end of her makeshift pole to swipe at the leaves to get more visibility.

As she continued, a patch of khaki canvas appeared. A duffel bag near the shoe?

She poked again. The branch hit something solid. "What the—"

She stepped back to assess the whole picture, a shape beginning to emerge. Then, in an instant, Esther understood what she was seeing. What she'd been poking at.

Khaki pants.

A leg.

No movement.

The bottom dropped out from her stomach.

It wasn't a discarded shoe. There was a person lying face up in the foliage. A very still, very unresponsive person.

She didn't bother looking for the face. She didn't have time. Her feet were moving before she could think.

Esther raced back to the car and slammed the door shut, heart thundering. She tore out of the parking lot, the car protesting in its old age as she applied more pressure to the gas. Without taking her eyes off the road, she plunged her hand into her purse.

She needed to call someone. She needed to call the police.

If the sickening churn of her stomach was any indication, Esther Bennett had just seen a dead body.

# CHAPTER 7

Esther covered her face. "So it *was* a dead person." She'd been semi-successful at convincing herself it could have been someone who'd drank too much or picked a strange place to nap.

"I'm afraid so." Detective Sabina Ali sat across from Esther at the dining room table, pen poised over a small notebook. She wore a neutral expression, but the intensity in her look suggested Sabina was as surprised about the discovery as Esther had been. "Can you think of any other details you might have missed?"

It had been a few hours since Esther found the body, but her hands were still trembling as she picked at a bead of dried syrup left on the table from breakfast. She'd have to ask Sveta for some of the wood-safe cleaning solution. When was the last time they'd polished the tables? Maybe Sveta could do that too.

"I know this is hard," Sabina said. "No detail is too small."

Working with Sabina on official police business felt wrong. Esther and Sabina had been in a book club together, had played side by side in the annual Lake Ezra Summer Games volleyball tournament. The inn had even hosted Sabina's celebratory friends and family brunch when she'd made detective.

She wore a gray-blue plaid blazer over a white turtleneck and subtly flared slacks. Someone could easily mistake her for a smartly dressed accountant or attorney, which Esther was grateful for, considering she didn't want guests speculating about why the police were visiting the inn.

Fortunately, the guests had already finished breakfast and most of them were out on a boat tour of Lake Ezra, courtesy of Justice. Esther vaguely remembered walking up to the reception desk when she'd gotten back, still shell-shocked.

Justice had looked her up and down and asked, "What do you need me to do?"

She must have looked as shaken as she felt.

Esther wasn't hard on her staff. She set a high standard for the guest experience, sure. But she also knew that the hospitality field was taxing, and ruling her staff with an iron fist would only eventually lead to absence and turnover.

In quiet moments, when guests weren't around, Esther wasn't upset by seeing a member of her staff checking their phone. She trusted that when they needed to put their game face on, they would. So far, she hadn't been let down.

"Keep the guests busy today," Esther had uttered. It was like she was talking through a fog, hearing the instructions come out, but unsure where they'd land.

Justice had replied, "You got it, boss lady," and started typing furiously into the computer.

She'd thank Justice later, maybe with a card or some of those white chocolates she was always sneaking when she thought no one was looking. Was it the strawberry or the raspberry filling she liked?

"Esther?" Officer Nolan Brown asked.

Esther had all but forgotten he was there. He leaned in slightly, exchanging glances with Sabina. Was that concern written on their faces?

Nolan was wearing a gray sweatsuit. Had he been off the

clock? How unfortunate. The last thing anyone wanted to be called into work for on their day off was a death. His eyes and skin tone were the same rich, dark brown.

Both Sabina and Nolan were illuminated by the wall of windows behind Esther. Maybe she, backlit by the sun, had an angelic halo cast around her head. Maybe it only highlighted her baby hairs.

"Esther, are you alright?" Sabina this time.

Esther blinked a few times, pulling her attention, like a sandbag, back to the present. "Sorry. I'm still trying to process all of this." What a wild twenty-four hours. First Kai, then a dead body. She let herself deflate against the back of the chair. "No. I've walked you through everything I can remember. I only got a brief look before I took off. I didn't exactly want to stick around."

Sabina capped her pen. "Thank you for sharing what you could. We have a lot of work ahead of us. We'd better get going."

That was it? "Hang on," Esther said. "What happens now? How soon will you know who it was? Or how they died?"

Sabina and Nolan exchanged another glance. Why did they keep doing that?

"What?" Esther asked, pushing up. "Do you already know something?"

Sabina slid her pen into the breast pocket of her jacket. She held her notepad with both hands and lowered it to her waist. "We won't know definitively until we get the autopsy and toxicology report back from the medical examiner in Yalfont. However, based on preliminary observation, we believe the individual died by a lethal dosage of an injected substance."

Esther raised her hands, in no mood for a science lesson. "Injected substance? What does that mean? Did they take drugs?"

Nolan responded slowly, looking at his superior for confirmation. "The individual had a wound at the carotid triangle. Soft spot to the side of the Adam's apple. Not a common site for self-injection."

43

Esther gripped the edge of her chair. "So what, then? You're not saying—" She looked between Sabina and Nolan. "They were murdered?"

Sabina lifted a steadying hand. "Like I said, we don't know definitively. We haven't recovered a weapon or any evidence to prove that."

"We have our work cut out for us, that's for sure. We'll need to turn over the crime area," Nolan explained. "A bunch of our folks are out on an Alaskan cruise. Booked it over a year ago. I don't think any of us were expecting...this type of eventfulness."

They were holding back. "But?" Esther urged.

Sabina eased out a breath. "But yes. So far, it reads like a homicide."

Esther was stunned. It couldn't be. A murder. In Oak's Rest. "Has anything like this ever happened here?"

Sabina looked upward. "It's rare. No doubt about it."

Esther fought the urge to stand and start pacing the room. "Do you know who the person is?" She corrected herself, "Was?"

Sabina looked out the window before meeting Esther's eyes. She said nothing.

"Tell me, Sabina. Was it a tourist? Was it someone we know?"

Sabina cleared her throat. "We were able to recover identification from the individual's person and have established a likely identity."

Esther raised her eyebrows. The anticipation was making her itch. "Well? Please drop the police jargon and tell me."

Sabina straightened and squared her shoulders. "We've identified the victim as Faris Holliday."

# CHAPTER 8

E sther had busied herself with bookkeeping and reviewing contracts after giving Sabina and Nolan her statement. Bunny tried to comfort her with sweet tea and scones, but she could only ride the blood sugar rollercoaster for so long before she'd crash.

Bunny and Kai had urged her to go home early. Bunny assured her lunch would be a breeze, and Kai offered to cancel her sessions for the day so she could help Justice with any guest needs.

Esther didn't doubt they could have handled the last few hours of the day without her. And she knew their advice was wise. Going home would have been the logical choice. The problem was, she didn't want to be alone.

It wasn't that she didn't feel safe—although the idea of a potential killer on the loose was unsettling—but that she felt a restlessness pent up inside her with nowhere to put it.

She didn't need to go home to stare at the walls. What she needed was fresh air.

Rows of shops and businesses, each different in height and

color, bordered the town square. What Esther loved about Oak's Rest architecture was how hodgepodge it all was. Every store, building, and home looked like it had been designed independently of its neighbors. Like each building was custom-built for its owners.

The car chirped as Esther clicked her key. From where she parked, she could see a small section of Lake Ezra, a straight walk a few blocks from the heart of the town square. A mint green paddle boat drifted by. On it were three people in yellow life vests, probably parents and a child. The water, glittering in the sunlight, parted for a beat before rejoining in the boat's wake, like it had never been there.

Esther spotted Dev Singh sweeping out front of Used Books & More. He looked deep in concentration as he meticulously removed every last leaf from his stoop before the wind picked up and blew them right back into place. It was a wonder how much he cared about keeping the outside of his store clear, given how cluttered the inside was.

The high school band was rehearsing under the gazebo at the center of the square. Trombones bellowed a soulful rendition of an R&B song Esther couldn't recall the name of.

A few of the band members sat on the steps, looking in Esther's direction as she crossed the X-shaped path through the square. It wasn't until she'd passed the gazebo that she could hear a snippet of their conversation.

"You don't go to jail for finding the body. You have to actually commit a crime."

"I would die if I ever came across a dead body. I can't even."

"You'll be lucky if interesting stuff is still happening to you when you're old."

Esther slowed but didn't stop. She wasn't sure which was more offensive—teenagers thinking of her as old, or them talking about her from less than twenty feet away.

The ache developing at the base of her head dulled her ability to care.

A doorbell jingled overhead as she walked into General Store. Behind the counter, Bethany Early was ringing up groceries with surgical precision. She placed an apple on the scale, frowned as she took it off and zeroed the measurement, then tried again.

Bethany was nothing if not consistent. She applied the same thoroughness to everything she did, whether acting as store owner or mayor. Esther called it rule-following. Some people used more colorful words, especially when their permits were denied on technicalities.

A few minutes later, Esther was deliberating between two bottles of pain relievers. She tried to remember which one she heard would destroy her liver and which would destroy her kidneys. She jumped when she felt a hand on her shoulder.

It was Molly Murphy, the town's florist. Her curly red hair was pinned back in a half-up-half-down style. "I heard about what happened," she said, looking pained. "I can't believe you found the body. Are you okay? I mean, the guy was hated, but I didn't realize he was *that* hated. Who do you think the killer is?" Molly was talking fast enough to make Esther's head spin.

How did she know all that? "I don't—I can't—" Esther put the bottles back on the shelf. "I have to go," she muttered before making a beeline to the door.

Had word already gotten out about Faris? Everyone knew everything about everyone in Oak's Rest, but did information always travel *this* fast?

Esther tried not to bump into any shoppers as she power-walked down the row of shops. She felt like all eyes were on her, which was surely ridiculous. Maybe it wouldn't hurt to slow down. Listen in on a few conversations. Confirm that no one was talking about her.

A woman fed the parking meter as she talked into her phone.

She explained she needed to hang up to save minutes for a call with her sister later.

Esther let out a breath. If people were still budgeting their cell phone minutes, they definitely weren't up to date on the latest breaking town news.

Esther slowed her pace. Jim White of J.W. Boating Supplies stood outside his store with a small group of other shop owners. He leaned on his cane, that and his uneven gait tells of a long-ago boating injury.

"It was one of my new ones too," Jim said. "I'd just polished her up."

"Sorry, Jimmy. I'm sure it'll turn up."

Jim didn't seem worried. "Happens every year. I budget for one M.I.A. canoe per calendar year. Ordinarily, it's the summer crowd tourists who *forget* to return a boat. I lucked out this season. Guess I was overdue."

"Esther!" called a woman's voice not far behind. "Yoohoo!"

Esther had nearly reached the crosswalk. She turned to see LouLou speed walking toward her.

Just her luck. Being accosted by Molly in the store hadn't been enough. No doubt LouLou wanted the inside scoop on what happened. She steeled herself.

"Listen, Lou," Esther said before LouLou could speak. "I've had the longest day of my life and I don't wanna talk about it. Can we let the police handle it, please?"

LouLou's lips parted in surprise. "Sweetie, I just wanted to let you know the Donnelly engagement party project fell through." She leaned in mischievously. "Turns out you *can* put a price on love. And six figures of student loan debt is too high. Anyway, I can get started on the yard sign for Makers and Merchants, if you'd like."

Esther felt a wave of regret for being rude. "That'd be great. Sugar Choo is going to hand paint the lettering, but some embroidery might really make the sign pop. Add a bit of texture."

LouLou nodded. "Sure, sure." She was waiting for Esther to elaborate on what was bothering her.

Esther didn't have the energy to fight it. "I'm sorry, LouLou. Bad day. I'm sure you've heard."

LouLou looked ready to burst. Clearly, she'd been waiting for the chance to talk about it. She swallowed Esther up in a hug. "Oh, honey, what a nightmare. I promised myself I'd wait at least forty-eight hours before calling you up. I do have some tact, you know." She released Esther from the embrace, but kept her hands on her upper arms.

Respecting privacy? Foregoing a good gossip session for "tact"? That was a first. Esther swallowed. "Wow. Thanks, LouLou. It's been—"

"So how did he seem when you saw him? Did the killer leave a note?" LouLou's eyes widened. "Do you think it was a crime of passion?"

There she was. "You know, I'm actually fighting a nasty headache. I'm gonna get out of here and take something for it."

LouLou looked disappointed as she let her hands slide off Esther's arms. "Alright. Well, come see me anytime." She lowered her voice. "I keep an emergency bottle of gin in my sewing kit." With a wink, she turned and tossed her pashmina over her shoulder, narrowly avoiding hitting Esther in the eye.

To make matters worse, Esther looked up and realized she was standing directly in front of Kai's spa. The memory of Kai crying came flooding back.

It was a Calliope day for Kai, so the shop was dark. The spa's logo was on the door, an intricate white outline of a pikake flower that read *Etana's Essence* in an elegant script font.

There had to be some way to help Kai pass the next inspection. It was the least she could do to repay Kai for contributing to the inn's local fame, not to mention having become a great friend.

Her head was still pounding. In all the chaos of the morning, she hadn't even stopped for her daily pick-me-up. The headache, lack of caffeine, and frayed nerves had her ready to curl up for a cat nap.

There was one tried-and-true remedy for a sour mood. And it was best served hot with a splash of cream and a spoonful of sugar.

# CHAPTER 9

The diner smelled like coffee and ketchup and toast all at once. The sizzle of butter hitting the hot griddle somewhere in the back was a lullaby.

Penny had cut through the order queue with Olympic agility, her bandana and pigtails a blur of red and black as she zipped from counter to tables and back again. She could run the place with her eyes closed and hands tied behind her back. Which was convenient, since Esther was coming dangerously close to jumping behind the counter and pouring her own coffee. Penny had insisted that was a one-time exception.

A family of three sat at the far end of the counter, high-wattage smiles ready for service. They wore matching Lake Ezra windbreakers, crisp, new, and coordinated with the diner's blue, beige, and brick red Victorian mosaic floor tiles, like they'd been styled for the front cover of *White Picket Fence Magazine.*

Penny wore her business-owner smile as she took her place behind the counter. A *No Wet Swimsuits* sign hung on the wall behind her. "Welcome! First time visiting town?" she asked, notepad at the ready.

The mother placed her hand on top of her son's head. "It is.

Our friends came here for their ten-year anniversary last summer. They couldn't stop talking about Oak's Rest. They swore they had the best coffee of their lives right here at Penny's Breakfast."

Penny glowed with pride. "Well, they have good taste. And staying married for ten years! What an accomplishment. My record is three."

The woman's smile faltered.

"Oh, not their wedding anniversary," the father corrected. "Ten years since surviving their IRS audit. It was choppy waters for a while there." He winked as if Penny were privy to the kind of tax gymnastics he was talking about.

This time, Penny's smile dimmed. She recovered quickly. "An inspiration to all of us. So, what can I get started for you?"

Without hesitation, the father said, "We'll take three Belgian waffles, one orange juice, and two coffees." He projected his voice like an announcer.

Penny pointed at the chalkboard menu above her head. "Sorry, breakfast stops at twelve. We don't all run on lake time around here."

The man looked up and squinted, as if noticing the expansive menu for the first time. He exchanged skeptical looks with the mother. "Oh...but..." he let out a small, humorless laugh. "You don't serve all-day breakfast? Isn't this place called 'Penny's Breakfast'?"

Penny's reply was automatic. "In name only. We don't—"

"—Like to limit ourselves." Esther didn't realize she'd spoken the words aloud until both Penny and the family turned their heads toward her. She stopped rubbing her temples. "Sorry, habit."

Penny put on a new smile. "Why don't I give you a few minutes? Pick something nice and filling after a morning on the water."

The father nodded glumly.

Esther heard her phone ding and extracted it from her purse.

*(1) Missed Call: Cameron Bennett*

Why did her sister keep calling? It didn't matter. She didn't have the energy for an awkward conversation after the morning she'd had. Cameron was a problem for another day.

"You look like you've been to the DMV, through an airport security line, and to the dentist for a root canal all in one day." Penny set a mug on the counter and poured steaming coffee into it.

Esther mustered up a mocking smile. "You really know how to make a girl feel beautiful." She rubbed her temples again.

Penny squatted, reached for something under the counter, then stood, producing a glorious white bottle. "My personal stash. Let me get you some water."

Esther was already reaching for the bottle. "Don't worry about it." She opened it, popped a capsule into her mouth and washed it down with a swig of coffee.

Penny's brows drew together like magnets. "Wasting a precious sip of coffee on an Aleve? Now I'm worried." She deposited the coffee pot back in its station. When she came back, she rested both elbows on the counter, casting an annoying, meaningful look from eye level.

Esther should have known. Of course Penny had already heard. The diner was like a train station. News traveled in every direction, but at some point, it all passed through. "I know you want to say something."

Penny scrunched her nose. "Don't get me wrong. Any death is a tragedy. But…if someone had to go…"

"Penny!" Esther set down her mug.

Penny leaned in closer. "You know I'm right. But seriously, if it was a—" she looked around, scanning for listening tourist ears. "—*murder*," she mouthed, "there could be a maniac running around Oak's Rest. How are we supposed to sleep at night?"

Esther rested her chin on her hand. Their elbows were just

shy of touching. "It's unsettling, for sure. When I gave Sabina and Nolan my statement, they tried to put up a professional front, but I could tell even they were spooked." She closed her eyes. "I wish this whole day never happened."

Without standing, Penny reached to lift the glass cover from the pastry display. She pulled a napkin from the dispenser and plucked out a blueberry muffin. "I'm sorry you had to see that. You okay?" She slid the muffin to Esther.

Esther rotated the napkin to view the muffin from all sides. It was a perfect golden brown. Penny baked in shallow tins so the muffin tops could spill over the edges, puffing up like tasty clouds. She knew her customers. "I'll be okay. I just can't believe it. You've lived in Oak's Rest forever. When was the last time something like this happened?"

Penny whistled softly. "I mean, we've had a few boating accidents over the years. But a serial killer running around? That's a new one."

Esther took a bite of the muffin. It was pillow-soft inside and had the faintest hint of lemon. It was the tiniest detail, but it added a certain sophistication to the flavor. "Please don't say that. They're not even sure there is a murderer, let alone a serial killer."

"I don't know," Penny said. "Faris must have crossed someone one too many times. Nine times out of ten, it's someone the victim knows." Her voice had a theatrical quality that suggested she'd practiced it plenty of times.

"You need to stop watching so many crime shows."

Penny scoffed. "You need to be watching *more* crime shows."

"Why? To resign myself to sleeping with a night light for the rest of my life?"

"It can't hurt to know what tactics bad guys are using these days. Besides, you can't tell me you've never fantasized about helping bring the swift hammer of justice down on people's heads. I used to pretend I was Judge Janice. Watching detectives track down criminals is fun too. You know, I could totally see you on one of those shows, chasing clues."

"Ha! Unlikely." Solving crimes wasn't something Esther could imagine listed on her resume. She *did* pride herself on being able to learn new skills, thanks to having held almost every job in hospitality, but she wouldn't encourage Penny by bringing that up now.

As a cleaner at Calliope Inn, she'd learned how to remove red wine from a rug with nothing but salt, club soda, and a hair dryer. At twenty-three, as an innkeeper, her record was getting a bed stripped and remade with military efficiency in under two minutes.

But solving murder cases? That didn't exactly correlate to her area of expertise.

Penny shrugged. "You're basically already on the Faris case. Plus, you'd look so cute going undercover in one of those old Hollywood headscarves. Oh, and you'll need gloves. And cat-eye sunglasses."

Esther tried not to spill her coffee. She couldn't tell if the woman was serious. "Woah. When did we go from talking about TV shows to a very real, very none-of-my-business case?"

Penny grew more animated. "I was kidding at first. But you *are* a great judge of character. You solve problems all day long. You could be an asset to Sabina and her folks."

"Naturally," Esther deadpanned. "Because my experience as an inn manager has *totally* prepared me to do police work better than the police themselves."

Penny ignored her skepticism. "I once witnessed a guest hug you at the end of a conversation that began with you telling them their room had been double-booked. At full capacity. You can get people to trust you. All the best undercover detectives do."

Esther was proud of that moment. A little finessing involving creative use of a family double-suite, a bonus spa treatment, and reallocating some of that month's budget to pay

Bunny to cook a private dinner had more than smoothed every-thing over.

Penny squeezed Esther's hand. "You make things happen. You're stubborn. You've got grit."

It was nice to hear those words. "Some people might use the word *determined* rather than stubborn, but thank you. I don't think I'll be fighting crime any time soon, but that means a lot coming from you."

Penny had been the first person Esther met when she showed up in Oak's Rest. At twenty-one, with one year of college left, Esther could no longer pretend to care about the things her parents wanted for her. So she dropped out.

She could still remember the look on her mother's face. First, a flicker of disbelief, hardening into anger, and finally, landing on a hollow, inevitable disappointment. They were all there. All the hopes her mother had dreamed up on Esther's behalf washed away in one sentence. The ivy-covered campus walks, the moments at dinner parties where she could make off-handed mentions of her first-born's attendance at some fancy graduate school. All gone.

It had led to the blow-up fight of the century, ending with Esther behind the wheel of her BMW, her suitcase in the passenger seat beside her.

She'd made it forty-five minutes down the highway when she pulled off for gas and some food in an unassuming town right on Lake Ezra. Oak's Rest? She figured if she'd never heard of the place, less than an hour from where she grew up, it must have been nothing special.

Esther stumbled into Penny's Breakfast, grabbed a menu, and took the first seat at the counter. She couldn't even read that day's specials through the tears welling up in her eyes, the reality of her predicament settling in. She was on her own.

Penny had appeared from nowhere. She placed a mug of steaming coffee on the counter. She hadn't asked any questions, hadn't told her to take her crying elsewhere. She'd simply said, "Refills are on me today."

Esther might have arrived in town by herself, but since that day, there hadn't been a moment she'd felt alone in Oak's Rest.

She finished the blueberry muffin and downed the rest of her coffee. "I better get back to the inn. We have a few check-ins this afternoon, and I want to make sure we have enough goodies stocked for turn-downs." She swung her feet over the barstool and stood.

"Hey," Penny said. "I'm waiting on a festival headcount. Need to know what ungodly hour I'll have to start brewing coffee that morning."

Esther considered her answer as she gathered her things. Between the vendors, townsfolk, plus as many tourists as they could attract to the event, she expected eighty to a hundred festival goers. Not all visitors would be coffee drinkers, but Esther always erred on the side of over-preparation. "I'd say one-fifty to two hundred cups' worth."

Penny nodded. "Alright. That's yours covered. And for everyone else?"

# CHAPTER 10

T he following week, Esther sat at the reception desk computer with her fingers hovering over the keyboard.

"Add a smiley face."

Esther swatted Justice's hand from the mouse. "I'm not adding a smiley face. We want to look professional."

The days since her discovery of Faris's body had passed in a blur. With an inn to manage and a festival to plan, it hadn't been too much of a challenge to keep herself occupied.

Justice went back to stroking Sesame, who'd made a comfortable home in the concierge's lap. "Don't you want people to know there's a human on the other side of the keyboard? Not some auto-reply robot?"

She didn't sound robotic. Did she? "I do not sound like a robot," Esther said. "I sound...polished." Yes, that was more accurate.

Justice sighed. "Fine. Read it back to me."

Esther cleared her throat. "Thank you very much for your five-star review, Linda. We are so pleased you enjoyed your stay. We'll give your compliments to our chef regarding the cream puffs." It was flawless. Professional but friendly. Take that, Justice. "See?"

Justice snorted. "Real polished. Shiny, even. Like a person made of stainless steel who says, 'Beep, boop, bop.'"

"Alright," Esther said, pressing the reply button. "This robot is officially not taking any more commands."

Justice reached for the mouse and clicked through the images the guest had uploaded. "The positive review is nice and everything, but she didn't do us any favors with these photos. We're already going to be up against the whole someone-got-murdered-in-our-town thing once news gets out. Can we afford for our rooms to look this creepy?"

Esther enlarged the first image, a photo of the Midnight Pine Room. The room was backlit so harshly by the window the forest-green walls and dark wood furniture looked more haunting than atmospheric.

She clicked to the next one, a motion-blurred image of what could barely be identified as the garden. "These are rough."

"Want me to upload new pics to bury them? I could steal some books from the living room. I'd stack them all cute on a bedside table and let Golden Hour do its thing."

"That could work," Esther said, thinking it over. "The Apple Blossom Suite recently got a fresh coat of mauve paint. Maybe some books with red spines? Or gold lettering?"

"I can already see it," Justice said, looking toward the ceiling.

Esther glanced at the photos again. Some extra proactivity couldn't hurt. "We should add a review incentive to our check-out thank you cards. Maybe anyone who leaves a photo review enters to win a giveaway of a Calliope Inn robe. We could have LouLou stitch their names on the back or the sleeve." She wouldn't mind one of those herself.

Justice tapped a finger to her temple. "That's why you're the head honcho."

A teenage girl approached the desk, two weary-looking parents trailing a few paces behind. The girl held up her phone like it had the plague. "I can't even use this. The Wi-Fi won't work."

Esther smiled. "That's an easy fix! Did you get the welcome email with the pass—" she made eye contact with the parents, both of whom were silently and vigorously shaking their heads behind their daughter's back. The mother gestured the 'cut' sign at her neck.

Esther blinked and turned her attention back to the teen. If she had to pick sides, she'd choose the paying customers who'd be spreading the word about the inn to their friends and coworkers. "You know what? The Wi-Fi is out today. I'm so sorry. We're working hard on it." She glanced back at the parents, who signaled their relief with thumbs up.

"But you're on the computer right now," the girl challenged, pointing to the desktop.

She had her there. Esther scrambled for a believable response.

"Landline," Justice said. "Hard wired into the modem by the ethernet cable. Only gets bars when the cell towers can cross-triangulate."

Esther tried not to let her face betray how impressed she was. But would the girl buy it? Silence stretched as her eyes ping-ponged between Justice, the girl, and her parents. Everyone seemed to hold their breath.

With a scoff, the teen walked away.

Her mother hurried over. "Thank you!" she whispered. "Maybe we'll actually get to enjoy our vacation without her friends joining every activity over the phone." She practically skipped away to catch up with her family.

"You're like a reverse tech expert."

Justice scooped Sesame off her lap and put her on the ground. "I bet her mom is going to leave a smiley face in her review." She stood and dusted off her shirt. "Now, if you'll excuse me, I'm gonna go see if Bunny's cream puffs need any quality control."

"As manager, I should sample some too," Esther said, turning back to the computer. She responded to a few more reviews before checking her email. She scanned the subject lines, breezing past invoices and vendor updates for anything time-sensitive.

An email from molly@busybeesfloral.com had the subject line:

*OK IF FESTIVAL DISPLAY ATTRACTS SQUIRRELS?*

Esther would respond to that later. Her cursor landed on an unfamiliar sender. Someone named Reese Williams had forwarded her an email with no subject. Willing it not to be malware, she clicked on the message.

Her stomach sank as a headshot of Faris Holliday filled the window. Esther skimmed over the words *RSVP* and *Celebration of Life* before jumping at a hand on her back. She looked up to see Kai. "You almost gave me a heart attack."

"Have you checked your email?"

Esther rolled back in her chair to let Kai see her screen. "Did you get this too?"

Kai tapped the screen. "Yup. According to his email signature, Reese is a director at the health department. I'm guessing he was Faris's boss. Check it out. He accidentally included the conversation history."

Esther scrolled down to the forwarded bit of conversation. A curt, *Can you help me get this out to my husband's client list?* was the only exchange between an Uma Holliday and this Reese person. Esther felt her eyes bulge. "Faris was married?"

"There really is someone out there for everyone," Kai said, looking like she'd seen a ghost.

Esther re-read the email. "Reese didn't even bother to add any context to the forward. He must have pasted the Calliope staff server list in and pressed send." She leaned in closer to read the event details. "And the celebration is tomorrow evening. He seems like a real sentimental guy."

"I guess that's the short notice you get when you're not family or friends. We're C-list guests," Kai said.

"Have you *seen* this?" a voice scream-whispered behind them, startling both Esther and Kai. Bunny was holding up her phone.

"We've got to work on our entrances," Esther said, placing a hand on her chest.

Bunny pointed to the phone. "The guy had so few friends his wife had to invite his clients? And the day before? That's kind of sad, is it not?"

Esther rolled out of the way as Kai positioned herself in front of the computer.

She used the mouse to scroll back to the event details. "Oh no."

"What?" Esther asked, suddenly nervous.

"It's in Yalfont. Faris is from Yalfont."

Bunny lamented, "Being invited to celebrate the life of a guy we barely know and who actively made our lives harder is one thing. Having to do it in snobby Yalfont is adding insult to injury."

"Alright, let's not be dramatic," Esther insisted, feeling the lie forming in her throat. "Is Yalfont the most neighborly place to visit? No. But—"

"They call us *Broke* Rest," Kai said, folding her arms.

"Remember the summer they held that 'Cocktails on the Lake' event?" Bunny asked. "They literally put out buoy dividers and a flag that said, *Yalfont Residents Only*. Like they owned that section of the lake!" She flapped her arms. "I'm still trying to figure out how they got those crystal pitchers to float upright on the water." She looked lost in thought.

Justice breezed around the front of the desk and set down a plate of cream puffs. Esther's hand was reaching for one before she knew it. Smart hand.

Bunny lifted the edge of the plate. "Are those my cream puffs?"

Justice ignored the question and leaned in conspiratorially. "Get this. Apparently, Faris died of something called botched-ism toxin overdose."

"*What*-toxin?" Esther asked, examining the pastry. The least she could do was admire Bunny's artistry before tearing into it. The top was dipped in shiny chocolate and dusted with fine powdered sugar. She took a bite. The sweet cream was as cool and fluffy as fresh sheets at the end of a long day.

"Botched-ism," Justice repeated. "I think." She seemed to be losing interest in favor of her cream puff.

Kai joined her around the front of the desk. "Do you mean *botulism* toxin? As in, Botox?"

"Yes!" Justice snapped her fingers. "That's it. Oh, and they're putting the time of death around ten-thirty that night."

"Wait. Hold on," Esther said through a mouthful. She held up her hand. "Slow down. Where did you hear this?"

Justice pointed toward the dining room. "They're talking about it in the kitchen. Someone has a second cousin who's best friends with someone who works in the medical examiner's office over in Yalfont."

Esther was having trouble processing. The kitchen staff was more in-the-know than she was?

"What kitchen?" Bunny asked. "My kitchen? The one I just came from and work in all day long?"

Justice gave an "mhmm," as she took another bite.

Bunny put her hands on her hips, the charms on the back of her phone case dangling. "Great. I'm so glad my staff is on their phones the minute I leave the room. I'll have to talk to them later."

"Well, you lead by such great example," Kai joked, pointing to the device in Bunny's own hand.

"Hang on," Esther said, swallowing the last of the distracting pastry. She needed to get the facts straight. "I'm having a hard time believing Faris died from too much Botox. I mean, the guy didn't exactly seem like the nip and tuck type. Also, Sabina seemed to suspect foul play. Where does Botox come into the equation? It doesn't make sense."

"Anything could be lethal in great enough quantities," Kai contended. "Botox is a serious substance, despite the fact that we use it all the time."

"So, what?" Bunny began. "Oak's Rest has a cosmetics-obsessed Barbie doll killer running around?"

Kai lifted an eyebrow. "Yes, please continue to reduce my profession to a steaming pile of stereotypes." She paused for a moment before adding, "But they *would* be the most beautiful killer in history."

Bunny grabbed a cream puff from Justice's plate and extended it to Kai as a peace offering.

"Hey! I was going to eat that," Justice mumbled through an already full mouth.

"I made 'em," Bunny retorted.

"Everyone, focus," Esther said, hoping to get them back on track. "Here's my question: are we going to this thing?" She pointed to the computer screen where Faris's headshot stared back at her, his eyes tracking no matter which direction she moved.

"I don't know," Bunny said. "Would it be weird if we did? Are we going to have to console his sobbing wife?"

"Wouldn't it be rude for us *not* to go after being invited?" Esther asked no one in particular. "Nobody deserves to die horribly. Even if we didn't like them."

They fell silent.

Kai pointed at Esther. "You're the boss. You make the call."

Esther rolled her eyes. "You're playing the boss card on me?"

Kai shrugged, standing her ground.

Esther noticed two couples make a quick exchange as they passed each other at the lobby entrance. One woman pointed at the front desk like she was giving directions. The other smiled appreciatively. "Okay, then. What would a boss say about three of her employees standing around gossiping during business hours?"

Kai grabbed the plate of desserts. "We'll let you think about that," she said before turning away.

Esther took a final look at the email invitation, still open on the computer. In theory, she did have a lot to consider. Was it their place to go? Would Faris have wanted them there?

In reality, though, she already knew the decision she'd make. But that didn't mean she was excited about it.

# CHAPTER 11

"You're sure this is it?" Bunny asked.

Esther shielded her phone from the sun as she checked the address one more time. "Yup, this is it."

"Faris Holliday was a lot of things, but I would not have expected *rich* to be one of them," Justice said.

Kai let out a low whistle. "Welcome to Yalfont, ladies."

Esther was at a loss for words. They stood at the edge of the manicured lawn, separated from the house by a circular driveway. A row of trimmed trees shielded the ground floor windows like knights earning their keep.

The neoclassical brick home had creamy white trim and columns on either side of the front door. Hedges demarcated the edge of the impressive property.

Esther tugged at her blazer. Underneath, she was wearing a floral wrap dress with pointed faux-leather loafers. She'd been unsure what to wear, but felt relieved when she saw another woman file into the home wearing a similar outfit. "Everyone ready?"

"Not really," Justice said as she began walking.

The interior of the home was equally polished. Simple wainscot ceiling panels drew the eyes upward, above the grand staircase, with their clean, deliberate lines. An orchestra played almost imperceptibly from a speaker somewhere out of sight.

A circular table greeted them in the foyer, displaying a photograph of Faris and a much shorter woman, presumably his widow, smiling at the camera. Faris was resting a hand on her shoulder. He looked...happy. Esther didn't think she'd ever seen him smile. He did look at least a decade younger in the photo, so maybe he hadn't smiled in as long.

"Do you think it was a hostage situation?" Justice asked. "Or a work visa that was about to expire?"

Bunny and Kai chimed in with their own theories.

"Let's try to be respectful," Esther said, despite the many questions she also had. She lowered her voice. "His wife could be anywhere."

The group straightened and kept walking. It was a light turnout. A handful of guests milled about, glasses of sparkling pale yellow liquid in hand, talking in hushed tones in pairs or small groups.

The house opened into a large living room, designed with muted tones and tailored furniture. It was the kind of understated elegance that whispered rather than shouted its value, but no doubt wanted people to be aware of it.

Against the wall, a white-draped table displayed framed photos and mementos Esther didn't have the chance to examine.

"Let's find the kitchen," Bunny suggested. "People always hang out in the kitchen."

"Do we *want* to join the crowd?" Esther asked. She already felt uneasy about being there. Was hiding away in a quiet corner the worst thing?

"No, but I want to see what kind of spread they have."

Bunny had been right. Four clusters of guests were gathered in the kitchen, sipping and nibbling and chatting. The kitchen was about twice the size of Calliope Inn's. Opened double doors led to a covered patio which very few guests were taking advantage of.

On the kitchen island, looped handle tasting spoons and shiny metal trays presented delicate appetizers. A bite of cherry tomatoes, mozzarella, and basil garnish looked tempting, but Esther wasn't in the mood to eat.

Bunny clasped her hands together. "I'm gonna go inspect. Anybody want anything?"

"Surprise me," Justice and Kai said in unison.

Bunny smiled and walked off.

"I think that's her," Kai said, tilting her chin upward.

Esther followed Kai's gaze to a corner of the kitchen where an older woman was whispering to a petite woman with long brown hair and patting her shoulder. It was the woman from the entryway photograph. "That must be Faris's wife. Widow," she corrected herself.

"What's her name again? Emma?" Kai asked.

"Uma," Esther reminded her, not taking her eyes off the small woman, who dabbed at the corner of her eye with a handkerchief.

Justice leaned in. "*Uma* is fake crying."

"What makes you say that?"

"I can tell. She's doing the Sniffle Down."

Kai snorted. "And what, exactly, is the Sniffle Down?"

Justice shifted, like she was about to divulge classified information. "When you can't get any actual tears to come, you sniffle a little—enough to suggest your nose is running, but not enough to gross anyone out—and look down, so no one can see how dry your eyes are. I used it to get out of a speeding ticket a week ago. Works maybe half the time."

"And you think Uma is doing the Sniffle Down right now," Esther deadpanned. When Justice wasn't looking, though, she glanced back at the woman. Even from a distance, her face seemed dry. And her eyes weren't red.

Justice pointed at herself. "I invented the Sniffle Down. I know it when I see it."

Bunny appeared, juggling a handful of small plates and glasses. She indicated for the women to help themselves.

"I don't know how you do that," Esther said as she reached for a glass balanced precariously in the crook of Bunny's elbow. "But thank you." She took a sip of the champagne, crisp and dry. Hopefully, it would settle her unease.

An expensively dressed man with a sharp, black goatee walked into the kitchen.

"Oh my gosh," Bunny said. "He looks like that actor from *New York Undercover*."

"You're so right!" Kai said.

Someone outside the kitchen said, "Hi Reese, good to see you."

The man smiled but didn't stop to talk. He looked determined as he strode across the kitchen, like he was on a mission.

Esther waited until he was a safe distance away to speak. "That must be Faris's boss, Reese Williams." Reese must have had a previous career in fashion, because he was wearing more shiny accessories than Esther. A little flashy for the circumstances. Then again, it was Yalfont.

Reese walked straight over to Uma, who was now standing alone, and gave her a hug. The hug was more clinical than heartfelt, like the hug someone would give their long-time accountant for fixing an error that saved them enough cash to go on vacation with.

"Should we talk to Uma too?" Justice asked. "Aren't we supposed to offer our condolences or something? Thank her for inviting us?"

Esther considered it. "Maybe we wait until people finish rushing her. This can't be easy."

"The invitation said there'd be a slideshow after refreshments," Kai said. "Maybe we can lay low in the living room until then."

Once there, Esther got a closer look at the table display. A miniature easel propped up the same headshot of Faris from the email invitation. In front of a small tray holding lined cardstock squares was a sign that read *Share a memory*.

Within seconds, Justice had picked up a pen and started writing on a card.

"Uh, Justice?" Esther asked.

Justice, apparently deep in thought, muttered, "Yeah?"

"What...are you writing? I didn't know you and Faris were close."

Justice didn't look up. "Remember the time I dropped my nametag trying to pin it to my shirt with fake nails? And then Faris picked it up for me?"

"Yes," Esther said, unsure of where the story was going. "Like three years ago?"

Kai added, "Wow. Faris doing a kind deed. Nice to think about."

Justice was still writing. "He told me to be more careful because if the vacuum had picked it up, it could have launched it across the lobby like a projectile."

That sounded more like him. "True. But is that memory card-worthy?"

"They're a little light in the memory department, so this will have to do."

Esther looked at the table. Justice was right. There was only one other filled out card, written in such chicken scratch it wasn't even legible. She didn't think about her own mortality very often, but she couldn't help but hope the end of her life required more cardstock.

Bunny picked up and was inspecting a wrought-iron candle holder shaped like the letter F. "Ooh, pretty. And lighter than it looks," she said, absentmindedly turning it over in her hands, then bouncing it up and down in the air. "We need to get these for the inn."

Kai brightened like a light bulb had turned on in her head. "We could get the letter C! For Calliope." She looked to Esther.

"I'll take that under consideration," Esther said. "But I don't think we should be touching—"

"Hello," a voice squeaked from behind them, nearly startling Bunny into dropping the candle holder.

Bunny set it back on the table and patted it twice. "I was just —we were—beautiful," she stuttered, pointing to the item.

Uma Holliday nodded without smiling.

"Thank you so much for inviting us," Esther said. "We work at the Calliope Inn in Oak's Rest. Faris always made sure we held ourselves to a high standard. So sorry for your loss."

Uma nodded again. Her mouth formed the words *thank you*, but no sound came out. She dabbed at her nose with the noticeably dry handkerchief.

Justice kicked Esther's leg. Esther took a step away.

"You have a beautiful house," Kai tried. As soon as she said the words, a woman approached Uma from behind, spun her around into a forceful hug, and whisked her away.

Esther blinked.

No one spoke for a few seconds.

"*That* wasn't awkward at all," Bunny said, breaking the silence.

"Definitely weird," Esther agreed. Had Uma come over just to get them to stop touching her decor? Or had she wanted to talk?

"She's reserved," Kai said. "But Mrs. Holliday was rocking that red lip."

"I was thinking the same thing," Justice said. "Brick red, but with an edge. I wonder if we're allowed upstairs. I need to know the shade."

"Oh my gosh, Kai!" A young woman appeared and gave Kai a double cheek kiss. She must have been in her early to mid twenties, and was wearing a long-sleeve backless dress that toed the line between daring and slinky. Either way, it looked amazing on her.

"Onyx! What are you doing here? You know Faris?" Kai asked.

"Health department, babe."

Kai slapped her forehead. "Duh. I totally forgot you work there." She turned toward the group. "This is Onyx Opal. She's one of the troublemakers that showed up on my doorstep when Stacey from the Face Bar over here in Yalfont went out on maternity leave."

"You're the only other person within a fifty-mile radius I'd even let near my face," Onyx said. "Speaking of, can you squeeze me in this week?"

"Of course."

Onyx turned her attention to Esther. She waved her hand once in a circular motion. "See, *this* is how I'm gonna dress when I get my skin clear and my credit score up. Sophisticated but fun. I love it."

Esther liked her already. "I'm glad you said that. It took me thirty minutes to decide what to wear."

Onyx widened her eyes in agreement. "To be honest, I wouldn't have come, but I thought it'd be weird to be the only one from the department not to show my face."

She didn't strike Esther as someone who was overly concerned with following the rules. She had the easy confidence of someone who'd been told they were beautiful and talented their whole lives, like their presence was more of a gift than a requirement. "Did you work with Faris? Are a lot of your coworkers here?"

"Nope," Onyx said, shaking her head. "Different teams, different floors. I'm a proctor for certification exams."

"That sounds like a rewarding job," Esther said.

Onyx looked confused. "How so?"

"Well, you must be working with people when they're at a crossroads. Getting certified with new skills, maybe a new job, new salary. Could be life changing." Esther imagined people finishing their exams with tears in their eyes, proud and hopeful about the next parts of their professional journeys.

"Never thought of it that way," Onyx said. "You're like a philosopher."

Esther laughed. "I like hearing stories about people forging paths on their own terms. It makes me feel like we're never stuck in life."

Onyx momentarily looked away like she was letting Esther's words sink in. "You know who's not stuck? Anyone from my team. Looks like I'm the only one who showed up after all." She looked around and pursed her lips. "It's kinda stuffy in here. Should we go outside?"

"Sounds good to me," Esther said, adjusting to the abrupt change in topic.

They turned back toward the kitchen when Esther saw a flash of light by the front door. She looked in time to see Reese leave and shut the door behind him. *Ducking out early? I take it Faris and his boss weren't close, then.*

Onyx exchanged her empty champagne glass for a new one as she led the way through the kitchen.

Justice, following right behind Onyx, spun to face Esther. *I like her,* she mouthed.

The outdoor seating area was paved with large stone groundwork. As the women took seats around a glass table, Onyx waved at someone across the backyard. Esther turned to see Ingram Ellis talking with two other men at the side of the house.

"He helped inspect the inn," Esther said. "He seemed nice. Much more laid back than Faris."

Onyx sipped. "Ingram's cool. And having to be within five feet of Faris all day? He deserves a raise more than any of us."

"Meow," Justice said, eyeing Ingram the way Sesame eyed catnip treats.

"Try to keep it together," Esther warned. It was not the time for Justice's antics. "Remember, we're here because a man died."

Justice raised both hands innocently. "I was admiring his tattoo. And his arms. They look...strong."

"Oh boy," Bunny said, taking a swig of champagne.

Onyx looked at Esther, confused.

"Our sweet Justice here thinks Ingram is handsome."

"Ew," Justice said, making a face. "That's how my mother would describe me having a crush."

Esther rolled her eyes and looked back at Ingram. She studied the tattoo of a roaring lion on his upper arm. "Do guys think tattoos like that make them seem tough?"

"No," Kai said. "They think wearing nothing but a short-sleeved polo in cold weather makes them look tough."

"I can hear my mother's voice now," Bunny said. "She'd be scolding him for tempting pneumonia and chasing him around with a jacket like she was trying to trap a spider under a cup."

Onyx glanced around like she was making sure no one was nearby. "Ingram was the last person seen with Faris before...you know."

That caught Esther's attention. "Do you know anything about what happened that night?"

"Not much. Just that the night Faris died, he and Ingram had been at a pub called The Speckled Stein in Oak's Rest."

"We love that place!" Justice said.

"That's our local watering hole," Bunny explained. "Anyway, he's a suspect?" she asked, leaning forward.

"Okay, Detective Bunny, let's not get ahead of ourselves," Esther said, trying to plug the curiosity springing up inside her.

Onyx shook her head. "He's been cleared by the police already. But it's got to weigh on him. I mean, what would have happened if he'd stayed with Faris a little longer? Maybe things would have turned out differently."

A few beats passed as everyone seemed to consider what she'd said.

Onyx picked up her phone and pointed it at the food and drinks on the table, the way people do when they took brunch photos for social media. "What?" she asked, looking up, realizing everyone was looking at her. "I could always use more B-roll for my YouTube videos. People like to see what I get up to in a week. Don't worry, I won't put anything death-y in there. Only cute drinks."

"What about the wife?" Bunny asked, shifting the conversation again. "Have you ever heard her speak at a discernible volume?"

Onyx raised an eyebrow. "If you ask me, she's who the police should be looking at. She's been fake crying her way through every conversation."

"That's what I've been saying!" Justice chimed in.

Ingram and his small group, along with a few attendees who'd been scattered around the yard, started making their way to the kitchen.

"Looks like the slideshow is about to start," Esther said. "Should we head in?"

The five women rose from their seats. Onyx downed the last of her champagne in a single swallow.

"Easy," Kai cautioned. "If you finish your drink now, what will you do with your hands while we stand around with a house full of people we don't know?"

"Please," Onyx said, tossing her hair over her shoulder. "Like I'm not getting another."

She *was* a troublemaker.

# CHAPTER 12

The next day, Esther's mouth watered as Bunny lowered a vegetable galette onto the dining room table. It was a glazed, bubbling masterpiece of caramelized onion and parmesan cheese.

Kai's stomach audibly growled. "I might have had a bit too much champagne at the celebration of life yesterday. This should revive me."

A kitchen staff member stepped out from behind Bunny and placed arugula salads with pomegranate on the table.

"Let's hope my meticulously crafted dish doubles as hangover food," Bunny said. "My mistakes have got to go somewhere. Better in your bellies than the trash."

Kai had already taken a bite of her galette. "If you call this a mistake, you'd be horrified to see the things I whip up for myself at home."

Bunny pointed at Kai's plate. "You don't want me to slice that up for you?"

Kai's words were less distinguishable this time, but a firm shake of her head as she took another bite conveyed she was perfectly happy.

Esther laughed as she admired her own. "What could be wrong with these? They look perfect." And they smelled even better.

Bunny pointed at Esther's plate. "Not enough thyme."

"And hers?" Esther asked, pointing to Kai's. Bunny was the most talented chef in the world. Being a perfectionist meant she noticed imperfections no one else ever would. She couldn't argue with Bunny's process, though, because her skills had earned her a reputation as culinary royalty throughout the region.

Bunny looked at Kai's galette. "I added the parmesan on top after I'd already assembled the galette. I should have tossed the roasted veggies with the parm from the start for a more even salt distribution." She looked wistful. "You live and you learn."

Esther couldn't imagine cooking with that level of consideration. "But you haven't even tasted these. How do you know there's something wrong with them?"

"Once something is baked, I can smell where I'm lacking or have overdone it with an ingredient. When I open the oven door, the steam rushes out right along with all the scents built up inside. Plus," she added, placing a hand on her hip, "That's what I have you guys for. Eat up. Tell me what it needs before I give it to guests. No pressure, but they'll either tell everyone they know to visit Calliope Inn or stay far, far away."

"It needs nothing," said Kai. "It tastes like my wildest dreams come true."

Esther laughed. As she was about to tell Bunny she'd prefer to eat without her watching her every bite, Justice crossed the threshold from the lobby into the dining room holding her phone. She looked out of breath.

"Everything okay?" Esther asked. "Did you join the guests on their hike?"

Justice loosed a breath. "Other than knowing you're sampling goodies without me, I'm fine. I'm very good at my job. When I want to be."

Esther extended a fork as an offering.

Justice waved it away. "I try not to eat anything I could get addicted to before noon. No, I caught a photo of our feathered friend out the window just now."

It took Esther a moment to realize who Justice was talking about. She felt her eyes bugle. "No! The cardinal from the parking lot? Let me see."

Justice handed over the phone. There was no mistaking him. Candy apple red with a shock of feathers on his head that resembled a tophat. He looked like trouble. "He's headed toward the parking lot, isn't he? Email me that," she said, handing the phone back to Justice. "I'm tempted to make a 'Wanted' sign."

"You know what the real crime at this inn is?" Justice asked. "Having to work in the depths of darkness."

"Lights go out in the basement office again?" Esther guessed.

"Did it ever," Justice said. "I was about to squeeze the lash curler. I could have lost my eyesight!"

Esther liked to stay accessible to guests and staff, so she spent most of her days on the first floor of the inn. If she needed a quiet space to focus or take calls from, she'd work from her makeshift office in the basement. It was essentially a storage room with a desk, chair, computer, and yes, pathetic lighting. She plugged in the space heater from time to time when it got chilly.

"Maybe this time you'll believe me when I say we can't plug the heater and the table lamp in at the same time. Mort said the electrical panel is full as it is." Esther took her first bite of galette, punctuating her final verdict.

It was wondrous. Crumbs fell to the plate as she bit into the flakey, buttery crust. The sweet caramelized onion balanced the tender, almost smokey vegetable medley. The parmesan cheese topped it off with a saltiness Esther never wanted to end. She gave Bunny a head nod as she patted the corners of her mouth with a napkin.

Justice crossed her arms. "But the overhead lighting makes me look like a ghost."

"You could always try doing your makeup at home," Bunny teased. "Or going a day without it."

"My makeup is my armor," Justice said. "But fine. I'll stop battling the circuit breaker if Esther agrees to at least fix the office door handle."

She wasn't wrong for asking. The thing threatened to fall off when someone so much as looked at it too hard. Esther was about to concede when she saw movement in the lobby.

Bunny was the first to offer a greeting. "Hey, Detective," she called out with a wave.

Sabina stood stiffly, hands planted on the reception desk, ignoring Sesame's swishing tail thumping against her arm. She was dressed more formally than usual in a solid navy pantsuit. The gold of her badge, clipped to her pocket, caught the sunlight from the windows and sent a beam of light bouncing off the lobby wall.

"Hello to you too, Bunny" Bunny muttered after getting no response. "What's up with Sesame? She has *don't mess with me* tail going."

Esther wasn't sure, but she was going to find out. "Hey, Sabina," Esther said, walking out to the lobby, the other women behind her. What's with the get-up? It's almost like you're a detective or something." She ran a reassuring hand along Sesame's humpback.

Sesame hopped down and headed off, like she'd done a full day's work luring Esther to the desk and was ready for a nap. Strange little kitty.

Sabina didn't smile. "Ladies," she said through tight lips. "I was hoping to speak with Miss Etana alone."

Kai let out a laugh. "*Miss Etana?*" She waved her arms like windshield wipers. "Hello? Where has Sabina gone and what have you done with her?"

Bunny and Justice laughed, but Esther felt a prickle of concern as she studied the detective's face. Sabina didn't seem to be in a joking mood.

She shifted on her feet. "What's up, Sabina? What's going on?"

Sabina looked at Kai like she was giving her one last chance to go somewhere more private.

Kai shrugged. "What is it?"

Sabina looked around, making brief eye contact with each of the women before reaching inside her jacket. She pulled out a pair of latex gloves. What did she need those for?

She donned the gloves, reached into the other side of her jacket, and produced a small brown paper bag. It had a strip of red tape across the top with the word *EVIDENCE* printed on it.

Everyone went silent. Esther's heart rate kicked up a notch. An evidence bag was never a harbinger of good news, was it?

Sabina unfolded the bag and reached inside.

Esther's mind worked at lightning speed trying to guess what she'd pull out. The world's tiniest gun? A bloody handkerchief?

When Sabina did pull the item out, it took Esther a moment to adjust her eyes.

"A needle?" Bunny asked.

Justice cringed and took a step back. "I don't do well with needles. Or blood. Or talking about needles. Or blood."

"Sabina, what is that? Why are you showing us a needle?" Esther asked.

Sabina rotated the needle so that the detailing on the opposite side was visible. The outline of a small pikake flower was printed at the top right below the plunge.

Esther's mouth went dry as she placed the flower.

"That's my logo," Kai whispered, her eyes fixated on the needle. She looked up at Sabina. "How did you get one of my needles? I don't even keep any here at the inn. Have you been to my spa?"

Esther looked from Kai to Sabina and back again, unsure who to focus on.

She could tell Sabina was growing uncomfortable herself, a crack in her professional facade revealing the slightest bit of something softer. Empathy? Sadness? She lowered her chin, fixed a stern expression on her face, and looked resolutely at Kai.

"Our comprehensive sweep of a recent crime scene turned up this needle, owned by your place of business. We believe the syringe contains traces of what was a lethal dose of Botox. Can you explain how it ended up at the location of Faris Holliday's death?"

# CHAPTER 13

"Your creations are coming along beautifully, everyone. Let your inner artist soar." Sugar Choo taught from the front of the Calliope Room, set up as a workshop room with long folding tables, waving her arms like a conductor.

Sugar had led art workshops at the inn for years, but this was the first all-adult squash decorating session. Still, the room could have been mistaken for a second-grade art class, the tables covered in glue, paint, scrapbook paper, buttons, and pipe cleaners.

Esther sat alone at the back of the room. She'd intended to participate in the class with her manager hat on. If she could pinpoint which aspects of the activity appealed to adult guests, she could feature them in their marketing, iterating on the fun in new and creative ways. Plus, maybe she could reuse the finished squashes for decoration at Makers and Merchants.

Of course, she'd laid those plans before Sabina had stopped by that morning and upended her day. In the hours since Kai and Sabina left for the spa, Esther had checked her phone no less than fifty times. No calls or texts. She felt queasy.

A guest raised his hand. He was an attorney for a big firm in the city, a fact he hadn't missed an opportunity to slip into conversation. He'd kept using that exact phrase—*big firm in the city*—as if posing as a lawyer was a cover for being an agent from some top secret organization. He wore cargo pants and flip-flops, hunched over his squash like a scientist titrating in the lab.

Esther used scrap paper to jot down a note to her future self:

*Purchase art stands for adult classes. Or strike partnership with local chiropractor.*

"Teacher?" the attorney began, raising his hand. "I think I added too much paint. My baseball is starting to look like The Joker."

Esther looked down at her own squash, a passable rendering of Sesame, ears made of pink plaid cardstock triangles and whiskers made from an old paintbrush at the end if its life.

Someone abruptly lowered to the seat next to her. "Bunny? What are you still doing here?" Esther asked quietly. "Lunch is over. You should have left at two." She had a feeling Bunny had stayed for the same reason Esther kept her phone face-up on the table next to her.

Bunny placed a bare squash on the table. "Are you kidding? We find out our friend might be implicated in Faris's death and I'm supposed to just go home and wait?"

Someone in the class shrieked. "I did it! I totally nailed the bow. Who's laughing now, glue-stained ribbon?"

Esther let out a breath. "I'm a nervous wreck too. I considered skipping this workshop, but I figured it would at least give me a view of the front door for when Kai comes back." Having something to do with her hands in Sugar's class beat camping out in the living room or Googling felony sentence lengths at the reception desk.

Bunny knocked on the squash. "How long does it take to ask some questions and look around the spa? Sabina must know Kai has nothing to do with this. Right?"

Esther startled when she felt a gentle hand on her shoulder.

"That, my friend, is a perfect kitty cat," Sugar said.

"Thanks," Esther managed. "I was thinking of setting it out on the reception desk, but we all know how Sesame reacted the first time she saw her reflection in a mirror."

Bunny shuddered. "Poor mirror."

Sugar's smile didn't falter. "Perhaps you can bring it home and put it in your window. It'd be lovely to see that cute little face every day." She scratched the squash with her pointer finger.

"What's it like being neighbors with a celebrity, Esther?" Bunny asked.

Sugar chuckled. "I wouldn't put prop maker in the celebrity category. Most people never know our names."

Esther tsked. "Which is a total shame, considering you've contributed so much to the entertainment they know and love." She'd seen some of the movies and shows Sugar had worked on over the years, everything from sci-fi dramas with alien-looking gadgets to rom-coms with fake pastries that looked good enough to rival Bunny's. The woman had serious talent.

Sugar nodded. "Yes, well, look at me now." She gestured to the group of guests scattered around the room. "Getting my time on stage."

"You were right about the squashes, by the way," Esther said. "I think it's the perfect challenge level for adults. They can carve, paint, decorate, whatever."

Bunny touched Esther's hand, turning her head toward the front door. Esther glanced over in time to see a purple streak of hair swish past the Calliope Room, headed toward the supply closet down the hall. She fought the urge to run after Kai. "I have to step out, Sugar. But this is so fun. Thank you a million times over for helping us get in touch with our creativity."

"My pleasure," Sugar said. "Thank you for giving this old lady a reason to get out of the house in retirement. Guy has convinced himself he can start stand-up comedy. He's been writing jokes." She widened her eyes and mouthed, *Help me!*

Esther gave Sugar a quick hug. "You're putting on a brave face. Tell him I say hi."

The last thing she heard Sugar say as she hurried out of the workshop was, "So, Bunny, tell me about your vision for this squash."

Esther found Kai frantically rifling through the supply closet. "What are you doing?"

Kai looked over her shoulder, hands on the top shelf, supporting a stack of white towels that threatened to topple over. "I have a session in a few minutes. I'm late. Gotta grab my stuff. I'll set up in their suite since the Calliope Room is booked. Could you help me carry my oils upstairs?"

Esther felt her jaw drop. Was she honestly worried about her next session? "Kai, forget the oils! What happened with Sabina?"

Kai gave up on the towels and lowered her hands. She looked exhausted as she tugged at the hem of her shirt. "It was a night-mare. Sabina's team basically ripped the spa apart. They looked through drawers, took inventory of all my stuff, asked me a million questions."

In all the time she'd known Kai, Esther had never seen her look like this. Tired, yes. Irritated, sure. But this was different. She looked…defeated. "What exactly did Sabina say?"

Kai let out an incredulous laugh. As she spoke, she seemed to be thinking out loud, describing a terrible dream. "'You're not under arrest, I'm just looking for some answers,'" she said, imitating Sabina's professional voice.

Esther didn't know what to say. She guessed it was a good thing Sabina had been forthcoming about their process, but the image of law enforcement pouring out glass jars of facial serums, rooting through treatment room drawers, and turning over trash cans wasn't exactly comforting.

"She actually used the word 'arrest,'" Kai said, her eyes turning glassy. "'Arrest.' In a sentence aimed at me." She looked toward the ceiling, blinking in quick succession. "I'm not allowed to leave town."

A person didn't have to be a crime show enthusiast to know that was a bad sign. Police never told people they thought were innocent they couldn't cross state lines. Esther stepped closer and placed her hands on Kai's shoulders. "You're not saying Sabina seriously thinks you had anything to do with this, are you?"

Kai swallowed. "I mean, it doesn't look good. She found one of my needles at the crime scene. And unless I can convince the police I didn't do it...what if they release my name publicly? The news would be everywhere. What then?" She started crying.

Esther embraced her. "Listen to me. There's no way we're going to let this come down on you. Absolutely not." She looked at the stack of white towels as she stroked the back of Kai's head, her mind already busy with how she'd be able to keep her word.

Kai wiped her face with her shirt sleeve as she stepped back. "If they release my name as a suspect, there's no turning back. It won't matter that I'm innocent. What can we do? It's not like we have any evidence to hand over proving someone else did it."

She had a point. In fact, hadn't Esther recently explained to Penny how unqualified she was to play the role of investigator? Despite that, Esther heard herself ask, "What if we got some?"

Kai squinted. "What do you mean?"

Esther didn't know where it came from, but she felt a confidence growing inside her, an urgency she couldn't, or didn't want to, fight. The one thing she was certain of was Kai's innocence. Which meant there had to be a way to prove it. "You said we need evidence to prove you didn't kill Faris. We can only do that if we find out who did. So let's find out."

Kai seemed apprehensive. "How would we do that? Where would we even begin?"

It was a good question. Esther tried to think logically. Where would a detective begin? They'd probably question the people who knew the victim. The people they'd spent time with recently.

She thought about all the people who'd attended Faris's celebration of life. Everyone who knew him intimately, or even distantly, had been gathered in that house. "We start with Queenie."

Kai looked confused. "Queenie from The Speckled Stein? What's she got to do with anything?"

"At the celebration of life, Onyx said Faris was at the pub with Ingram the night he died. That Ingram was the last person seen with Faris."

"Onyx also said the police have already cleared him," Kai reminded her.

*The police are also entertaining the idea that Kai could be a murderer, so their judgment might be off.* "Well, we haven't cleared him. Is there a chance either Faris or Ingram could have stolen Botox and a needle when they inspected the spa?"

Kai looked around the closet as she thought. "No. I was following them around like a complete stalker because I was so nervous. I wanted to make sure everything was perfect. We were together the whole time."

"Who else had access to the spa? Could one of your other clients have taken it some time that week without you noticing?"

"No," Kai said, shaking her head. "One of my part-time girls does inventory every day. As of that morning, the inventory must have been perfect, otherwise she would have told me. And I seriously doubt any of my clients that day were thinking about anything other than smooth skin." She thought for a few moments. "But anyone could have broken in after hours. There's a long stretch of time from closing to Faris meeting his end."

"That's fair," Esther said. They needed to pick a starting point, though. "I still think we should begin with our inspection team."

Esther wondered what the men's relationship had been like. "How were Faris and Ingram acting during your inspection? Did they seem to get along? I didn't get to spend much time with them." On her own inspection day, Faris had grown tired of her quickly and the feeling was mutual.

"They seemed friendly enough," Kai said. "Faris was being bossy and criticizing Ingram's note taking and stuff. Faris being Faris."

No surprise there. "I want more details about that night at the pub. We should go see Queenie tomorrow at Open Mic Night."

Kai sniffed and looked at Esther, a hint of a smile on her lips.

"What are you smiling at?" Esther asked, surprised to see Kai looking positive.

"Should I start calling you Detective Esther?"

"More like Very Amateur Sleuth Esther," Esther said. "Doesn't have quite the same ring, though."

Kai reached her arms out again. "In case this is our last hug before I get sent to the slammer."

"Don't even joke like that," Esther said. She laughed it off, but she felt uneasy. What if she couldn't prove Kai was innocent? What would happen to her?

And how would she lead dozens of employees one day in her own business if she couldn't even fight for one now?

# CHAPTER 14

The Speckled Stein smelled like onion rings and old oak. Neon beer signs cast a soft, colorful glow over the dark wood walls.

Guy Choo stood on the pub's tiny stage platform, gripping the microphone so hard his knuckles blanched. He blinked sweat from his eyes.

Open Mic Night had an impressive turnout, even for a Thursday. So far, Clint had played "Ain't No Mountain High Enough" on the flute, Dev Singh had worked lines from ten of his favorite Shakespeare sonnets into a rap, and LouLou sang an Italian opera that had dazzled everyone.

Guy cleared his throat. "My wife and I have been married thirty-five years. At this point, we finish each other's sentences. Mostly with, 'That's not what happened.'"

A smattering of laughter from patrons tipsy enough to laugh at anything.

Esther leaned toward Sugar, seated next to her in the cozy booth. "He's been practicing for this all week?"

Sugar whispered, "All month. Imagine how I feel," before clapping enthusiastically.

Esther scanned the pub again. Queenie stood behind the bar wiping it down. No customers at the moment. She nudged Kai's arm and motioned for her to follow.

The shiny, red-brown upholstery squeaked as they scooted out of the circular booth. Sugar didn't seem to notice them leave. Her sight fixed on Guy, she held both hands near her mouth like she was watching a toddler carry a full glass of grape juice across a white carpet.

"So, you really think Ingram could have done it?" Kai asked as they weaved through tables. "Is Faris criticizing the guy's notes a reason to want him dead?"

"No," Esther admitted. "But having to spend eight hours a day with him might have been."

Queenie looked happy to see them. She rocked a short, blunt bob with bangs that could have made her seem too-cool to people who didn't know her well. "Hey, Esther! If you've come on official festival business, don't worry, I already vetoed Jim's idea to serve cocktails out of a canoe."

"Perfect. You just saved me three weeks of negotiations with him."

"Happy to help. What can I get for you ladies?"

Esther tilted her head in consideration. "Shirley Temple for me. Same for this one—" she said, motioning to Kai, "—but with vodka."

Kai laughed. "Do I look that bad?"

"No. But you've had a heck of a day, and since you're not addicted to Penny's coffee like me, I figure a different type of drink might do you some good."

Queenie gave a tight smile. "I heard about what happened, Kai. We're all rooting for you."

Kai looked alarmed. "We?"

Queenie's eyes shifted past Esther and Kai. Esther turned around in time to see a few Oak's Rest residents quickly avert their gazes, pretending they'd been watching Guy Choo the whole time.

"We need to move to a bigger city," Kai said.

"Maybe get fake names and new social security cards while we're at it," Esther said. "Gotta love a small town."

Queenie scooped ice into two skinny glasses. She poured grenadine straight from the bottle, the red liquid making its way through the ice like lava working its way down cracks of a volcano.

"We were hoping you could tell us about that night, actually," Esther started. "We heard Faris and his coworker, Ingram, were here at the pub."

Queenie glanced up as she poured ginger ale into one of the glasses. She slowed the pour as the fizz reached the top of the glass. "Shoot. What do you wanna know?"

Esther opened her mouth to speak, then shut it when she realized she didn't know what to ask. She looked at Kai, who seemed equally stumped. They should have prepared more thoroughly for their first interview. "How were they acting that night? What time did they come and go? That kind of stuff."

Queenie dropped a cherry into one drink, then filled a shot glass and poured it into the second.

"I think I know which drink is mine," Kai said with a smile.

Queenie slid the two glasses forward on napkins. "They came in around dinner time. They sat in a booth at the back, so I didn't have eyes on them most of the time. But they were ordering pitchers of beer, and I stress the 's' on pitchers."

"They were drunk?" Esther asked.

Queenie shrugged. "After a while, they got up to play pool with a couple other fellas. The dinner rush was over by then, so the pub had cleared out a bit. Faris was…loose. Leaning on the table for support. His buddy? I couldn't tell. But you know, people handle their liquor differently."

"How long did they stay?" Kai asked.

Queenie wiped her hands on a white towel. Esther wondered how The Speckled Stein kept their laundry so pristine, given their menu of colorful drinks. Did the pub have its own Sveta?

"Until fifteen or twenty minutes before closing time. Maybe around nine forty-five? The Ingram guy came over for water. I commented about hoping they weren't driving home. He said his neighbor was a cab driver, so he'd leave their car in Oak's Rest overnight and call the cab to pick them up. He and Faris didn't live too far from each other, so it'd be no problem."

Esther looked between the booths and the front door, trying to imagine the scene. "And that's all you saw? They went home in the cab?"

"They did..." Queenie said, looking bashful.

Esther leaned forward on her elbows. "Queenie? Did you see something?"

Queenie set the towel down. "I whistled and got the guys' attention when I saw the taxi pull up. They made their way outside. I was going to kick out the other patrons a few minutes early too..."

"But?" Esther asked, eager to hear more.

Queenie sighed. "But it was quiet, and my shift was almost over anyway, so I took a little break. Out back."

"I thought you kicked your smoking habit months ago," Kai said. "Oh, honey, you're so young. You have so much mileage left in your skin. Wait until you're seventy and already wrinkled. Then give smoking a go."

Esther made eye contact with Kai.

"What? I'm being practical."

Queenie groaned. "I gave up bagels. I need *something* to live for. Anyway, pretty much everyone was gone by the time I came back inside. It's not like anyone stole anything while I was gone. No harm, no foul."

Esther paused. The timeline didn't make sense. "So, if they

both went home to Yalfont, how did Faris end up back in Oak's Rest?"

Queenie looked around, tossed her hand towel over her shoulder, and leaned in. "According to Nolie—"

Kai put a hand up. "Hold on there, Miss Thing. Do you mean Nolan Brown? As in, *Officer* Nolan Brown? Sabina's star pupil?"

Queenie giggled like a little girl. "We've been seeing each other. It's no big deal."

Esther managed a few seconds of supportive smiling, not wanting to ruin Queenie's bliss. "Too cute. But you were saying?"

Queenie nodded. "Fine, but please don't repeat anything I say. Nolan could get in trouble for sharing details about the investigation."

Someone in the crowd called out, "You're doing great, Guy!"

Esther disregarded the background noise and extended her pinky as a promise.

Queenie took it. "Ingram told Detective Ali that he did, in fact, get driven home by his neighbor. But without Faris."

"What?" Kai asked. "I thought you said they went home together in the cab."

Esther waved her quiet.

Queenie went on. "Ingram said he tried to get Faris into the cab, but Faris refused and said he wanted to find another bar. Ingram got fed up and took off without him."

"Wow," Esther said. "So Faris never went back to Yalfont. He was here the whole night."

Kai blew out a breath. "I see what Onyx meant. Ingram must feel guilty about not being there. If he's innocent, that's got to eat at him."

Esther tried to recall more details of their conversation with Onyx. "Do you know anything about him talking to the police? We heard he's been cleared already."

"They were able to track his phone's location on that night.

He offered it up to the police without a warrant or anything. GPS put him at his house in Yalfont at the time of Faris's death."

Esther rested her chin on her hand. So, Ingram had a weak motive and a verified alibi. When did she start using words like 'motive'? Maybe she'd be better at this whole investigating thing than she thought. "If Ingram didn't do it, who did?"

Queenie lifted a shoulder. "Seems like you'd need to figure out what Faris did after leaving the pub."

"There won't be many witnesses," Esther said. Oak's Rest would have been quiet at ten o'clock on a Monday night.

Kai groaned.

"What's wrong?" Esther asked.

Kai slouched on her stool. "Our only suspect has already been cleared by the police—the *actual* police—and we have nothing else to go on. We're never going to catch the killer."

"Hey, chin up," Esther said. "This is only the beginning. We're not quitting that easily. We're going to find out what happened." She'd make sure of it.

Kai gave her a sidelong glance. "Yeah, I guess."

Queenie dropped an extra cherry into Kai's glass. "Drink up, sister. Have you ever known Esther to fail at anything she set her mind to?"

Esther felt herself smile. It was nice to have someone acknowledge her stubbornness as an asset rather than a source of frustration.

Kai smirked and sat up straighter. "That's a good way to think about it," she said before biting a plump cherry off its stem. "Never."

# CHAPTER 15

The next morning, Esther stretched her legs under the blanket, lingering in the space between sleep and wakefulness unique to Sundays. The scent of wet pine and overnight rain seeped in through invisible cracks in the window seals.

Reluctant sun, filtered by thick, puffy clouds, brushed her bedroom with soft, hazy light. She peeled back the blanket and swung her legs over the side of the bed. She pulled off her satin bonnet and exchanged it for her tortoiseshell glasses, which she only wore at home or on days she was too tired to bother with contacts.

The floorboards creaked as she padded over to the window. Esther turned the crank until practically the only thing standing between her and the lake was the ground floor of her house.

The first time Esther had seen this view, she was twenty-one years old, freshly dropped out of college. Tracey Harriet, the owner of Calliope Inn, had taken pity on her and given her a cleaning position.

Tracey owned what she described as "a little cottage in the woods" she'd been considering selling. Curious, Esther had asked so many questions Tracey invited her to come see it for herself.

Esther began renting the house from Tracey at a very generous price as a temporary arrangement. A place to land until she figured her life out, her unfinished degree and incredulous family frozen in time where she'd left them. But a year passed, then another, until Esther officially signed the papers that made the house hers, nine years into living there.

Esther was still amazed she got to call this place home. She looked out at the never-ending expanse of water, lapping gently against the rocky sand at the foot of her yard, leaves floating on the surface. Not a single boat motor or voice carried along the water. It felt like the lake reserved this part of itself just for her, and she did her best to honor that by joining its companionable silence.

She made her way downstairs, stepping over the yellow rain boots by the back door, not bothering to straighten the books balanced riskily on the coffee table.

The kitchen was modest but updated with warm, gray-beige inset cabinets and a double farmhouse sink framed by a window overlooking the gravel driveway.

Esther moved through the motions she knew by heart: filling the reservoir, scooping the grounds she faithfully restocked from Penny's every month, bending over and waiting patiently for the first trickle to fall and fog up the pot.

By the time she'd stepped out onto the patio, wiped down the Adirondack chair, and sat, coffee in hand, the sun had peeked out from behind the clouds, warming the air so slightly she wouldn't have noticed the shift if she hadn't experienced it so many times.

The curtains were still shut at the Choos' house. They were late sleepers on the weekends. Only her, the lake, and the crisp fall air. She loved this weather, but she longed for warmer days when she could take a dip. Water always cleared her mind.

Between sips, Esther held the mug up to the lake to see the steam rising off the surface of the coffee.

Her cup was halfway empty when her phone rang out from her bedroom.

"No way." She went in for another sip. "Whoever it is can wait."

Quiet fell when the call went to voicemail. Perfect. She went back to watching the water, her legs curled up in the chair, when the phone rang again.

She groaned. *This better be good.*

She set her mug down and headed inside. The phone rang for the third time as she was cresting the stairs. "Hold your horses. I'm working on half a cup of coffee here."

Esther jogged the last few steps to the ringing phone on her night table. She stopped when she saw who was calling.

She closed her eyes, drew in a deep breath, and swiped to answer. "Doctor Cameron."

"Oh, please," her younger sister replied. "Call me Doctor Bennett. I insist."

"I hope you're calling to tell me you won the lottery and want to split the profits. I ran up the stairs to take this." *Ran* might have been a bit of an exaggeration, but she'd never pass up an opportunity to play the guilt card.

Cameron snorted. Of course she did. How could Esther's time possibly be as valuable as the golden child's? "You don't have to sound so grumpy. I'm the one who's been calling you for almost two weeks with no response."

The wind picked up and lashed at the open window. Esther rolled her eyes as she turned the crank counterclockwise. She tried to dial in the irritation in her voice. "I've been busy with the inn. Today's my first guaranteed day off in a few weeks, and I'm trying to soak up every minute."

"Then you'll love to hear what I have to say," Cameron said.

Not a promising start. "Just tell me who died, please." She hoped the uncertainty hadn't crept into her voice. What could Cameron have been calling about so persistently?

"You've always been one for dramatic effect. Obviously, I'm not calling to drop some morbid news on you. I'd do that during business hours so I could tell you over voicemail."

"Okay," Esther said, mildly relieved. Maybe it wouldn't be so bad. "Then what is it?"

Cameron paused for a moment. "We're having dinner at Mom and Dad's house tonight."

Esther didn't understand. She'd called to brag about her dinner plans? "Congrats? Tell David and the kids Auntie Esther says hi."

Cameron heaved a breath. "Not us, Esther. *Us*. Me and you."

Esther pulled back to look at the phone screen before putting it back to her ear. "I'm sorry, what? The last time I talked to Mom was last February when she mailed me a birthday card with a fifteen-dollar visa."

"So?" Cameron asked. "That's a thoughtful gesture."

Cameron taking their mom's side. Shocker. "The woman's Chanel collection alone is worth more than my house. I didn't even think they let you buy fifteen-dollar gift cards. She probably had to call the company and ask for a special one to be made up for her sad, under-credentialed daughter."

Esther could almost hear the disapproval coming from the other end of the call.

"I don't know why you have to be like that, Esther. Look. They invited us over for dinner, no kids or spouses. I told Mom I'd make sure you came, so here I am. I didn't realize it'd be such a life-altering ask."

Esther bit back the first responses that came to mind. The worst part of talking to her sister was that Cameron knew exactly why she felt the way she did. She had to. That their mom had invited Esther to dinner through Cameron was proof of that.

And Cameron's insistence on playing clueless about being her parents' favorite child was enough to make Esther want to scream. But she wouldn't scream. There'd be nothing to scream about. Because she wasn't going to dinner. "I can't," she said, determination in her voice. "I have work."

"You *just* said you have the day off."

Esther looked around her room as if she'd find a better excuse waiting in some forgotten corner. She sat on the bed. "Oops, sorry, that's my maintenance guy calling on the other line." She held the phone farther from her mouth. "I think it's an emergency. I'm gonna have to call you back."

"ESTHER," Cameron said firmly enough for Esther to drag the phone back to her ear. Her voice was measured now. "Dinner is at six o'clock. Be there. On time. Dressed appropriately."

It was like she was talking to their mother. Memories of being scolded for trying to wear a tutu to school came flooding back. "I'm always dressed appropriately. I'm an adult. I'm older than you!"

"See you at six," Cameron said. The line went dead.

Esther blew raspberries at the darkened screen. "Nice talking to you too, sis."

# CHAPTER 16

It could have been her imagination, but Esther swore her car was making a faint jingling sound, like there was loose change in the engine, as she inched down her parents' quiet residential street.

She patted the steering wheel. "I know, girl. I know. I'll try to keep this visit short."

Esther's heart was racing as she turned onto the property. Light posts along the cobblestone drive were already illuminated as the sun threatened to sink below the horizon.

From the street, the Bennett house was hardly visible. Even from different vantage points on the property, its white facade and slanted copper roof was shrouded by tall trees with far-reaching, full branches.

The mystique made the house a status symbol. People in her parents' echelon signaled their wealth through exclusivity. It was exhausting.

Esther stood in front of the house, craning her neck to look to the top. For a long time, Esther maintained the routine of visiting her parents at least twice a year. Over time, twice a year had faded to once, or less.

She took a deep breath. *You're a grown-up now. You can handle this.* She checked the time. Five minutes early. A Penny's coffee would have helped.

"Hey," a voice called from behind.

Cameron was making her way to the front door. Under her jacket, she wore an elegant, navy blue button-front dress and short pumps. Esther could see Cameron simultaneously assess her own black jeans, leather booties, and cowl-neck sweater with distaste.

"I told you to dress *appropriately*," Cameron angry-whispered.

Esther lifted her brows and waved a hand over Cameron's outfit. "You told me to dress appropriately for dinner at Mom and Dad's house, not to be photographed on the Red Carpet."

Cameron crossed her arms. "Fine, wear whatever you want. Don't say I didn't warn you." She breezed past Esther and rang the bell. Even the way she pressed the doorbell was polished. Assured, but not too eager.

Esther's outfit choice was perfectly reasonable. It was too early in the evening to let Cameron get in her head. "Mom's not even going to notice what I'm wearing. She'll be too busy asking us to raise donations for her WONSE group or whatever she asked us here for."

"Pfft. The Women of New York Societal Engagements don't need our money." Cameron glanced sideways at Esther, giving her another once-over. "And she notices everything."

Esther wouldn't admit it, but she knew it was true.

The door swung open. Anna, the Bennetts' long-time house-keeper, smiled warmly. Instead of her housekeeping uniform, she wore smart khaki trousers and a black top.

Anna hugged both sisters, but lingered a few extra seconds on Esther, to Esther's small delight. "I'm so happy to see you," Anna whispered, pinching Esther's cheek. "Beautiful as ever."

Esther couldn't help but smile. "Please. You're aging in reverse. You look younger than me." Anna's skin had somehow become even more glowing in the time since she'd last seen her.

Anna opened the door wide and ushered them inside, taking their jackets.

The marble floors were shined even more severely than Esther remembered. As a kid, she'd hop to the black diamonds, pretending the white marble was lava. Her mother always accused her of scuffing the floors. It wasn't until she was older that Esther realized, guiltily, Anna had probably cleaned them every time.

The house was lit with layers of ambient and accent lighting. Sconces lined the walls, framing each imposing piece of artwork, of which there were many. Esther paused in front of a Renaissance-style painting. At its center, a dark-skinned man posed, draped in crimson velvet, one hand resting on a gilded harp, the other holding a scroll.

His eyes met Esther's with a calm authority that made it hard to look away. Around the man, cherubic children floated on clouds, offering laurel crowns and golden fruits. The longer Esther looked at the image, the smaller she felt.

Esther's father appeared beside the staircase. She remembered him towering over her like a skyscraper. Today, though, her heeled booties closed a good portion of the height difference.

His suit hardly moved as he strode over to Esther and Cameron. He clapped his hands together. "Girls. I'm happy you could make it over here."

He took Esther's hand like she was royalty. Ah, stifled affection. They'd never been a family of huggers.

He patted Cameron on the head, careful not to muss her neat, low bun.

She laughed and swatted him away. "Stop, Dad!"

Esther felt like she was standing on the outside of an inside joke.

"I'll meet you in the living room," their father said. "Can I get either of you a drink?"

"I'll have the usual," Cameron said.

He looked at Esther, expectant.

"Oh, um, I'll have what she's having."

"Follow me," Graham said, leading the way. "Your mother will be down any minute."

The living room had always felt like a museum. No half-empty mugs, no threadbare pillows. Nothing to hint that people actually lived there. All fragile, irreplaceable heirlooms and over-priced art.

Esther sat next to Cameron on the sofa as their father disappeared into the parlor to fix their drinks.

"Stop bouncing your leg," Cameron whispered sharply. "You're stressing me out."

"Blood flow is the cornerstone of cardiovascular health. Shouldn't you know that?" Esther hadn't realized she was, in fact, bouncing her leg.

Cameron turned to her. Esther had sat on the couch in that exact position enough times to recognize incoming snark. "Thank you for that reminder. Always good for us internal medicine docs to stay up to date on the most cutting-edge health discoveries."

Esther smiled sweetly. "No problem. I'm not totally against helping Big Medicine every once in a while, if it's for the good of humanity."

"For the last time, there's no such thing is Big—"

"Graham?" their mother's voice called.

"In the living room," he called back, handing them each a martini glass with olives.

"Thanks, Dad," Esther said, grateful for something to take the edge off. She took a sip and instantly regretted it. She made a split-second decision to swallow the battery acid rather than spit it out, but started coughing.

Cameron and Graham both looked at Esther like she was an alien.

Esther's mother walked in at the end of her coughing fit. Veronica Bennett was timelessly beautiful. She'd started going gray prematurely, so in true Veronica fashion, with the help of a hairdresser, she took control of her hair's destiny. Tonight, her hair was perfectly curled away from her face, the thick gray and white-streaked locks resting on her shoulders.

She wore a simple white blouse tucked into a pencil skirt and a pearl necklace. Simple. Definitely expensive.

"So rude of me to keep you waiting," Veronica declared. "One of my earrings broke. Cheap things."

"I told you, not everything that says 'genuine' is to be trusted when you're shopping out of the country," Graham said.

Veronica disregarded his comment as her eyes met Esther's. "Hi, darling," she said, crossing the room.

"Hi, Mom. It's good to see you." Esther leaned in to reciprocate a double-cheek kiss.

As they stepped back, Veronica looked Esther up and down as her hands hovered next to her shoulders, close enough to resemble an embrace to an untrained eye. "You look well." She picked at the fabric of Esther's sweater. "Is that polyester?"

*So it begins.* "Mind if I give myself a tour?" Esther asked with a tight smile, clutching her drink with both hands.

Her mother had already moved on to greeting Cameron.

Esther started on a lap around the room, lingering in front of a tall marble display case.

Her eyes landed on a cluster of three photos of herself: her as a baby swallowed up by a fluffy dress, her in her middle school winter formal dress, her smiling in her high school graduation photo.

She wished she could tell them all that it would get better one day, that the crushing pressure and impossible standards wouldn't be forever.

Higher in the case was a photo collection of Cameron's children at every age. Had her parents asked for them, or had Cameron just offered? She didn't know why it mattered.

The focal point of the display came into view. Three doctoral degrees—her father's, in business administration, her mother's, in education, and her sister's medical degree—all lined up like soldiers. Her mother and sister's degrees bore matching Colborne University insignias.

"Dinner is ready," Anna announced.

Between bites of salad, Esther found herself counting the prisms on the chandelier above the dining room table. She'd never landed on a definitive number.

"You don't like your poached salmon?" Esther heard her mother ask, startling her back to reality.

"No, everything's great," Esther lied, using her fork to break a piece off. "Thanks, Mom."

Her mother, seemingly appeased, shifted her attention. "So, how was the drive in?" she asked, looking from Cameron to Esther. "I hope those dreadful leaves didn't muck up your tires. I told the landscaper to have them gone by the time you arrived, but you know how hard it is to find reliable contractors. Absolute nightmare."

"Well, I guess that's why they call it 'fall.' Can't stop the leaves from doing it," Esther joked.

"What?" her mother asked, confused.

Swing and a miss. "Nothing. The drive was fine."

"The drive was nice, Mom." Cameron said. "Your neighborhood is so scenic this time of year." Of course Cameron had the perfect answer. "Are the Johnsons still using that leaf blower?"

Esther's parents both erupted into laughter.

"Oh my goodness," Veronica said, covering her mouth with a cloth. "That awful thing. I still hear it in my dreams."

"I don't know what would possess them to attempt their own landscaping," Graham said, chuckling.

Esther let her thoughts wander. She wasn't sure how long she'd been pushing the food around on her plate, dreaming of a cheeseburger, but when she brought her attention back to the table, the conversation had landed on her mother's upcoming charity event.

"I just hope Betty Roberts and Sally James don't botch the flowers again," Veronica said. "Gardenia centerpieces for an indoor event," she scoffed. "The place smelled like Grandparent's Day at a retirement home."

"Aren't you a grandparent, Mom?" Esther asked.

Her mother looked startled by the comment, not as though she was offended, but like she'd forgotten Esther was there. She reached for her glass and took a slow slip. Esther recognized the stall, the practiced expression her mother wore when buying herself time to recall the name of a donor she'd met more than once. "How's that little motel of yours?"

A familiar heat crept up the back of Esther's neck. "It's an *inn*, Mom."

Her mother wrung her hands like she was putting on lotion, her signature passive-aggression move. "Sorry, dear. Close, though."

Esther dabbed at the corners of her mouth. "Right. Except one is where you stop when your foot cramps up driving on the highway. The other is a destination."

"No need to get upset, Esther. I was only trying to make conversation."

"Calliope Inn was featured in the New York Times last year. Our chef was in a Netflix documentary."

Veronica dropped her napkin. "Graham? Can you please tell your daughter she's overreacting to a benign question?"

Graham looked unsure of how to disarm the conversation from either end.

Esther decided to show mercy. "We're preparing for a big

festival in a few weeks. It creates a lot of awareness about our local businesses. The inn is hosting it for the first time."

She inwardly cringed at her own tone. She'd meant to sound confident, nonchalant, even, like hosting an important town event was any other day on the job. But it came out like a little kid telling their parents she'd gotten an "A" on her report card, waiting for a big hug and a celebration.

"That sounds lovely," Veronica said. "Who knows? Maybe one day, some of those hobby shops will be able to afford real advertising campaigns."

There it was. Esther should have known her mom could turn anything sweet sour.

"So, Mom, Dad," Cameron said, cutting in. "Any special reason you invited us to dinner tonight?"

"Great question," Esther said dryly.

Veronica flipped over the palm of her hand as though she were the only level-headed one in the room. "Can we not invite our daughters over simply to enjoy a meal together?"

"You could, but that doesn't feel like the case. What's going on?" Esther asked, any semblance of politeness used up.

"Your manners could use some work, Esther Bennett," Veronica said, the rest of the sentence lingering on her lips. "But yes, there is a reason we called you here today."

Finally, they were getting to it.

"Your father and I would like to have family dinners. Weekly."

Esther wasn't sure she'd heard that right. "Come again?"

Even Cameron looked concerned. "That's very kind of you to offer, Mom, but is everything okay? Are you sick?" She looked between their parents.

Graham closed his eyes for a long blink. "Everything is fine."

"We're a family," Veronica said. "We should behave like one."

Everything inside Esther told her to run. There was no chance she'd return every week for more of the same delightful banter. Best to shut it down quickly. "Sorry, Mom, my schedule can be chaotic with my new position. I'm on-call a lot, and—"

"We'll write you out of the will if you don't come," her mother blurted, crossing her arms. "Either of you."

Esther shut her mouth. Even her father looked caught off guard, like her mother had gone off whatever script they'd agreed on.

"Don't you think that's a little extreme?" Cameron asked.

Their mother stood firm. "No, I don't. And I want the two of you to prepare a dish and bring it with you each week."

Now that was downright comical. "Mom. Come on," Esther said, laughing in disbelief. She looked to her sister for confirmation, who was also laughing. "You have a personal cook who prepares you fancy foods I've never heard of. I don't think my world-famous pizza toast would exactly fit the menu."

"This is not a joke," her mother said, sounding defensive. "You'll prepare the dish together. I don't care who brings it. Do it. Or the only worldly possessions your father and I will be leaving you are my broken earrings."

Silence fell over the table.

Esther had never given much thought to what she'd inherit once her parents were no longer around. She'd been living independently for so long it hadn't even occurred to her. As much as she rebelled against it, maybe some part of her had always taken leaps knowing she had the safety net of a wealthy family to catch her.

Veronica took one last sip and stood from the table. "Thank you for coming tonight, girls," she said, looking at her feet. Was she fighting back tears? Had they actually hurt her feelings? "I will see you next Sunday evening." With that, she headed for the staircase.

After dinner, Esther and Cameron absently followed Anna to the front door, Esther too stunned by what she'd just experienced to speak.

She slipped into her jacket and burrowed her hands in the pockets as she crossed the threshold of the front door, chilly air rushing inside. She felt something hard in her left pocket.

She pulled out three foil-wrapped chocolate peanut butter cups and smiled. Her favorite post-dinner-she-didn't-eat treat. She looked up at Anna, who winked before closing the door. It wasn't only unhappy memories that stood the test of time.

Esther shut the car door and rested her forehead on the wheel. "You told me to run, and I didn't listen," she admitted. "Remind me to listen next time."

# CHAPTER 17

Esther relished the scent of laundered sheets and lavender as she smoothed the freshly fluffed pillow. The guest room, with its soft cream paneling and sunlight spilling into the bedside window and across the floor, offered a sense of calm she desperately needed.

Monday mornings always energized Esther—the hum of the inn, the purposeful rhythm of routine. But today, especially, the inn felt like a respite.

Framed paintings of trees and wildflower fields hung in a gallery above the headboard, not too dissimilar from the real-life greenery outside the room's window. Floral shams and a quilted coverlet, folded neatly at the foot of the bed, added pops of rose red and mossy green, like a cottage garden blooming indoors.

Calliope Inn's themed suites were all the rage, but Esther secretly loved their standard rooms even more.

"Thanks for making the pillow sachets, Kai," Esther said, brushing her fingertips along the embroidery on a pillow. "It's almost Sesame's snack time, and I didn't want to get lavender oil on my hands."

"You're aware you have a housekeeping team, right?" Kai asked as she parted the curtains on the far window.

"But it's so much more fun to do it with a friend."

"It's what Esther does when she's stressed," Bunny's voice bellowed through the phone speaker. "She nests."

Esther gasped in mock surprise. "I'm not stressed. I'm being threatened into a weekly commitment."

Kai laughed. "Your mom is bold. But seriously, this might be a chance to get to know your parents again. It could be a positive thing. Healing, even."

Esther could feel the weariness in her expression. "What more is there to learn? I lived with them for twenty years."

"You could finally figure out what your dad does for work," Bunny offered.

"I know what my dad does. He's a—" Esther concentrated on the floral detailing of the vase on the bedside table. She squinted as she tried to conjure up the job description she'd heard so many times.

"'Business executive' isn't a description. It's a title," Bunny interjected.

"Whatever. I cannot go back there. Did I tell you my mom made the *motel* comment?"

Kai snapped and pointed at the phone. "Told you, Bunny! You owe me five bucks."

"Oh, good," Esther said, "I'm glad my personal misery is so entertaining."

"Oh honey, I'm sorry," Bunny said. "It sounds—" loud crashing metal in the background cut her off.

Esther plugged her ears. "Is it a bad time? I can fill you in later."

"No!" Bunny shouted. "Hang on a sec."

There was muffled talking on Bunny's end, as if she'd stepped away. After a few moments, her voice came through again, all command. "Use the tongs with your non-dominant hand. These babies are delicate. If you treat them like stress-balls all the flakes will flake off. Do you want the flakes you worked so hard on flaking to flake off? Forget it. Hold this."

"Bunny?" Esther said, almost afraid to ask. "Are you taking my employees hostage again?"

"Technically," Bunny retorted, "Luis is a member of *my* kitchen. Which means he assists me, the chef, when I need help. Sometimes that means holding the phone for me so I can stir."

Kai stifled a laugh. "Hi, Luis," she called out.

"He can't hear you. I have my headphones in. They're kind of broken, though, so I have to talk directly into my phone. Oh, and they only pick up loud sounds. And high-pitched dog barks. Kai and Esther say hi, Luis."

"Hi, Kai and Esther," Luis said.

"Luis, you're not a part of this call, my dear," Bunny said. "Just hold it and tell me if my sauce is getting too thick."

Esther walked over to the far window, looking out onto the front lawn, where a pair of robins were pecking at a patch of grass. "Anyway, I need you two to help me think through this Faris stuff."

"Yes," Kai said, "We need all the brain power we can get. Bunny, guess who knows all about my needle at the crime scene?"

"Who?"

"Everyone," Kai said with a sarcastic smile. "Everyone in Oak's Rest. I was getting stares at The Speckled Stein."

"Accusatory stares or nosey stares?"

"Nosey. But still! I can't even get a drink without the paparazzi gaping at me."

"That's awful. I'm so sorry, Kai," Bunny said. "So, now what?"

"Well, it seems like suspect number one is a dead end," Kai said.

Esther stepped closer to the phone. "Was there anyone else at Faris's celebration of life we should think about? Was anyone acting weird?"

"I mean, the wife didn't seem too upset," Kai said. "We're pretty sure she was fake crying. That's weird."

"It could have been a coping mechanism," Bunny said. "Or maybe she prefers to do her crying in the shower to Whitney Houston, like the rest of us."

"Maybe," Esther said. She thought back to who she'd observed in the Holliday house that day. "What about the boss? He made a beeline right for Uma and then snuck out early. Like he came just to show his face."

"Very strange," Kai agreed. "If one of your employees died, wouldn't you at least stick around for the slideshow?"

"So, we start with Reese?" Bunny asked. "How do we learn more about him? Show up at his house? We don't have many reasons to be over in Yalfont."

Esther thought for a moment. "Except maybe we do." She made eye contact with Kai.

"Why are you looking at me?" Kai asked.

"Doesn't your client, Onyx, work at the health department?"

"Yeah?" Kai said, looking confused. "So?"

"So, Reese works in the same building. Maybe Onyx can get us in so we can talk to him. We pretend we're there for some other reason." It seemed like the kind of thing a sleuth would do on a TV show, but it was the best idea Esther had.

"Okay," Kai said, nodding like she was starting to understand. "But when would we go? It'd have to be during the day."

"Tomorrow?" Esther proposed. She saw no reason to wait.

"Tomorrow's a heavy baking day," Bunny said. "My dough has a mind of its own when I'm not here to coddle it."

Kai scrunched her nose. "I'm at the spa in the morning. And in the afternoon, I'll only have a few pockets of time between clients here at the inn." Worry flashed over her face. "My schedule would be full, but someone cancelled. Looks like my reputation is already suffering."

"A guest cancelled because of what happened?" Esther asked.

If visitors somehow knew that much about the case, Calliope Inn would have more to worry about than cancelled wellness bookings.

"Well, she said it was because she had to cut her trip short," Kai said.

Esther let out a sigh of relief. "Oh, Mrs. Jones? That has nothing to do with you. Her son was in a motorbike accident."

"How do we know she's not using that as a polite excuse?"

Esther gave Kai her best stern look. "Mrs. Jones said the doctors described his leg as a *skin bag full of loose marbles*." It'd take a long time to erase that visual from her mind.

"That doesn't sound like something a real doctor would say," Bunny chimed in.

"Don't add to her anxiety," Esther said into the phone. "We can't all be gone, anyway. I'll go alone. Just connect me with Onyx. And don't tell her why I need to get into the building." Onyx seemed laid back, but it felt safest to keep their investigation close so early on.

"What about you?" Bunny asked. "When will you have time to slip away?"

Esther pulled up the calendar on her phone. "Guests have birdwatching in the morning, so I'm sure they'll finish up breakfast by nine. Painter is coming back at ten-thirty. We have a check-out at eleven. I should be able to sneak out after the breakfast rush for an hour or so. I was going to create some social media graphics, but I'll work on that during lunch today."

"What if a teen needs help with the Wi-Fi while you're gone?" Kai teased.

Bunny laughed. "Justice's ability to deflect amazes me."

"We all have our skills," Esther said. "I'll tell you two the same thing I told Justice: any time a guest asks a hard question, nod enthusiastically and make a show of writing it down. Tell them you want to make sure they have the most accurate information, so you'll have the manager reach out to them personally." Esther had learned that customer service was more about making people feel understood than actually being able to meet all of their requests.

"Do hard questions include, 'Why can't I take a pack of your turkey bacon home with me?'" Bunny asked.

"That fits the bill," Esther confirmed, although she did understand the inclination. Bunny's turkey bacon was an enlightening experience.

"Alright, so here's the plan," she said, refocusing. "Kai, you'll connect me with Onyx. I'll run into Reese at the health department and try to get a better feel for the guy. I'll start thinking of ways to get in touch with Uma, the widow. I also might take another look around the crime scene after work today. I didn't stay very long the last time I was there."

"Do you think you're ready to go back?" Bunny asked. "It won't be too upsetting?"

Esther looked from the phone to Kai, considering. "I think it'll be okay. What's more upsetting is the idea of Kai never being able to enjoy a Dirty Shirley again."

Kai smiled. "Because my reputation, business, and freedom being in jeopardy are minor details."

Esther admired that Kai could have a light-hearted conversation about the situation. She admired everything about how strong Kai was. She hoped to be like her some day. A fearless business woman. "All of those things are safe," she assured, patting Kai's shoulder.

Just then, she clocked movement out the window. Molly Murphy had emerged from the parking lot and was carrying a metal letter M twice her size across the lawn. "I better go check on that." They'd agreed on the following week to test run the display size for Makers and Merchants, but apparently, it couldn't wait. *We also agreed to start with the smaller size.* "But listen," Esther said before leaving the room, "We're going to sort this out."

Now, all she needed to do was figure out how.

# CHAPTER 18

"Thanks again, Penny!" Esther called over her shoulder as the diner bell gave a cheerful jingle overhead. The savory smell of onions wafting from the back had almost lured Esther into staying for an early dinner, but she'd forced herself to keep moving.

"Don't blame me when you can't sleep tonight!" Penny hollered before the door closed.

Esther stepped onto the sidewalk, cradling the hot paper cup in her hands. Who cared if she stayed up late? She'd need a clear head and sharp eyes if she hoped to spot anything useful at the crime scene. *And maybe a little delusion to think you'll find anything the police haven't already.*

She shook the doubt away as she reached her car at the end of the block. Paws wasn't far from the town square, but with only an hour before she needed to get back to the inn, driving had made more sense.

Esther took the first sip. She tilted her head back as she savored the deliciously hot coffee, right below burnt-tongue temperature. She lowered the cup just as a woman in a floppy sun hat hurried past her, narrowly missing a collision.

"So sorry," Esther choked out, amazed she hadn't dropped the cup.

The woman kept power-walking, the black ribbon tied around her hat flowing behind her in the wind. She gave a one-handed wave, like she was too busy to stop, but wanted Esther to know no serious harm had been done.

"I'll wait until we're not in motion to drink you," she said, patting the lid of the cup like a puppy's head.

Just as she pulled her car door handle, a commotion across the square caught her attention. Bethany Early was mid-rant, gesturing animatedly to a visibly exhausted Detective Ali, in front of General Store.

Sabina massaged her temples as Nolan scribbled notes. This would be good. Esther strained to listen, but could only make out something about writing up a bike for using an unsanctioned lock.

Sabina, no doubt looking for a mental escape from the conversation, looked around the square. Her sight landed on Esther. She gave a brief dip of her head in acknowledgement.

Esther waved. Should she ask about the case? Find out just how likely it was Sabina would publish Kai's name as a lead suspect? No. Sabina knew Esther was close to Kai. Asking her too many questions might only make Kai look guiltier.

There was also the fact Esther was on her way to snoop around the crime scene, which Sabina would have very much disapproved of. She ducked into the car and started it up.

The Paws parking lot was semi-full, but no one was outside. Esther strode past the front door, hoping to avoid being seen through the windows. She headed straight for the clearing where she'd found Faris's body.

Esther tried to steady her breath. Even though she'd assured Bunny coming back wouldn't be a big deal, her stomach was doing somersaults the closer she got.

The only sign of its former crime scene status was a small

torn piece of yellow tape caught on a tree branch. Much of the tangled brush had been cleared, probably by the officials who'd searched the area.

A fresh pile of leaves had settled into place, as if the earth was gently patching up a wound. If Esther forgot about what she'd seen, she could almost imagine children playing there, pretending they were entering a forest portal to another world.

Esther didn't know exactly what she was looking for. Maybe something small had gone unnoticed during the police's official sweep. An item fallen from the killer's wallet. A button. A shoe print that would lead her to a clue. Anything.

She'd come prepared. She pulled a latex glove from her back pocket and slid it on. The wind picked up, sending the leaves into a frenzy of motion close to the ground. Esther cautiously stepped further into the clearing, retracing her steps from before.

She scanned the ground, pausing every few feet to sweep leaves aside with the toe of her boot. Her heart pounded, not from fear, but anticipation.

She shifted her sight to a patch of browning leaves when a streak of color snagged her attention.

Esther pulled up the camera on her phone as she approached. A real detective would document the scene before moving anything, right?

She snapped a photo, then crouched to sift through the leaves, her eyes fixed on the fragment of color.

Her fingers closed around something flat and hard. Esther stood and held the item at face level. Recognition bloomed in her gut like ink in ice water.

It felt light in her hand. A little dirtier than the last time she'd seen it, but nothing a quick rinse wouldn't fix.

A rainbow-colored house key stamped with a black palm tree.

The key Kai had made for Lani.

What in the world was Lani's key doing at the murder site?

# CHAPTER 19

E sther had tossed and turned all night, debating whether to call Kai about what she'd found at the crime scene.

Ultimately, she'd decided against adding any more stress to her friend's plate. If Lani was hiding something, Esther would find out herself. Her next order of business, though, was learning more about Faris's boss.

The Ezra County Health Department, a forgettable brick building equipped with a fleet of government vehicles, rested on the outskirts of Yalfont. There was a decorative fountain out front—it was Yalfont, after all—but glossy touches couldn't mask the fact it was still a government building.

Esther took down the knitted daisies hanging from her rearview mirror and tossed them into the glove compartment. She'd already look out of place. No need to make it worse.

Her phone buzzed with a text from Justice. She'd sent a screenshot image of camping chairs. The backs of the chairs read, *If You Can Read This Leave Me Alone I'm Napping.*

**Justice:** OK to order these for the festival?

Esther looked around before typing out her response.

**Esther:** Nothing better than passive-aggressive furniture. Add the Calliope logo and order twenty.

She knew Justice would understand she was joking, but she set a reminder to check in on the status of the chair rentals later.

A few minutes later, she spotted Onyx strutting across the lot without so much as a glance over her shoulder to make sure Esther was following. Esther switched the car off and speed-walked to close the gap.

Just as they'd planned, Onyx punched in her employee code to get into the building, a perfectly normal arrival to work. She held the door for Esther behind her, a kind gesture for an apparent stranger.

Esther knew exactly where the inspections department was, thanks to Onyx's prior directions. She just hadn't specified *why* she needed to know. Onyx had asked surprisingly few questions. Her only comment was that she'd take any opportunity to "shake things up in that hamster wheel." The girl was downright likeable.

In the elevator, Esther pressed the button to the third floor. *Look confident, like you belong here.* She spread her feet, hands on hips, chin high. *Does this really work?* She felt as powerful as a paper straw in a smoothie. She lowered her arms, hoping there wasn't a security feed recording the show she'd put on.

The scent of stale coffee and printer toner greeted her as she stepped into the office. The air was somehow both cold and humid. People were typing away on thick computers, referencing papers, talking into phones. Not a smile as far as the eye could see.

Esther occasionally pictured working in an office, but the idea of buzzing fluorescent lighting and hand-washing posters were too sad to bear.

She loved getting to meet new people, face new problems every day. It was like every time she imagined herself working somewhere other than the inn, she could see people working around her, but couldn't quite place herself in the scene.

There it was. Esther laid eyes on Reese's name card mounted to the wall next to his office. His door was open, which was promising.

Esther patted her stomach, willing the butterflies to settle down. Having a tough conversation with an inn supplier who wasn't holding up their side of an agreement? Not a problem. Dealing with a guest on the verge of an adult tantrum? No sweat off her back. Questioning potential murder suspects? Not her area of experience.

*Just look at it as a new challenge.* She could take on a challenge. She took a deep breath, stood tall, and crossed the office floor, veering around the perimeter so Reese wouldn't see her coming. The dull gray wall-to-wall carpet muted her steps.

She slowed a few paces to the side of his door to mentally review her questions one last time.

Did he have a motive to kill Faris? What kind of boss-employee relationship did they have? Had there been something happening behind the scenes?

Esther exhaled as she took the final step. She knocked on Reese's door, plastering on a camera-ready smile.

Reese scratched his beard, eyes glued to the screen. He looked up a few seconds after her knock, like he'd been waiting for her to talk first.

"Hi! Reese, right?" she asked, lingering by the door.

His expression was blank. "I'm Reese. Can I help you?"

"I'm Esther Bennett," Esther said, placing a hand on her chest. "I'm the manager at Calliope Inn over in Oak's Rest."

Reese's expression didn't change. Clearly, neither her name nor the inn's rang any bells.

"I was one of Faris's inspection clients," she added.

Reese nodded tentatively, like he still couldn't place her but didn't want to admit it. "Gotcha. Have a seat." He motioned to the chair on the opposite side of his desk.

She was in the office. So far, so good.

"Sorry to intrude. I was downstairs getting..." She thought quickly. What had she planned to say? "A license renewed. And I thought I'd pop up to thank you for inviting me to the celebration of life. I don't think I saw you there?"

Reese didn't flinch. "I was only there for a bit. Had a family emergency come up and had to leave early." He switched gears. "Did Emerson tell you I was in?"

Esther had no clue who Emerson was, but she smiled and looked at the office full of employees behind her. "Mhm," she said brightly. If she was about to get an underpaid college intern fired, the least she could do was suggest her interaction with them had been a positive one.

Before Reese could say more, Esther steered the conversation back to Faris. Reese wasn't the only one who could switch topics.

She started with condolences, trying to gauge his reaction to her talking about Faris. Reese was hard to read. He didn't seem flustered, but he didn't seem comfortable either. He kept fidgeting with his gold watch. If the way it shone even under office lighting was any indication, it must have cost a small fortune.

Was it wishful to hope Reese would openly admit he'd always hated Faris? "I'm sure Faris was an easy employee to manage," Esther prodded. "I wouldn't be surprised if he had the whole health inspection manual memorized front to back."

Reese laughed softly and made a *you're telling me* face. "Faris was a good kid. It wasn't all sunshine, though. I had to check his work."

"Check his work?" Esther asked.

"He could take things to the extreme," Reese explained. "People would complain, so I'd step in. If I let his peer review reports go through to HR before reminding him to take it easy, everyone would have resigned by now. Especially the new guys."

"I see," Esther said, remembering to lean back in her seat a little. She didn't want to seem too eager. "Faris was critical of his coworkers."

"You could say that." Reese folded his hands on his desk.

Esther fumbled to keep the conversation going. "So, he and Uma's house was beautiful. To be honest, I was kind of surprised. Not to be rude or anything. He didn't strike me as..." she waved her hand in the air, trying to come up with the right word.

"A rich Yalfonter?" Reese suggested, smirking.

Esther eased out a laugh, relieved he was showing some sign of humor. "Your words, not mine."

Reese smiled. "If I had to guess, I think we'd need to give Uma a lot of the interior design credit. As for the house itself," he said, "the guy had the means. Why not use 'em?"

Esther raised her eyebrows. What did he mean by that? "Either Uma is a high-powered business mogul, or I need to fill out a job application here at the health department."

Reese shook his head. "I think we both know no job at the health department compensates *that* well."

Then what paid for Reese's consistently sharp wardrobe? Maybe directors got paid more? Had he gone into credit card debt trying to keep up appearances? Esther filed those questions away for later.

Reese leaned back, lacing his fingers over his stomach. "No, he came from a well-off background. Probably why he had such a *particular* set of standards," he muttered, almost to himself.

Esther's ears perked up. Reese's demeanor had shifted. He seemed more open than when she'd first arrived. Was he letting his true feelings about Faris show?

She gave it a few beats, not wanting to push too hard. "I'm guessing he was still taking an allowance from his parents?"

Reese snorted. "More like a trust fund."

Esther consciously stifled a gasp. "Faris had a trust fund?" she asked, keeping her cool an afterthought. "So, he was *wealthy* wealthy."

Reese shifted upright again, snapping out of whatever thought bubble he'd been in. He cleared his throat.

*Crap.* She'd hit a nerve. Either the conversation was about to end or Reese was about to start lying. Neither boded well.

"You know," Reese said. "I have a lot of work to do. Thanks for coming by." His tone wasn't unkind, but there was no mistaking he was done talking.

"Sure," Esther said, standing to leave. "It was nice to meet you, Reese."

"Sure, yup," he said, already pretending to be engrossed by his computer again.

Esther pressed the elevator button to the ground floor, replaying the conversation over in her mind while it was still fresh. It was like he'd realized he said too much and gotten spooked.

People didn't get spooked unless they had something to hide.

What was Reese Williams hiding?

# CHAPTER 20

E sther cursed under her breath as she jammed the *save* button. *Come on, come on.*

Beside her, Sesame lay unbothered on the reception desk, paws tucked neatly under her chest. Light streamed in from the dining room behind, casting Sesame's shadow across the wood, nearly twice as big as she was.

"You know pressing it harder won't fix it, right?" Justice said, spinning in her chair.

Esther sighed in frustration. "What good is a fancy staff scheduling and note-taking system if the thing can't even save our notes?"

One of Esther's favorite tasks was collecting all the special requests and accommodations future guests submitted with their reservations. It was a well-oiled machine, her tagging system: allergy information to kitchen or housekeeping, special activity interests to Justice.

A few clicks later, Justice rolled her chair closer and batted at Esther's hand. "Let me try." She clicked a few times, but the screen didn't change.

"See?" Esther gloated. "Not just me."

Justice shrugged. "Just plop Sesame on the keyboard and let her stomp around. She normally ends up deleting whatever is annoying me."

Esther shot her a look. "I think I'll try restarting it." She turned the computer off and faced Justice, her back to the quiet lobby. It'd be a few minutes before the desktop was booted up. "Got any good jokes while I wait?"

"Sure," Justice said. "What do you call a manager with the attention span of a goldfish?"

Esther pretended to think. "Drop-dead gorgeous?"

Justice rolled her eyes. "Tell me more about your suspect interview this morning. I heard our dear ol' health inspector was rich."

Esther wasn't sure what to make of it herself. "I'm still processing that one. The first time I saw his house, I just assumed his wife must have been the breadwinner."

"And then you met her."

"Shy women can be powerful too," Esther said, though Justice had hit the nail on the head.

"Sure they can. But Uma Holliday wasn't shy. She was an apparition."

Esther couldn't argue with that. "I don't think I caught even twenty percent of what she said. But...she did recently lose her husband." She held Justice's eye for a moment, aware of what the other woman was thinking. Esther relented. "The fake crying was weird."

Justice threw her hands up. "Told you! Okay, so give me the suspect list. Uma Holliday and who else? The emotionally repressed boss?"

Sesame nudged her head against Esther's palm, insisting on more pets. Did she know how cute she was? "It seems that way. We have two whole suspects."

Esther hadn't told anyone what she'd found at the crime scene. Especially not Kai. She hated even thinking of Lani as a suspect, but he'd been there, and Esther couldn't come up with a single good reason why.

"If Faris had a trust fund," Esther continued, "Uma would have been the beneficiary, right? That gives her a motive."

Justice pointed at her like she was exactly right. "Money is always the motive."

"And she could have had the opportunity. Maybe Faris and Uma shared their phones' locations with each other." There was one problem niggling at Esther. "She's tiny, though. I don't know if she's physically capable of it. Even if she'd snuck up on him, wouldn't he have fought back?"

"Motive and opportunity, but no means." Justice held an invisible pipe to her lips like a detective from a black-and-white movie.

"Pretty much," Esther said. She kept thinking. "But Queenie did say Faris had been hitting the beer pitchers hard that night. If he was drunk, it probably wouldn't have taken much strength to catch him off guard."

"Maybe Uma pretended she was going in for a kiss and then WHAM!" Justice made a jabbing motion.

"Possibly," Esther said. "I need to talk to her myself. I just need a reason to strike up a conversation with her. But I don't think she works a typical job, so I wouldn't even be sure where to 'run into' her."

"Why don't you invite her to the inn tomorrow? Treat her to lunch or tea."

Esther hadn't considered that. "Do you think it's a good idea to have a potential murderer here at the inn, around our staff and guests?"

"Isn't it kind of the perfect place? It's not like she's going to attack anyone in broad daylight. And your suspects already know you work here, so it's not like you're taking on any additional risk. But maybe stay away from the wine in case she's still in a killing mood."

"I try not to drink wine while I'm on the clock, but thanks for the tip," Esther said. "But if she's truly grieving, do you think she'll be up for driving to Oak's Rest and having lunch with someone she barely knows? And on short notice?"

"Well, if she is bushy-tailed enough to come meet with you," Justice said with an arched eyebrow, "doesn't that further prove she needs to be at the top of the suspect list?"

"You might have a point."

Justice's eyes shifted past Esther. "Hey, I got another joke for you."

"Hit me."

"A housekeeper and a groundskeeper angrily walk into a lobby…"

Esther looked behind her to see Sveta and Mort arguing across the lobby, Sveta flailing her arms in exasperation. She couldn't hear what they were saying, but their voices were distinct. Somehow, Sveta's Russian accent seemed to grow thicker with every passing year.

Esther turned back toward Justice. "Now would be a great time to practice those conflict resolution skills I'm always teaching you about. What do you say?"

Justice smiled. "I'm pretty swamped right now, boss. Sorry. Maybe another time." She scooted closer to the desktop, suddenly very interested in getting back to work.

Esther blew out a breath, preparing for the storm making its way to reception. Even Sesame lifted her head, ears twitching at the tension, before abandoning the scene.

"Show her," Sveta said when they reached the desk. She grabbed one of Mort's hands and held it up for Esther to see.

Mort yanked his hand away and crossed his arms. "You're being cockamamie, you know that?"

Esther must have looked confused, because Mort put his nose in the air and said, "What? I've been practicing my dictionary game. I'm addicted to the thing. Or should I say, *inveterate*. Betcha can't spell that, Svetty. I-n-v—"

"Anything I can help with?" Esther broke in.

Sveta exhaled through her nose. "He use white towels for hands. After oiling door! Now black oil on my nice white towels. Always same!"

"Don't be so operatic," Mort said. "I got a teeny-tiny drop of oil on *one* of your towels. Do you want the doors to squeak? Besides, isn't that what bleach is for?"

That had apparently been the wrong thing to say, because Sveta's face turned redder. She looked at Esther. "Every week he do this. When it will end? No bleach in whole world can fix this oil. I almost pass out from fumes trying to make towels white again!"

Esther's brain shifted into problem-solving mode. "Mort, could you use the dark hand towels we specifically bought for maintenance?" Esther had denied Bunny's request for butter dishes that month to budget for those hand towels.

Mort looked bashful. "The white towels are softer. Make me feel like I'm wiping my hands on clouds. I deserve luxury too."

Not what Esther had expected, but he wasn't wrong.

"Thank you," Sveta said with a nod, still on the defensive. "My towels are softest ever. I am queen of laundry. I know what I'm doing."

Esther clasped her hands together. "Sveta, how about you give Mort the hand towel he stained and I'll replace yours? Mort, you can get this one hand towel as dirty as you want, and Sveta will wash it with the darks, but will at least keep it nice and fluffy for you." She looked between her two staff members. "Does that work for everyone?"

"Thanks, boss," Mort said, smiling.

"Yes. Thank you, Esther. Very good idea," Sveta said.

"Of course," Esther said. "I need you two on good terms for

Makers and Merchants. I'm going to be leaning on the both of you."

"That remind me," Sveta said. "I would like to be front of house staff. Say hello to visitors. Offer friendly face."

"You want to be a greeter?"

Sveta crossed her arms. "Give me reason to put on lipstick in the morning."

Esther bit back a smile. "Okay, you got it. You'll be our festival welcome committee." She turned to Mort. "Any requests from you?"

Mort wrinkled his nose. "I'm more of a special-ops, behind-the-scenes dude." He sniffed and looked toward the kitchen. "Aw snap, I think I smell chocolate chip loaf." He shifted, offering Sveta the crook of his elbow. "Shall we?"

Sveta linked her arm. "*I* shall. *You* need to watch figure," she said, patting Mort's belly. They passed the reception desk and headed through the dining room.

"See, that wasn't so hard, was it?" Esther asked Justice.

Justice tilted her head. "Sure. When a child throws a tantrum and you give it candy, the tantrum fizzles out pretty quickly."

Esther slumped in her chair. "Remind me again why I don't make you work from the basement?"

"Then who would be here to give you honest feedback on your conflict resolution practices?" she asked innocently.

Before she could reply, Esther clocked the corner of Kai's spa cart as it descended the last step of the staircase. It turned down the hallway right off the front door, headed toward the Calliope Room. Lani was scheduled to help out that afternoon.

Esther quickly made her way around the desk, hoping she could get a moment alone with Lani before he and Kai's next session.

A guest stepped into her path, looking worried. "You're the manager, right?" the woman asked. She was wearing a fitted lilac workout top with matching leggings.

"That's me," Esther said, craning her neck to see where Kai and Lani had gone.

"I lost my fitness watch. I had it on when I woke up this morning. I think. I don't remember, to be honest," she said, shaking her head. "The point is, I need my watch to tell me how many steps I've taken. If I don't get enough physical activity, I won't be able to sleep well tonight. If I don't sleep well tonight, my anxiety will spike tomorrow. Then I won't be able to sleep tomorrow night. Then I—"

Esther placed a gentle hand on her shoulder. "See that lovely woman behind the front desk?" she asked, pointing to Justice, who was looking right at them. "That's Justice, our concierge. She can help you retrace your steps. All over the inn. Have her show you around the garden too."

The woman placed a hand on her chest and smiled. "That's such a relief. Thank you so much."

"My pleasure," Esther said sweetly, waving at a nervous-looking Justice. "If you'll excuse me, I've got my own mystery to crack."

## CHAPTER 21

Esther found Kai and Lani in the Calliope Room. Kai had creating a serene, calming environment down to a science. Aside from a few folded tables and chairs stashed in the corner, it was hard to tell the space was only temporarily serving as a spa suite.

LouLou had made them custom double-layered curtains that let in soft, filtered sunlight when the first layer was pulled back, but bathed the room in darkness when closed. The ambient sounds of soft piano notes, trickling water, and distant wind chimes made the room feel like an oasis.

"This place looks great," Esther said by way of announcing herself.

Lani looked up from where he was folding a blanket on the massage table. "Thanks," he said, smiling proudly. "Auntie Kai did a lot of it. I helped, though."

"It takes me twice as long without him, though," she said, winking at Esther.

If anything, Kai almost certainly worked faster on her own. She was a master. But Esther knew she loved having a buddy to work with. "So, Lani, still enjoying Oak's Rest? Not sick of us yet?"

Lani patted the neatly folded blanket. "No way. It's been dope. Everyone is so cool here."

"This one already lost the key I made him," Kai said, pointing at Lani with her thumb. "I put all my artistic integrity into that key, you know. That tree design? Straight from the heart." She balled her fists and rubbed her eyes, pretending to cry.

Esther measured her reaction. "Is that right?" she asked, looking at Lani. He must have realized the key was missing not long after leaving the crime scene.

"Where was the last place you remember having it?" She might have been pushing it, but she wanted to see what kind of poker face he had.

Lani didn't miss a beat. "Must have fallen out of my pocket by the lake or something. I got into a race with a couple pups at the dog beach a few days ago." His hands were still on the blanket, like he'd had to pause to concentrate on the memory. "I ended up in a pile of face licks and wagging tails."

So, that's how he was going to play it. Esther smiled half-heartedly, observing him carefully. Was he lying? Could Kai's own nephew have done something horrible and framed her for it?

"That's right," Kai said, snapping. "We're running low on massage oil. I'm gonna go grab a second bottle from the supply closet."

"No worries," Lani said. "If the client shows up early, I'll tell them you'll be right back."

Esther waited until she was sure Kai was out of earshot. She pulled the house key from her pocket and opened her palm.

Lani's eyebrows furrowed. "Where did you...?" he began, looking up at her. Recognition dawned on his face. "You know." It was a statement, not a question.

"I don't know anything," Esther said. "But there are plenty of things I'd *like* to know. Starting with why your key was at the scene of the crime the police seem to think my friend committed." Her voice was steady, sharp, almost rehearsed, like she'd been cross-examining suspects her whole career. Maybe she should have gone to law school.

Lani stepped toward her, the creak of the original wood floors the only sound in the room. His voice was soft. "I know what you're thinking, and it's not what it looks like."

Esther raised her eyebrows. "Then what's it like? Because I remember you joking about killing Faris after your Aunt Kai failed her inspection. Tell me you were joking."

"I was doing a little digging around, okay?" Lani said, sounding like a little kid in trouble. He looked guilty, but not *left-a-body-in-the-woods* guilty. More like *please-don't-tell-my-mom* guilty.

Esther shook her head, confused. "Digging around? Have you been trying to find out who did this too?"

Lani nodded solemnly. "Of course I'd never do something like what happened to that Faris guy. But I take my family duties seriously. If my aunt is in trouble, I can't sit back and watch." Confidence returned to his voice at the mention of his family. He seemed sincere.

Esther let out a sigh, relieved she wouldn't have to break more bad news to Kai. She handed Lani the key.

"Thanks," he said. "I'll say I found it under the couch cushion."

"Smart thinking," Esther said. "Now, doing your own investigating? Not the best idea."

"Aren't you?" he asked, tilting his head toward the key. The unspoken indication was clear: she had to have been at the crime scene to find it.

"Fair point. However, you're only here for a few months. Try not to get on law enforcement's bad side. They tend not to appreciate people sneaking around crime scenes." She hesitated. "This is a safe town, but there's a very real chance the killer is still out there."

She couldn't bring herself to say it out loud, but there was no telling what they'd do next. And she couldn't stomach the thought of something happening to Lani.

Lani seemed to understand that. "I guess I just wanted to help."

"I get it," Esther said. "I do. But you getting into trouble would only make things worse. I'm going to help Kai out of this mess. I promise."

Lani smirked. "I'll stay out of it. If you ever need some muscle, you know who to ask."

Esther laughed. "If you're offering, we got a heavy shipment of laundry supplies with your name on it."

"Happy to help," he said. "I'll check on that right after our session here. Where should I put it?"

"Just ask around for the head housekeeper, Sveta. Super sweet woman. She doesn't mind people touching her supplies at all."

# CHAPTER 22

The next day, Esther poured herself a cup of English Breakfast, steam pouring out the spout and curling up and away into the cool air behind the inn. Gravel crunched underfoot as she shifted to carry out the pour.

She and Uma sat at the only occupied table in the garden. Esther wondered whether sunlight damaged teacups. She took another look at the set, white with a blue and pink floral pattern and silver trim. On second thought, she moved it under the shade of the table umbrella.

The nearby lounge chairs and pair of chaises, which guests enjoyed sunbathing on, lay empty and perfectly positioned like they were holding their breath, waiting to eavesdrop.

Across the small table, Uma clutched her own teacup as if it was trying to run away from her. She'd yet to taste it, though. Esther hoped it wasn't too hot. Bunny had insisted on waiting until the moment Uma arrived to start the tea, explaining that if she let it boil too long, too much oxygen would leave the water, and the flavor would be sacrificed.

Uma finally took a sip, then parted her lips from the teacup, leaving behind a kiss of bright red lipstick. The bold color clashed with the tiny woman, whose teeth chattered like she'd been dropped into a snowstorm without a coat.

It seemed like Uma was never caught without her makeup. Which was probably for the best, since Esther would have bet her lips were turning blue under the makeup.

Aside from the soft gurgle of the water fountain and the scrape of porcelain on saucer, the backyard was quiet. Guests had already eaten lunch and were out and about on their afternoon activities or preparing for their evenings. The garden nestled against the dining room's outer wall, a small patch of gravel on the expansive lawn.

Justice had given her some assurance about inviting a potential murder suspect to the inn, but Esther still wanted to remain alert.

If she needed to make a quick escape, her best bet was getting back inside the house. She had three good options. The obvious choice was the dining room door, but Uma would anticipate that. Beyond the backyard, the gravel split into two winding paths, each curving around the inn to a set of porch stairs, one leading to the living room, the other to the kitchen's delivery entrance. Either way, she'd have to watch her step and avoid the neatly arranged potted plants.

Bunny had outdone herself. A two-tiered tray of delicate finger sandwiches and bite-sized pastries, varied in color and texture, looked positively regal on the table between them.

Uma's tiny designer purse seemed almost curated to complement the luxurious spread. Esther could understand why Uma had placed it there. If she'd spent a month's pay on a bag, she wouldn't have put it on the ground either.

"You have to try our chef's smoked salmon tea sandwiches," Esther said, adding two to her plate. "Whatever she puts in the herb cream, I'd bathe in it if I could."

Uma smiled weakly. She took another sip of tea, but made no moves for the food.

Esther couldn't tell if Uma was shy, grieving, or flat-out didn't like her. Whatever the reason, it would not be an easy-going conversation. "You know, I learned that in England, pouring tea before milk used to be a sign of wealth. Cheap china couldn't handle boiling water without cracking. So the order of events was sort of a class distinction."

Uma nodded twice, looking marginally more interested in Esther's presence than she had before, which was encouraging. "I did know that," she said.

Esther capitalized on the momentum. "Thanks again for coming all the way here. I didn't want to impose, given everything you've been going through, but I wanted to properly introduce myself. We didn't have much of a chance to talk at Faris's celebration of life." She took a small bite of the sandwich, fighting the instinct to close her eyes and sing in delight.

Uma opened her mouth to respond. "It—" she squeaked, her voice giving out. She cleared her throat and tried again, this time clear and steady. "It's nice to get out of the house. This place is..." She looked around, clearly searching for a word that wouldn't offend. "Quaint."

Esther had to stop herself from doing a double-take. It was the first time she'd heard Uma talk at a reasonable volume. It almost distracted from the subtle jab.

Uma continued, eyes downcast. "I know my husband wasn't always a crowd pleaser. I don't exactly have many people to share my grief with." She took another sip.

Was that a thank you? "Well, you're welcome here any time," Esther said. She needed to coax out Uma's alibi, to pin down where she'd been the night of the murder. "How are you holding up? I can't even imagine getting a call like the one you must have gotten. Waiting all night for him to come home, worrying..." She left the sentence hanging, hoping she'd guessed accurately and that Uma would fill in the rest.

Uma set the teacup on the table. "I actually wasn't home that night. I was staying with an old college friend in Manhattan. She bought this beautiful apartment on the upper west side."

Did she sound rehearsed? She'd sprinkled in just enough detail for the story to seem real, but not enough to be difficult to remember. Esther needed to keep prodding. "Do you mind me asking how you found out?"

Uma sighed. "It was all a daze. I got a call from a number I didn't recognize. All I know is I left for home right away, but I barely remember the train ride." She fiddled with her teacup, turning it to the side by its handle. "I don't even remember what I said to my friend before leaving. I was in her apartment one moment, and sitting on the train the next. I remember the cold window feeling nice against the side of my head. I never put my face against windows on public transportation. But, alas."

Someone was in the talking mood now.

Esther considered the alibi. Claiming to be out of town felt convenient. Maybe too convenient? The kind of alibi someone would offer if they wanted to stay as far from a crime scene as possible.

"Wow," Esther said. "That's awful. I'm so sorry." She took a sip of her tea. She tried to sound nonchalant as she asked, "Have the police been nosing around much, bothering you?"

Uma puffed out her cheeks. "It was almost nonstop at first, like they were suspicious of me or something. Especially that detective, Sabrina something. She made me give her my train ticket and everything. A total invasion of privacy."

Esther decided against correcting Sabina's name. It made sense Uma would have been one of the first people the police cleared. That didn't mean she was off Esther's suspect list, though. "Sounds like they're being pretty thorough. I can imagine how that would feel invasive," Esther consoled her, silently wishing she could get ahold of that train ticket herself.

Uma crossed her arms and muttered, "It's ironic. Faris was the one who did all the sneaking around, and here I am, having to prove *my* late-night whereabouts."

Esther paused, finger sandwich halfway to her lips. "Sneaking around?" She took a bite, hoping she was still coming off casual.

Uma looked away. "I think he'd been seeing someone. For a while."

Esther nearly choked. "Faris was having…an affair?" The man had a knack for offending just about everyone he met. And he'd been in not one, but two romantic relationships?

Uma stiffened. "He was."

"Do you know who he'd been seeing?" Esther asked. "Did you tell the detective about your suspicion?"

Uma shrugged. "I told her. She said they'd get a warrant to look through his phone, but they haven't yet."

"Did you find something in his phone to suggest an affair?"

Uma scrunched her nose. "I couldn't stand seeing that kind of detail up close. But I did find a pink scrunchie in his work bag. I'm guessing she was young and dumb."

"That's terrible," Esther said, not mentioning she had her own collection of scrunchies at home. She found herself feeling a flicker of empathy for Uma. She really hoped she wasn't developing a soft spot for a murderer.

Uma picked up her cup. Before taking a sip, she said, "Unless, of course, he was seeing more than one woman." For the first time, Uma looked Esther directly in the eye and held her gaze.

Esther felt thrown by the shift in tone. She felt like she was supposed to catch the meaning in that look, but she didn't, so she changed topics. "Yeah, hopefully not…so, have the police given you any new information? Any new evidence or findings from the crime scene?" She hoped she wasn't being insensitive, but she wanted to be certain they hadn't discovered anything she couldn't have found out on her own.

"Nothing yet," Uma said. "But I doubt they'll find much of anything under all that foliage. It's a mess over there."

"You've been to the crime scene?" Esther asked, surprised. Was it normal for a widow to visit the place where her husband had been found dead?

"Oh, I haven't—I'm going off what they told me," Uma stammered.

She was definitely lying about something. Esther remembered her conversation with Reese, the moment he realized he'd said too much and needed to backtrack. It seemed like Uma had just made a similar realization.

"Right," Esther said. "Of course."

# CHAPTER 23

"An AFFAIR?" Bunny flicked suds from her hands, glancing at the kitchen staff bustling behind them, likely aware she'd been louder than intended.

Esther had barely waited for Uma to close her car door before rushing inside to relay the conversation. And when Esther had turned from the parking lot, Sesame had been sitting in the front window, tail swishing. Maybe Uma hadn't passed the feline instincts test.

Bunny, already deep in her kitchen routines, had put her to work mid-story. Esther had almost been led off course by a tray of cooling sugar cookies.

She stood beside Bunny at the three-compartment sink, inhaling the fresh lemon dish soap as she caught her breath. "I couldn't believe it either. I'm desperate to know who it was. One, because hello, *have they met Faris*? Two, because they could be another suspect."

Bunny passed a dripping plate. "And Uma *just happened* to be out of town that night?" She raised a skeptical brow.

Esther dunked the plate under the surface of the sanitizer. The heat of the liquid seeped through her rubber gloves, warm and oddly calming. Her heart rate slowed. "I'm telling you, Bun. Something's off. Between the trust fund and the affair, the motives are stacking up." She slotted the plate into the drying rack.

Bunny counted on her fingers, her wet gloves squishing with each tick. "Husband is an insufferable grump, husband is rich, husband is a cheater. That's three strikes." She looked at Esther. "Home run."

Esther gave her a flat look. "Let's leave the sports references to people who own gym shoes. But yeah, there's a lot to unpack."

Droplets fell from Bunny's glove to the floor. The checker tile was wet. Esther imagined Faris snipping at her about occupational hazards. She'd wipe it up as soon as they were done.

"Uma also made a weird comment about all the foliage at the crime scene. When I asked how she knew that, she got all cagey."

A timer screeched somewhere in the kitchen. "Got it!" A staff member called out.

"I should hope so!" Bunny yelled over her shoulder before turning back to Esther. "What if she got weird because she visited the scene while it was blocked off for investigation? Maybe she thought she'd get in trouble. Or maybe she knows her way around Oak's Rest."

Esther gave Bunny's points some thought. Why would Uma be afraid to tell her she'd snuck into the crime scene? Esther wasn't a police officer. And it was possible Uma was familiar with Oak's Rest, but what were the chances she'd know so many details about the landscape around the vet? The creamery wasn't open in the fall, so that took a potential ice cream addiction off the table. "Nah. I don't think Uma Holliday spends much time around here. She looked around the inn like she half expected our guests to be staying in tents. She called us *quaint.*"

Bunny squinted. "Did she say it in that fake-nice way?"

"Yup."

"She's hiding something."

"Exactly. If she'd just said she saw a photo, or didn't act like I'd caught her shoplifting, I wouldn't have thought twice."

"So, is Uma Holliday our number one suspect?" Bunny asked.

Esther rested her hand on the edge of the sink. "For now, yes. But I want to know more about the boss. Reese is still in the race."

Bunny smirked. "Who's using the sports references now?" Her eyes widened. "Oh my gosh. What if the killer strikes again? What if they pick their next victim at the Makers and Merchants Festival?"

Esther felt a pang of worry. She pointed to the plate in Bunny's hand, prompting her to keep washing, buying herself a moment while her mind raced. What if Bunny was right? The festival *would* be the perfect opportunity—lots of visitors, busy staff, chaos.

She felt a little selfish, but she couldn't help imagining the news headlines:

*Disgraced manager of quaint inn puts on deadly event.*

*Inexperienced motel manager tries and fails at hospitality career.*

She forced the images out of her mind. "I think we should follow the money. But we also need someone with inside information. Someone who knew about Faris's personal life." Esther racked her brain for anyone who could have known Faris personally. "Remember the last town hall? When someone said Dev Singh was the only business owner Faris got along with?"

"Yeah," Bunny said. "It surprised me. Dev doesn't strike me as the kind of guy who would be friends with someone so…"

"Right," Esther said, not needing to hear whatever unflattering word Bunny was thinking. "Maybe Dev knows something we don't. About Faris. Or Uma. Or their finances. I think I need to pay a visit to our bookstore."

# CHAPTER 24

Oak's Rest was a fall postcard come to life. The air carried the scent of leaves reaching the ends of their seasonal lifecycle.

Lake Ezra, only a few blocks from the town square, shimmered in the sunlight like cut glass. The wind sent leaves dancing along the sidewalk, skittering past storefronts adorned with decorated wicker baskets and plant arrangements alight with burnt oranges, whites, and yellows.

Esther sipped her coffee and savored the heat in her chest. "You're a miracle worker, Penny," she told the cup. She'd slipped out of work a little early, determined to find answers, but she didn't want to let her mission overshadow the beautiful day.

A familiar voice pierced through her moment of peace like a sharp needle. "Esther?"

Esther took a deep breath before responding.

"Esther Bennett." The voice was closing in from behind. "I need to talk to you about Makers and Merchants."

Esther turned around and mustered up the warmest smile she could. "Hi, Bethany."

Bethany Early was wearing her General Store apron, but

somehow, Esther could sense she was approaching on mayoral business.

Bethany panted lightly as if she'd been chasing Esther for blocks. "I'm collecting signatures for the parking adjustment approval." She pulled a notepad from her apron pocket. "To show the county."

"Parking adjustment approval?" It was a new term for Esther.

Mayor Early looked impatient. "So we can temporarily block off parking spaces around the town square during the festival. People will have to go looking for other places to park. If that means they happen to stumble upon the inn…" She straightened her apron and jutted out her chin. "Well, that wouldn't be the worst thing in the world."

"You're going to squeeze tourists out toward the festival so they come spend money with us," Esther said. She wished she'd thought of it herself. "Mayor and savvy business person. How did you get so talented?"

Bethany looked embarrassed. "So far, I have signatures from J.W. Boating Supplies, Louisa's Fixes, Penny's Breakfast—"

"And you need Calliope Inn to sign off on allowing additional parking on the premises?" Esther guessed.

"Precisely," Mayor Early said, extending the paper and pen.

"Okay, I'll ask her," Esther said. "But she's notoriously crotchety about doing business after four p.m."

"Who?" Bethany asked.

"The inn," Esther replied, trying to keep a straight face.

Bethany allowed her shoulders to sag for one brief moment. "Esther, sign it, please. This is serious."

Esther did as she was told. "How many more signatures do you need?"

Bethany examined the new name on the page and beamed. "Thank you. Just forty-seven more."

"Easy-peezy," Esther lied, looking around for a way out of the conversation. She glanced in the direction of Used Books &

More, where she was headed to talk to Dev Singh. A few spaces over from the bookstore, Ingram Ellis, Faris's prior inspection buddy, was loading a bag into a county vehicle. "I'm sorry, Bethany. Gotta run," Esther said, already walking away.

"Okay," Bethany called after her. "But don't forget to obtain waiver of liability signatures from all the vendors. Oak's Rest cannot be found liable for any damage to booths, tents, or merchandise!"

"I won't forget," Esther called over her shoulder before muttering, "How could I? Collecting signatures is so much fun."

Esther waved at Ingram as she approached the bookstore.

He smiled. "Calliope Inn, right? Esther, was it?"

"That's me," Esther said. She pointed to the health department car. "Still working hard to get us all in compliance, huh?"

Ingram laughed. "Yeah, well, someone's gotta do it."

"What got you into this work?" She couldn't imagine many little boys dreaming of being health and safety inspectors when they grew up.

"I was a contractor in another life. I took over the family business after my dad passed. But running a business is hard, and running a profitable one? Even harder."

"Hence the stable government job," Esther said, understanding. "Hey, how are you holding up? You know, since..."

Ingram smiled sadly. "Kinda weird being solo for a job I used to have a partner for. Faris and I didn't agree on much, but, you know, it was nice having someone to make conversation with during car rides and stuff."

Esther could see how that would be sad. "That's gotta be tough. Could you request a different service area? To avoid the constant reminder of being here?"

"Actually, I kind of feel a sense of responsibility to this town to finish the job right. And to Faris." Ingram looked pained. "I don't know what happened that night, but I was with him before it did. I can't stop thinking maybe I could have stopped it, or...I don't know." He paused. "I left him." He looked at Esther like whatever she said next had the potential to crack him wide open.

Esther decided not to mention she already knew all about the timeline of events from that night, and had dissected it in detail with multiple people. "You can't beat yourself up for something that was out of your control."

Ingram nodded. Was he getting choked up?

"Are you from the area?" Esther asked to change the topic, even though she already knew he lived in Yalfont.

He seemed to brighten. "Born and raised. I'm a lake boy through and through."

"I'm surprised," Esther began. "I wouldn't have taken you for a Yalfonter. You seem more…"

"Normal?" he asked, his forehead wrinkling in question. "There are some humble pockets of Yalfont. We don't all own yachts."

"Good to know," Esther said. "In fairness, I haven't spent a ton of time over there. The limited interactions I have had with Yalfonters have been…interesting enough."

Ingram laughed. "I totally get it. Hey, I gotta head to my next appointment. But it was nice chatting with you, Esther from Calliope Inn."

"You too," Esther said, before heading toward the bookstore. Ingram seemed like a much more agreeable inspector than his former coworker. Hopefully, that meant the business community of Oak's Rest was safe from any more excessively thorough inspections. Hopefully, Kai would be safe on her next try.

Used Books & More smelled like an old cedar chest opened up after years in the attic. The shop was stuffed to the gills with merchandise. Books, lamps, and other vintage keepsakes lined every surface. Even the ceiling beams were used to hang picture frames.

"Welcome," Dev's voice called out from somewhere undeterminable. "Have a look around. I'll be right with you."

Esther chuckled at the greeting reserved for tourists and store newcomers. "Thank you," she responded, playing along.

She circled a tall, revolving postcard display, fingering through the old images. She paused on a sepia-toned postcard with an old-timey automobile loaded with suitcases. A rooster perched on the roof. The caption read, *Headed for the Big City!*

A couple browsed on the far side of a nearby shelf. "This place is kind of chaotic," the woman said.

"You're telling me," the man said. "I thought this was supposed to be a bookstore. It's more like some weird book-antique-shop hybrid."

Esther held back a snort. *It's called Used Books and MORE, not Used Books.*

"Hey, Esther," Dev Singh said, appearing from deep in the store. He was carrying a stack of books up to his nose. "This is a nice surprise. What can I do for you?"

"Oh, you know," Esther said, trying to sound casual, and not like she'd come by for the sole purpose of fishing for clues. "I was in town and thought I'd stop in."

Dev set the books on the checkout counter, sighing in relief. "I don't suppose you want to help me with inventory, do you?"

Esther smiled. "I would, but I already have a full-time job. Plus, if I got poached to work here, I'd have to replace myself."

Dev raised his hands in surrender. "It was worth a try. I might point out, however, it is a business day and you're here at my store."

Esther lifted her cup of Penny's. "Even managers need their coffee breaks sometimes." She opened a book and flipped through. "Planning on selling any of these at Makers and Merchants?"

"I'm saving some special ones for the festival," Dev said. "Only real history buffs will understand. Weed out the casual window-shoppers."

"Interesting strategy. Your goal is to not make any money, then?"

"Very funny."

It was time to get down to business. "I just ran into Ingram Ellis out front. Have you had your inspection yet?"

Dev spoke as he typed on the computer. "I have. Luckily, he came alone this time. A much more friendly fellow than his predecessor. Faris always had a field day in this place." He stopped typing and looked at Esther. "We all support Kai, us Oak's Rest business owners. We know she'd never do something so terrible."

"I know," Esther said gratefully. She guessed people felt responsible to show their allegiance since Kai was her part-time employee.

She was about to say more when she heard a thud. Someone yelled, "Ow! Who put that there?"

"Footstool?" Esther asked.

"Floor lamp," Dev replied without looking away from the screen.

"Speaking of Faris," Esther said, looking for an inroad, "Did you know him well? You know, outside of inspections?"

Dev frowned slightly. "I wouldn't say that. He'd come in sometimes looking for vintage almanacs. He said he used to read them as a child." Dev looked away from his screen. "Which didn't exactly scream 'lots of friends,' if you ask me. But I'm an old man. What do I know about the pastimes of today's children?"

Esther nodded. "I think it's safe to assume those almanacs kept little Faris company."

"But I did grow to appreciate the young man's taste in reference materials. Anyone who still seeks information from books gets points with me." Dev opened a book cover, ran his finger along a string of numbers on the page, and typed with the other hand. "I think he grew fond of me too. Especially after I gave him a ride home."

"You drove him home?" Esther asked, intrigued. "When was this?"

"Not too long ago. Earlier this year. He came into the store and just…stayed.

He lingered longer than usual, as if he didn't want to go home. I know a man in the doghouse when I see one."

"You think he was having relationship issues?" Esther surmised.

Dev tilted his head. "I can't say. Relationship, something else, I don't know. But it was something. He told me his car died at the edge of the town square. So I offered to close up early and give him a lift."

Esther had a hard time imagining Faris asking anyone for help. "What did you talk about on the drive?"

"Not much of anything. It was a mostly quiet trip. Like I said, the young man was going through something. I didn't want to press it. Anyhow, I had to drive a roundabout way due to the bridge construction. We ended up passing a casino. I made a joke about us stopping in and gambling away his worries. That was when I knew something was very wrong."

"Why? What did he say?"

Dev pursed his lips. "Not so much *say*, as much as *cry*."

"He cried?" Now *that* was an interesting mental image. "What was he so upset about?"

Dev huffed. "Apparently, the lad had come from quite an affluent background. Trust fund. That sort of thing."

Reese was right. "I did know about that, actually. I've been trying to get to know more about Faris's wife, since that seems like quite the motive for…." she widened her eyes, not wanting to throw around words like "murder" in the presence of shoppers.

"Well, I don't suppose there's much motive left," Dev said.

"What do you mean?"

He crossed his arms. "From what I gathered, he spent most of it. Although he mentioned something about making the money he had left count."

Esther felt her jaw drop. "Wait, what? How could he have spent it all?"

Dev gave a small shrug. "I couldn't say. But when I asked him about the casino, he indicated he was having financial issues. Oh, how I hoped he'd invest what he had somewhere safe. They ought to teach financial literacy in schools, I'm telling you."

Esther thought about Faris and Uma's large house, her designer purse. Could Uma have known Faris had spent the money? "I'm shocked. I guess that does away with my gold-digging motive. I wonder what that means for his widow, Uma. I wonder if she'll have to sell their house."

"I don't know," Dev said, thumbing through a book like it was the most fascinating thing in the store, though his eyes kept darting to Esther's. He was all in on the gossip, and was hiding it poorly. "But if you ask me, Faris throwing away Uma's secure future, Uma perhaps trying to claim it early, both sound like viable motives."

Esther considered that. "You know, you could be right. Uma was definitely accustomed to a certain lifestyle. I can't imagine she would have reacted well to the news that it was all gone."

Worse yet if Faris hadn't delivered the news at all, and she'd happened to find out on her own.

Had Uma reached her breaking point?

# CHAPTER 25

The next evening, Esther lingered on her sister's porch with a container of fresh-baked vanilla wafers, courtesy of Bunny. In the golden light of the waning sun, the cul-de-sac looked like a movie set featuring identical houses with shuttered windows, manicured hedges, and two-car garages.

Cameron had first suggested a layered chocolate cake for Sunday dinner at their parents'. Esther countered with something simpler, something without awkward stretches of wait time while the cakes baked. They'd agreed on banana pudding.

Esther rang the bell. She braced herself as footsteps raced toward the other side of the door. *Get in, get out. That's all you have to do.*

Cameron opened the door as her son, Eli, wrapped himself around her leg. He hid his face behind her.

It took the wind out of Esther's lungs. He was so big. She'd half expected him to still be in diapers.

"Hi, Eebie-Jeebie," Esther said, hoping he remembered the nickname she'd given him when he was still cooing and drooling out the side of his mouth. "You're huge! What are you now, twenty years old?"

Eli spoke quietly from behind Cameron. "Nooo, I'm four."

His shyness made Esther want to tear up. It wasn't just her sister's life she'd been on the outside of.

Esther hoped her guilt didn't show. "You're *forty*?"

Finally, a grin broke across Eli's face. "No!" he said, letting a giggle escape. "Four!"

Cameron smiled. "Alright, E. Can Auntie Esther come inside, please?"

Eli untangled himself from Cameron and ran inside.

"Tell Daddy to get your sister her blue coat. *Not* the pink one," Cameron called after him.

Esther hadn't been to her sister's house in nearly two years, but some things never changed. The living room was spotless. Unnaturally so, considering there were two kids under six in the house.

A woven toy basket rested in the corner, brimming with plush animals, the frilly limbs of a well-loved doll, and picture books. A race car track curled on top, coiled like a snake. Not a single toy had dared touch the floor. It was like the toys knew they had a standard to live up to.

Cameron looked from Esther to the container of wafers. "Thanks for bringing those. I'm sure they're way better than the store-bought ones."

Good. Talking about the food was neutral territory. "The curse of having a chef best friend is that nothing prepackaged can ever compare."

As they started toward the kitchen, Cameron's husband, David, ran down the stairs holding their five-year-old daughter, Tamara, who did not look happy. "Eli's not going to touch your dollhouse, honey. He's coming with us. You'll see him the whole time." David pointed to Esther as they reached the bottom of the stairs. "See? Auntie Esther is here. Don't you want to put on your happy face for Auntie Esther?"

Ugh. She'd sprouted up too. Esther pushed down the second

wave of emotion rising in her chest. "Hi T.T.," Esther said, about to reach for a hug, but thinking better of it.

"Hi, Auntie Esther," Tamara said gloomily. "I can't talk. Eli touched my dollhouse."

"Oh, I see," Esther said, making eye contact with David. "That's serious business. Hey, I'll keep an eye on your dollhouse while you're gone. I'll make sure no one touches it. Deal?"

"Promise?" Tamara asked.

Esther held out her pinky. "Promise."

"Where has Eli gotten off that fast?" Cameron asked, peering around the staircase. "Eli? Come on buddy, the train is leaving the station!"

"All aboard!" the boy called out from another room.

Cameron turned her attention back to David. "Remember. No extra parmesan on top. They'll have plenty of artery-clogging goodness as it is. And make sure Eli doesn't slouch in the booth. I'm worried about his muscle tone."

David gave Cameron a peck on the cheek and set Tamara down. "We're going out for pizza, love. Not Navy SEAL training."

It was like watching a sitcom about the perfect family, only without the commercial breaks.

Right on cue, Cameron rolled her eyes—half resignation, half affection—the patented look of the female lead amused by the charming fool she'd married. "When our child can't sit at his school desk because his core muscles have weakened to mush, you're answering the call from his principal."

"We're outta here!" David bellowed to his son, winking at Cameron.

Eli darted past them all and landed at the front door. He wrapped his little fingers around the knob like he'd been waiting for them the whole time.

"Have fun," Cameron said, kissing Tamara on the forehead.

"Nice to see you, Esther," David said, corralling the children out the door. "We'll be back in a bit."

Esther didn't have a chance to reply before they were out on the porch.

"Sorry about the mess," Cameron said, walking over to shut the door behind them. "Two young kids and one grown one means it can be a bit of a circus around here."

Esther looked around the home that was tidier than her own, without kids to blame. "No worries, Veronica."

Cameron looked at Esther sharply. "What?"

Esther clasped her hands behind her back. "Nothing. It's just, apologizing for an immaculately tidy home is a pretty Bennett thing to do, don't you think?"

Cameron looked upward, clearly exasperated, then led the way to the kitchen. "Don't start. Can we make the banana pudding, please?"

"I'm not starting anything," Esther said, following behind. "But I took an oath as your big sister to remind you whenever you started aging faster than me. So I'm telling you. You're turning into Mom."

"We never made that oath," Cameron said, opening the container of wafers. The kitchen island was full-on *mise en place*, every ingredient and supply already lined up, ready to go.

"I may have forgotten to mention it," Esther said, surveying the kitchen. "You didn't have to do all this before I got here. I would have been happy to help."

Cameron shrugged. "I didn't know if—I didn't know how long you'd be able to stay." She avoided eye contact.

Esther and Cameron hadn't done an activity alone together in years. In fact, other than their brief conversation in front of their parents' house before the previous Sunday dinner, Esther couldn't remember the last time they'd been alone in the same room. There had always been parents or kids around.

Then, something about Cameron's efficiency clicked into place. She was rushing because she didn't think they'd be able to go thirty minutes without snapping at each other. She was worried it might be too uncomfortable.

Sure, Esther had gone through the same thought process when she suggested banana pudding instead of a complicated cake. But knowing her sister felt the same way still stung. Was she being hypocritical?

"I see," Esther said, narrowing her eyes. "And it was purely out of concern for my schedule."

"Yes," Cameron said, pretending to check the expiration date on the carton of whole milk.

Esther snorted. "Your lying face hasn't gotten any better."

Cameron rolled her eyes and poured the milk into a measuring cup. "You said you'd help me. So, help."

As they settled into the flow of measuring and whisking, conversation came more naturally than Esther had expected. Perhaps having things to do with their hands was the key to keeping the atmosphere light.

Cameron told Esther about a recent patient who'd come into the hospital with stomach pains, only for the x-ray to reveal she'd swallowed two whole sets of press-on nails.

"Painful *and* a waste of a good manicure," Esther said. "Two sets of dollar store press-ons would have lasted at least three days."

Cameron laughed. "What about you? How's the *motel*?" she asked, imitating their mother's snide comment. She glanced at Esther as she said it, like she was testing the waters.

Esther crossed her arms and widened her eyes, leaning into the performance. "Wow. Those are fighting words." She paused long enough for the bit to land. Cameron smiled. "But honestly? It's going great. I feel like I'm starting to get my footing as a manager."

Cameron tossed utensils into the sink as she finished using them. She was a clean-as-she-went person. Could those types of people ever be trusted? "Tell me more."

Esther pulled the stringy bits from a peeled banana as she thought. "Like, the other day, we were finalizing details about an upcoming guest trip to our local orchard and winery. I was able to negotiate the rates down enough to afford each guest a complimentary bottle of wine to take home with them."

"Now *that* sounds like a trip worth taking," Cameron said.

Esther flung a string from her fingers. "It's weird being an authority figure to my coworkers now, though."

Cameron started lining the baking dish with wafers. "Don't be ridiculous. You've been a leader for a long time."

The unexpected compliment caught Esther off guard. "What do you mean?"

"Esther, come on. You were the assistant manager before getting bumped up to the big leagues. Was it a surprise you're doing well as manager?"

"Yeah, but I was more assistant *to* the manager. I basically handled the manager's emails and waited for her to go out on maternity leave." Esther couldn't pretend she was upset to find out the woman decided not to return to work.

Cameron gestured to Esther with a wafer. "And when she left, you took the initiative to tell Tracey Harriet you were the right candidate for the job."

Esther paused her banana-slicing. It was true. She'd been so nervous her knees had buckled as she walked into that meeting. But she did it. And it was one of the greatest kindnesses she'd ever given herself. She didn't remember telling Cameron all of that, though. "How do you know all this?"

Cameron wiggled her eyebrows. "I listen. I may only hear from you once every thirty years, but I piece things together."

Esther studied the side of Cameron's face as she doled out equal numbers of wafers in each row. Maybe the whole making dishes together thing wouldn't be as torturous as she'd thought. Was it possible they were...getting along?

Esther opened her mouth to speak, but chickened out. *Just say it.* "You know, if you're interested in that winery trip, I could get us in on it." She rushed to add, "I mean, I know you're busy with work and everything. But if you wanted to." What good was being a manager if she couldn't pull strings for herself now and then?

Cameron looked up, pleasant surprise written on her face. "I'd have to get Dr. Patel to cover my patients, but he owes me for covering for him when his daughter had a gymnastics competition in Buffalo. Sure, why not? That sounds really lovely."

Esther pulled her phone out of her pocket. "I'll email our concierge right now to put us on the list."

A short while later, Esther scattered the final layer of wafers across the top of the dessert. It smelled sweet and comforting. She looked at Cameron. "Want to do the honors?"

"It would be my honor to do the honors," Cameron said, topping it all with thin slices of banana. She took a step back to admire the dish. "And just like that, they had dessert."

Esther had to admit, with each layer of cream, banana, and wafer distinct through the glass, Bunny would have been proud of her. "I guess you should store it here, since you're a short drive from Mom and Dad's. Think you can keep this beauty safe for three days?"

"That works," Cameron said, reaching for the refrigerator door. "I'll just have to move some of my green juices around."

Esther was about to make a joke about people who drank liquified lawns until she saw the bottles in the fridge, filled with unsettling shades of swamp green and neon pea. She cleared her throat. "So, my place next time?"

Cameron closed the refrigerator, banana pudding placed safely on the second shelf. "For what?"

Esther laughed. "What do you mean, *'For what?'* For this—" she motioned to the kitchen. "Making something for next week's dinner."

"Oh—I didn't—you want me to come over to your place?" Cameron asked, wringing her hands like she was suddenly chilly.

Esther knew that gesture. It was the same thing their mother did when she was either about to insult Esther or was pretending she hadn't just insulted her.

"Cameron."

Cameron busied herself with rinsing the dirty dishes. "Mhm?" she asked in a high-pitched voice, her back facing Esther.

Esther wasn't going to let her dodge it. She walked over and shut off the faucet, forcing her sister to focus on her. "Why don't you want to come to my house?"

Cameron wiped her hand on a dish towel and walked back to the island. "I never said that."

Esther followed. "No, but your body language did." She pointed to Cameron's hands. "If you pull another Mom tonight, you're gonna have to start wearing pearls and heels to the pharmacy."

"That happened once, Esther."

"Because she realized it was ridiculous or because she stopped running her own errands?"

Cameron threw her hands up. "What's your problem with pearls? They're timeless. And can you please stop comparing me to Mom? I never said I didn't want to go to your house. I don't know why you're reading so much into it."

*No need to get upset, Esther.*

*You're being dramatic, Esther.*

*Not everything is about you, Esther.*

Esther hated that those words still rang in her ears, even with so much time and distance. She hated how thinking about them made her want to shrink smaller and smaller until she was invisible. Not this time. "Okay, then I'll see you at my place next week," she said definitively, keeping her voice steady.

Cameron nodded. "Fine. I mean, we'll need to plan what we make around what you have available."

Bingo.

Esther blinked. "What I have *available?*"

"Yeah. I'm not sure what ingredients you have at your local market or whatever."

"I live less than an hour away. We do have access to food over in Oak's Rest, you know. The relief effort flies it in once a week by helicopter."

"Please don't make this a thing," Cameron said. "I was just trying—"

"Trying to do what?" Esther asked. "Trying to remind me how much better your life is here because you stayed near Mom and Dad? Because I ran off to the middle of nowhere without an M.D. or a Phd after my name?" The words had flown out of her mouth before she'd even chosen them.

Cameron finally looked her in the eye. "Maybe it is, Esther. Maybe I consider having a relationship with my parents a good thing. Sue me."

Esther's phone started ringing before she could respond. It was one of the after-hours maintenance guys. "I have to take this," she said before stepping into the living room. She forced out a breath before answering. "What's up, Toby?"

"Hey, Esther. Sorry to bug you. Remember that no-show earlier? Well, they showed. The family wants to check in now. Said they were having car trouble and couldn't get here sooner. Should I turn them away?"

"No, no," Esther said. "The room is still empty and prepped." Official policy stated late check-ins without a phone call could be cancelled. Esther had re-opened the family's room in the booking system, but it was still available when she'd left for the day.

"I'm not exactly sure how the check-in process goes," Toby said. "Do you want to talk me through it over the phone?"

Esther placed a hand on her hip. She could see the weekly meal whiteboard on the far wall of the kitchen, but Cameron was out of sight. "Don't worry about it. I'm on my way. Give them their room key and let them know I'll call them from the front desk when I get there. They'll need to come back downstairs to verify everything."

Most people would gripe about having to go back to work, but Esther couldn't exactly complain about the timing. She ended the call and returned to the kitchen. "I got called back into work. I have to go."

"Okay, fine," Cameron said, the tension in the air still palpable.

"Okay," Esther said, turning to go. She took a few strides, then backtracked. "Make sure no one touches Tamara's dollhouse."

Cameron said nothing.

Sunday dinner was going to be lots of fun.

# CHAPTER 26

"This is the best customer service I've ever gotten," the woman said, placing a hand on her son's shoulder. "We've had this trip planned for months. We would have hated to lose it because of the old lemon this one—" she looked in her husband's direction, "—insists on working on himself."

Her husband gave a weary smile, taking the dig. "We're here now, honey. That's all that matters. After the day we've had, I'm about ready to kick my feet up."

Esther smiled, heartened by the family's gratitude. She made a note on the guest ledger. She'd log the details in the system first thing in the morning. She slid a second copy of the room key, brass with a magenta leather fob stamped with a calliope hummingbird, across the reception desk. "No chance I was going to send you driving all the way home in the dark. Get a good night's sleep. And in case you didn't already see it, there's a selection of bath salts on the rim of your tub. I highly recommend lavender, citrus blend, or cedarwood. Take your pick."

The woman beamed. "That's so thoughtful. I love lavender."

"We try to make things feel like home, only with fluffier

towels," Esther said. "Breakfast runs from eight to ten. Tomorrow is gingerbread waffles with cinnamon butter. Chef de la Mora is a local legend, so save your appetites."

"Yum!" the little boy said, taking off across the lobby. "Waffles! Waffles!"

"That sounds divine," the woman said. "Be careful. You may never get rid of us."

Crisis averted, Esther walked through the dining room, her sight set on the kitchen. It was strange being alone there. It was typically alive with the symphony of pots and pans clanging, bells dinging, steam whooshing, and Bunny shouting orders.

"Let's see what kind of trouble I can get into." With any luck, Bunny had left some goodies lying around. Esther opened the refrigerator and her eyes immediately landed on several flutes of Bunny's latest concoction—poached pear praline parfaits.

One flute had a sticky note: *set longer.* Another read: *close. try over-steeping tea.* Esther grabbed the second flute, found a spoon, and dug in. If this was "close," Esther couldn't even imagine what Bunny's idea of perfection was.

Bunny's made-from-scratch cream was still fluffy. The Earl Grey-poached pears complemented the vanilla in the cream perfectly. Candied walnuts added a satisfying crunch. "Remind me to never cross Bunny. I need her in my life forever," she cooed to the flute.

Snack finished, Esther gathered her things from the reception desk and headed for the door. The soft crackle of the fireplace drew her into the living room. Firelight flickered over the stone surround and across the faces of a half-dozen pajama-clad adult guests, curled up on floor cushions like kids on their first camping trip.

Mrs. Carter, a retired school librarian, sat proudly in the wingback chair closest to the hearth, a thick novel propped on a lap pillow. Her glasses were poised at the tip of her nose. She read aloud with professional cadence, her voice drawing out warm and low.

Behind her, the bookshelves were packed with novels of every kind: faded paperbacks, hardcovers without dust jackets, and a scattering of golden nugget finds from library sales.

One woman listened with a blanket clutched to her chest, while an older couple leaned together on the couch, fingers entwined. The husband's eyes were closed, not quite asleep, but content. Sesame was curled up next to his leg, and perked up when she saw Esther.

Esther caught herself smiling. Adult storytime had sounded a little silly when she'd first pitched it, like something more suited to an elementary school than an inn. But here it was, already feeling like a long-beloved tradition.

Sesame leapt off the couch and made her way to Esther. Only, she didn't stop for a body rub or head butt like Esther had anticipated. Instead, the cat breezed right past her. She stopped at the entrance of the hallway toward the Calliope Room and looked back at Esther, as if checking she was following.

In fact, Esther did hear a faint sound from the direction of the Calliope Room. Who could it be? The candle-making workshop had ended hours ago. She drank in one last sight of the cozy living room before easing away on quiet feet.

She trailed Sesame to the Calliope Room, where she discovered a frazzled-looking Kai rifling through her bag on the ground. There were papers scattered all over the spa bed and floor. Esther didn't know what to ask. "If you're going for a 'creative-genius-mid-meltdown' aesthetic, you nailed it. But I don't think your clients are going to find it very relaxing."

Sesame lowered into loafing position by the door, apparently settling in to watch whatever chaos was unfolding in what was previously a calming space. Esther was going to have to start paying her if she kept helping her monitor the inn so well.

Kai looked up from her bag in surprise. "What are you doing here?"

Esther put a hand to her chest. "Me? I could ask you the same thing, lady."

Kai stood, holding a paper. "I was at the spa tonight with Sabina."

A bucket of cold water on a warm mood. "If the ORPD is still bugging you, they must have not made much progress in finding the real killer."

Kai waved the paper around as she vented. "This is the most interaction I've ever had with our police department. They keep asking me the same questions. It's like they're hoping I contradict myself at some point."

Esther felt her head tilt as she tried to see what Kai was holding. "What did Sabina want? How many times can they dust the place for fingerprints?"

"She wanted to see the inspection paperwork Faris had given me. I don't know why, but my guess is, she's desperate for any lead she can get." She sighed. "I probably should have read through it all before handing it over…"

"Kai!" Esther admonished. Paperwork was no delight, but sometimes it was a necessary evil. Like when a business was on the line.

Kai ducked her head. "I know, I know. Don't get me wrong, I read the important stuff. The things I failed on. There were just so many papers. And they always use that tiny font."

Esther couldn't argue there. "I think companies use that font to break down our will until we sign whatever they give us. There's no other explanation."

"Agreed," Kai said. "But that's not the interesting part. I was combing through the paperwork before giving it over to Sabina, and I found this." She handed Esther the page she'd been holding. "I was going to wait until tomorrow to show you."

Esther glanced down at it. There was an official-looking New York state seal and a lot of jargon. "Is this a business registration?"

"It sure is," Kai said. "Check the contact name on it."

Esther held the paper up to read more closely. Her heart skipped a beat. "Faris Holliday."

"I don't know what this is, but I don't think Faris meant for me to have it."

"I can't imagine he did," Esther said, scanning the page. "The name of the entity is Kinghead Properties." She looked up, thinking. "Properties? Was Faris applying to start a business in real estate?"

Kai didn't have an answer. "I searched the business address online but nothing came up. Maybe he was planning to buy another house and wanted the deed to show a company name instead of his own."

"It would make sense to want to stay anonymous. He certainly made enough enemies over the years," Esther said. "He probably didn't want his address to be public record."

"Talk about sleeping with one eye open."

"Wait!" Esther said, remembering her conversation with Dev Singh. "I have to update you. I talked to Dev yesterday after work. Get this: Faris spent most of his trust fund money. So, I doubt he would have been purchasing a new mansion any time soon."

"No!" Kai said, eyes wide. "Spent it on what?"

"Dev didn't know. But Faris said he only had a little money left and needed to make it count. I'm guessing that's where this comes in." She waved the paper. "Last ditch effort to bring in some income?"

Esther noticed something written on the back of the page. "R.W. Zoning Compliance," she read aloud. It was circled. "Is that the name of a company?"

"Search it," Kai said, pointing to Esther's phone.

Esther typed *R.W. Zoning Compliance Yalfont New York* into the search bar. She clicked on the first search result. It was a *Yalfont Gazette* article about a recent gala for a major construction project.

She scrolled down the webpage, then paused on the first photo. A group of men in suits sat around a banquet table, smiling at the camera. Esther locked eyes with a familiar face. "Is this who I think it is?" she asked, holding the phone up for Kai to see.

"Woah—" Kai blinked rapidly like she was seeing double.

"Is there a caption?" Esther pressed.

Kai grabbed the phone for herself and scrolled down. She glanced at Esther before reciting what she saw. "Members of Ezra County Board of Zoning and Compliance gather to celebrate breaking ground on newest development."

"R.W.," Esther said.

Understanding struck her and Kai at the same time.

"Reese Williams," they said in unison.

"What does Reese have to do with Faris's real estate business?" Kai asked. "Do you think he wanted to start a development project and needed the board to sign off?"

"Maybe. But why mention Reese specifically? Why not any of the other members?" Esther's mind was racing with possibilities. "There must have been something Faris needed approval on that he only felt comfortable bringing to someone he knew."

"Something shady," Kai suggested.

"That's what my gut tells me," Esther agreed. "I knew that Reese was hiding something. Maybe we can have a real estate agent look over the documents. She could tell us if there's anything obvious we're not seeing here."

"My old agent, Cindy, lives on Bunny's street," Kai offered. "We can ask Bunny to drop it off."

"Good idea," Esther said. "And do you think Onyx might have any dirt on Reese? She didn't bat an eye at smuggling me into the health department. I get the sense that if anyone knew about shady business, it'd be her."

"It's worth a shot. I'll ask if she can meet us tomorrow."

"Perfect," Esther said. "There might have been more to Faris and Reese's relationship than boss and employee. We need to find out what."

# CHAPTER 27

The late morning sun heated the back of Esther's neck. She felt like she was trapped in a Dutch oven. She sat behind the reception desk, nodding along to the guest's story, wondering how much longer she could fake engagement without saying a word.

It was ten fifty-seven. Any moment now, the person she was waiting for would walk in.

She caught movement by the entrance and let her eyes drift. A guest ushered a single kayak paddle down the stairs and out the front door. It was against policy to store sports gear in rooms, but Esther could pick that fight later.

The man placed both hands on the desk. "And with the October tax deadline done and dusted, I'm ready to sit back and relax." His wife stood a few feet off, flipping through a Lake Ezra brochure. Apparently, she'd already heard all his riveting stories.

Esther felt a twinge of guilt for half-listening, but the man had spent ten minutes detailing the world tour highlights of his accounting career. Between working late and tossing through much of the night, she didn't have the energy to spare.

"I'm so glad to hear that," Esther said, mustering a smile.

"We're excited to have you. Please let me know if there's anything at all you need during your stay. Happy Friday!"

Conversation blissfully over, Esther reached for her Penny's cup like a lifejacket. She took a generous gulp, hoping the caffeinated liquid gold would revive her. A happy Friday it was. Until she spotted the stack of festival flyers sitting half-hidden under Justice's activity guide for the day.

Esther reached for the top page. It was printed in black and white, though she'd triple-checked she ordered color copies. They were meant to be posted inside all the local shops, to entice passersby to stop and take notice. The drab greyscale document looked more like a contract than an event flyer.

There was a small yellow sticky note at the top corner of the paper, a message written in Justice's handwriting: *This doesn't look good.*

*Real helpful, Justice.* She put the flyer back on the stack. She'd get that straightened out on Monday.

More movement by the entrance. Sveta emerged from the far hallway carrying a cleaning tote. Her lips pursed to whistle as she started up the stairs.

Not ten seconds later, in she walked. Onyx Opal was perfectly punctual. Esther fired off a text to Kai to meet them in the dining room.

Esther greeted Onyx and walked her back through the lobby.

"This place is so cute," Onyx said, surveying the space like a home-staging expert. "Like one of those celebrity Architectural Digest features where the home actually looks like people could live in it."

Esther was fairly sure it was a compliment, but limited her response to a smile. She snagged her Penny's cup as they passed reception. "I know you're busy. Thanks for meeting up with us."

The dining room smelled like bacon and freshly baked croissants. She chose a table with a clear view of the lobby in case she was needed.

Onyx took a seat. "My next proctored exam isn't for another hour. I'm supposed to be taking notes on our new handbook for my boss, but she's out sick today. I was mostly planning to catch up on *British Bake Off*."

Her dark brown hair brushed over the table as she brought it in front of her shoulders. It had an ethereal effect that somehow made her look even younger. She couldn't have been older than twenty-four.

"If that's not our tax dollars in action..." Esther said, taking another sip of her coffee.

"Huh?" Onyx asked, her jaw working over her chewing gum.

Kai breezed in and took a seat. She gave Onyx's hand a light squeeze as she sat.

"Nothing," Esther said, smiling at Kai in acknowledgment. "So, we wanted to pick your brain about what Faris and Reese's relationship was like."

"We've learned enough to make us think they might have had...other connections," Kai added. "Outside of work."

"Interesting," Onyx said. "I mean, Faris was not Reese's favorite person. Faris was always gunning for more special certifications. I can't even tell you how many times I'd proctored the guy. The thing is, Faris wouldn't just get the certification and get on with his life like a normal person. He'd convince HR that his entire team, Reese included, needed to get the certs too. And Reese would back him up."

"Faris could do that?" Kai asked. "Dictating what his coworkers did?"

"Technically, no," Onyx said. "But departments are always looking for ways to spend every last cent of their funding so their budget won't get taken away. Continuing education is an easy way to spend it. Plus, I'm sure it wouldn't have looked good for one of Reese's employees to be more qualified for his job than he was. He might have done the education to secure his seat on the throne."

"Normally, I'd applaud someone wanting to be a pro in their field," Esther said. "But something tells me Faris was after more than a passion for enforcing maximum microwave wattages in break rooms."

"Yeah, he was after ruining business owners' days everywhere," Kai added.

"If you want the scoop on Reese," Onyx said, looking around to make sure no one was listening, "I think I know why he really hated Faris. And it wasn't only how uptight he was."

"Do tell," Esther encouraged, hoping Onyx was about to spill something juicy.

Onyx leaned in. When she did, her blouse dipped, revealing a small butterfly tattoo under her left collarbone.

"Pretty," Kai said, pointing it out.

Onyx looked down. "Oh, thanks," she said, adjusting her shirt. "Butterfly is a nickname my favorite person in the world gave me. I thought the tattoo was inoffensive enough that if my parents ever saw it, they couldn't hound me too much."

"Practical," Kai said.

Onyx continued. "I've heard rumors that Reese has been taking kickbacks from higher ups. Making sure enough businesses in the county pass inspection every year. So they look good on paper for federal grants and stuff. I don't know how it all works, but totally shady."

"Faris definitely wasn't involved in that operation," Kai said. "He got stricter every year. He failed my spa!"

Onyx pointed to Kai in agreement. "True. If anything, Faris would have been a major roadblock between Reese and his cash."

Esther looked out the window as she thought through what Onyx had said. "If Faris knew about the kickbacks, he could have tried to use that against Reese." She turned to Kai. "For instance, if he had a big project he needed the green light on."

"Blackmail," Kai said, pointing. "Illegal, but timeless."

"From Reese's point of view, that's a pretty compelling motive to want Faris out of the picture," Esther said. She turned back to Onyx. "Who are these 'higher ups' Reese has been answering to?"

Onyx shrugged. "Not sure. All I know is these big wigs look out for each other. Their bonds go deep. They make sure their kids get into the best schools, take vacations together, all of it. By the way, have you seen how Reese Williams dresses? No health department salary is treating any of us that well."

"I noticed that!" Esther said, glad she wasn't the only one to find it notable. "I was almost blinded by one of his watches."

"Right? The guy must have dirty money."

"What now?" Kai asked. "How do we find out for sure where Reese is getting his funds?"

Esther thought for a moment. "If Reese has new money, I'm sure he's burning some of it. We've already seen some evidence of that. What else would he be spending on that would give us clues about who he's in cahoots with?"

Onyx perked up. "There's this restaurant in Yalfont where some of these power players go every Monday night. A real fancy place. Food, drinks, live entertainment."

"Aren't all restaurants in Yalfont fancy?" Kai asked.

It was a valid question.

Onyx let out a quiet chuckle. "This isn't a place that sees a lot of generational wealth. Old money prefers more lowkey estab- lishments where they won't be gawked at. This is where new money goes. You're seen there, people know you could use dollar bills as napkins. If Reese is getting kickback money, he's there."

"Got it," Esther said. "You know, I've been meaning to try out some new places to eat," she said, a plan forming in her mind. "Haven't you, Kai?"

Kai nodded. "Oh, for sure. In fact, I think I'm free this Monday night!"

"It's settled," Esther said. "I'll start picking an outfit."

# CHAPTER 28

"Coffee?" Penny asked as Esther collapsed onto a stool. Penny's Breakfast was characteristically busy on a Sunday night. It was an unofficial tradition for Oak's Rest residents to eat out after a day of grocery shopping and chores.

"And a cheeseburger," Esther mumbled. "Extra cheese." She burrowed her face into the bend of her elbow, careful not to damage her glasses. "Extra burger too," she grumbled against her arm.

Penny whistled. "Either you embarrassed yourself on live TV again, or you found out I've been serving you decaf this whole time."

Esther shot her head up. "Excuse me?"

"I'm kidding, sweetie," Penny said, pouring from a full pot. "Drink up." She was pure nineties in pigtails, a bandana, and a cassette graphic T-shirt.

Esther brought the mug close, shut her eyes, and inhaled. "You are the best thing in my life, you know that?"

"Love to hear it," Penny said, putting the pot back. She mouthed the word *cheeseburger* to her cook and held up two fingers. "Almost as much as I love being called a 'thing' by someone half my age."

Esther eyed Penny above her glasses. She knew the woman basked in praise for her diner. "Come on now. You don't look a day over sixty-five."

"What!" Penny said, a hand flying to her hip.

Esther giggled. "You're not the only one with jokes."

Penny grabbed a napkin from the dispenser, crumbled it, and threw it at Esther. "Very funny."

"And for the last time, the TV debacle wasn't my fault. They tell you they're doing a short local piece on the inn. They don't tell you they're arriving with a full crew, hair, makeup, and lights. Sesame was well within her rights to hiss at that reporter. The crew catching it on camera was just an unfortunate coincidence."

"That's sweet," Penny said. "Sesame likes you the way you are. She wasn't a fan of the beauty team messing with your curls?"

Esther blew on the coffee. "I'm not the one whose hair they were trying to do."

Penny looked upward, clearly trying to imagine the scene before shaking it off. "Anyway, what's with the sulky act? Cheeseburger and coffee spells trouble."

Esther sighed. "The Bennetts."

"How could I forget? I take it tonight's dinner didn't go any better than last week's?"

"My sister and I hardly said a word to each other after the failed Mission Banana Pudding. And that was only the start."

"I'm sure your mother was pleased about you two doing exactly what she asked, though," Penny offered.

The dessert had elated her mother. She even had Anna transfer it to a special serving dish. Veronica didn't eat any, of course, but she'd been happy. "Oh, she was thrilled. She didn't even pick up on the weirdness between Cameron and me." Esther realized, in that moment, the reason was simple. Her mother didn't know her well enough to spot when she was upset. "As long as everything is going according to her plan, nothing else matters."

Penny nodded, quietly polishing an empty glass with a cloth. She wore her *I know better than you* face.

"Yes? I can hear you thinking from here."

Penny put the glass down. She looked at Esther for a long few seconds before saying anything. "I'm wondering what your game plan is."

"My game plan?" Esther asked. "For what?"

"Your Mom. Your sister. Your family dynamics. What's the plan?"

Esther's heart rate picked up. Was Penny suggesting she was responsible for how her family behaved? "My mom asked me if I had a reliable source of running water at my house, Pen. She thinks I've been bathing with lake water this whole time."

Penny broke into a smile. "Your mom's imagination has never failed to entertain me." She swallowed a chuckle. "Fine. What are you going to do about it?"

Esther looked from side to side. "What am I missing here? What *can* I do?"

Penny frowned. "You know, you are one of the most intelligent young women I've ever known."

What a kind thing to say. "Aw, thank you—"

Penny held up a finger. "But you are completely dense when it comes to your personal life."

That wasn't true, was it? "Explain," Esther said, shifting in her seat.

"Esther, honey. You showed up in Oak's Rest over a decade ago with no connections here. You worked your way up to your dream job. You're a pillar of the community. In every other aspect of your life, you kick butt, take names, and don't care what anyone has to say."

Esther wanted to be flattered by the highlight reel, but she wasn't sure where Penny was leading her. "Okay...but?"

"With your family, you suddenly forget you're a professional problem-solver. You let them get right under your skin. Why?"

Esther could feel herself wanting to shut down, wanting to change the topic. She fought through it. "I have a two-decade history of living with them. It was like a pressure cooker. Being around my family has always made me feel…" she swallowed hard as further realization set in. "Like a failure." There it was. Being around her perfect doctor parents and sister made her feel like a failure.

The confession hung in the air. Penny softened. "I can understand why you'd feel that way. But I think you've been waiting all these years for your family to validate your accomplishments, when it might be something you have to give yourself."

Esther looked away. What if Penny was right? Maybe Esther was so affected by her mother and sister's comments because, deep down, she was worried they had good reason to look down on what she did. "What am I supposed to do in the meantime?" she asked. "While I'm getting the hang of all this self-validation? I can't stop seeing them. My parents will write me out of their will."

Penny thought for a moment. "If you can't change the circumstance, you'll have to change how you look at the circumstance."

Esther felt a weak tilt at the corner of her mouth. "I'm sure whatever ancient book of wisdom you got that from is a great read, but please translate."

Penny smiled back. "You need to make a choice. Are you going to let your family make you feel like crap? Or are you going to try to change how you feel in their presence?"

Esther let out a long sigh. "Are you sure I can't move out of the country and change my name?"

Penny patted the countertop. "Welcome to adulthood, babe. You're in the driver's seat now."

LouLou materialized next to Esther at the counter, startling her out of her thoughts.

"I'm gonna go check on that burger," Penny said before disappearing in the back.

Esther blinked a few times, reorienting after the heaviness of her conversation. "Hey, LouLou."

LouLou placed a hand on Esther's forearm. "You're getting too thin, darling. I hope you ordered something deep fried."

It was worth a shot. "LouLou, remember we talked about not commenting on people's—"

LouLou turned to look in the direction she'd come from. "Jim?" she called. "Be a gentleman. Give Esther some of your fries before she floats away like a balloon with no string."

Esther swiveled on her stool. Across the diner, Jim was sitting around a table with a few other business owners. There was a blue streak along the edge of their table, like a child had used a crayon to mark their path.

Clint sat alone at the next table over. He was reading a book and pushing his salad around with his free hand. He had a napkin tucked into his shirt and another in his lap.

Jim dabbed at his mouth. "You see, I would, but I'm not a gentleman. Sorry, Esther," he said, smiling. He scrunched his shoulders to his ears, bracing for impact as LouLou power-walked back to the table, waving her fist in mock anger.

Esther couldn't help but laugh. She looked around at the people in the diner. Colleagues, neighbors, friends. No matter what happened with the Bennetts, she'd always have the family she'd made in Oak's Rest. It was a great feeling.

Her chest tightened at the thought of Kai being pulled out of that community. What would happen if the police decided they couldn't come up with a more likely suspect?

She wouldn't let that happen. She couldn't.

"Clint," LouLou said, "You've been pushing that salad around for an hour. Just get a grilled cheese, sweetheart."

Clint closed his book. "I'm expanding my palate. I'm learning to be more adventurous so I can woo a woman."

"Atta boy," Jim said through a bite.

"Try ditching one of the napkins," Esther suggested. "You're wearing more white than your future bride."

The group laughed. Clint patted his shirt napkin in defiance and resumed reading.

Jim sipped his soda, then set it down. "Hey, Esther, how are we looking for Makers and Merchants? People haven't been pulling out on account of..." he trailed off, looking around for help.

"The fact that a young man was murdered in our backyard?" LouLou supplied.

"I wasn't gonna put it like that," Jim said. "But yeah. Margins are already thin this time of year. Relying on discounts to get people to stock up on gear for spring and summer. It'd be a real punch to the gut if the festival fell through."

Esther felt a spike of anxiety at the idea. With two weeks to go, she was well past the point of tempering her hopes for the perfect day. "We're looking good from our end," Esther said. "Have any of you noticed decreased foot traffic in your shops? Visitors expressing concern about what happened?"

They all looked at each other, each shaking their heads. Esther was relieved, but she knew they weren't out of the water. There was still time for out of towners to decide not to attend the event.

She pictured the booths set up on the freshly cut lawn, everyone eager for visitors to arrive, then the morale slowly fading as the hours dragged on. How disappointed everyone would be.

LouLou looked around furtively, even though all the diner patrons were locals. "I asked Sabina where she was in the investigation. She's tight-lipped, that one. Anywho, I told her to blink once if they had a name yet, and to not blink at all if they didn't."

"What did she do?" Esther asked, having a hard time imagining Sabina going for that.

"She said she wouldn't do it," LouLou said. "But then she

blinked. Twice. To be honest, it could have been an eyelash in her eye. But who knows? It could have been something."

"What does twice mean?" Clint asked, showing interest in the conversation again.

"I don't know," LouLou said. "Maybe that's how many suspects she has?"

"Maybe it's how many decades the killer is going to serve in prison," Jim

offered.

"Oh my goodness," LouLou said, placing a hand over her chest, fighting laughter. "Do you all remember when Sabina first joined the force, that time she caught Clint and his cousin stealing from the town hall vending machines? She had them both by the shirt collars. Clint called her 'Ma'am' for the next ten years."

"She only caught me because my arm got stuck inside the machine," Clint said. He hung his head. "I still think about that KitKat bar."

Fifteen minutes and one and a half cheeseburgers later, Esther left Penny's Breakfast with determination. She had planning to do.

She stepped out of the diner and turned left toward her car when something caught her eye further down the block. A woman who looked remarkably similar to Uma Holliday in a floppy sun hat spun and disappeared around the corner.

"Uma?" she called out, jogging to the corner. The woman had disappeared.

That was odd. Who wears a sun hat at night? Esther stopped in her tracks when she realized she'd seen that hat before. The day she discovered Lani's keychain at the crime scene. She'd been coming out of Penny's when she'd almost collided with the woman.

Was Uma Holliday following her?

# CHAPTER 29

The Aureum Room was warm, with gold leaf accents framing the large windows. Outside, string lights shimmered across the ripples of Lake Ezra, the water blending with the velvety indigo of the restaurant's walls. It was mesmerizing.

The thrum of conversation mingled with the smooth sounds of jazz from a band playing at the front. The air smelled like expensive perfume and garlic bread. Servers circulated like shadows in black vests over crisp white shirts.

Something hard knocked against Esther's shin, sending a thunderbolt of pain up to her knee. "Stop kicking me," she scolded.

"I'm sorry!" Justice said, squirming in her seat. She placed her hands flat on the white table linen, seemingly trying to calm her nerves. "I thought wearing these heels to work all day would break them. It half-worked, because my feet are numb. Plus, you know I get fidgety around rich people. I feel like they can read my net worth by how I part my hair."

It was nice seeing Justice dressed up outside of work. She wore a long black wrap dress and slender, strappy heels. Esther had also committed to full glam, in a forest green satin maxi dress with a pleated lower half. The seats were so plush, her dress might not even wrinkle. Were they memory foam? Maybe that's why people ate there.

Bunny raised her second glass of red wine by the stem and tilted it. She squinted. "Are those particles?" She placed the glass back on the table and swirled. She took a sip, took in some air through puckered lips, then swallowed. "Nope, this is good stuff. Here," she said, passing the glass to Kai. "Try this."

Esther intercepted the glass. "Let's focus up, ladies. I said you could all come, but we need to keep a low profile." She looked pointedly at Justice, who was making a swan out of her cloth napkin.

It took the concierge a few moments to notice the silence. "Okay! I hear you. But I'd avoid checking the balance on the company card tomorrow. I plan on ordering the most expensive, pretentious thing on the menu."

Esther ignored her, searching the sea of faces again. "I see him," she said, trying not to stare. Reese Williams and his wife sat across the restaurant, his back to their table.

"Are you sure you don't want one of us to come with you?" Kai asked.

"I think I should go alone," Esther said. "He might recognize you all from the celebration of life." If she needed an out, she could pretend she was on a date she needed to get back to.

"He would have had to stay at the celebration of life for longer than five minutes to have seen us!" Bunny said, laughing at her own joke.

"How about we slow down with the wine, Bun?" Esther suggested. Cracking-herself-up territory was only a few steps from asking diners at other tables what they'd ordered and switching around their side combinations.

Kai patted Bunny on the back. "Yeah, let's wait to get some food in your stomach." She reached for Bunny's glass and took a swig. "What?" she asked when she noticed Esther glaring at her. "Someone's gotta drink it."

Esther took a final sip of her own liquid courage. She wasn't sure what made her nervous—feeling so out of place at the ritzy restaurant, or that her last conversation with Reese had ended with him politely kicking her out of his office.

"Loosen up," Justice said. "You're making *me* nervous."

"I thought your lack of net worth was making you nervous," Esther replied.

Justice groaned. "I had just forgotten about that. Back to square one."

Bunny reached across the table to place a hand on Esther's arm. "You'll be fine. It's like acting. You act every day. Remember when that artist group stayed, and the painter asked you if her piece looked like swiss cheese?"

"I remember that," Esther said, easing out a laugh. "I could tell she wanted me to say no, so I did. But I was craving a turkey deli sandwich all day."

"See?" Kai chimed in. "You've got this."

Esther stood, smoothed her dress, and set her shoulders. "Okay. Here goes nothing."

She approached Reese's table from behind, and pretended to be texting as she walked by, glancing up every few seconds to make sure she didn't run into anyone. She did a fake double take as she passed the table. "Reese?" she asked.

Reese and his wife looked up. Esther could track the progression of his reaction from confusion to vague recognition to the moment it clicked in. He smiled and stuck out his hand. "Esther."

Esther shook it. "Not a bad memory." She turned to his wife, whose facial expression had not changed. "Hi, I'm Esther. I don't think we've met. I was a client of one of Reese's former employees."

She placed a hand on her heart. "Was it that poor guy who

passed? How sad." Only her mouth moved, as if the rest of her face hadn't gotten the memo. "I'm Kyla."

Esther had a hard time parsing the woman's kind tone from her lack of a smile.

As if reading her thoughts, Kyla said, "Don't mind the face." She held a hand to the side of her mouth like she was telling a secret. "Just got my touchup done."

Esther smiled diplomatically. That explained it. Which response would Kyla prefer: *couldn't even tell*, or *trust me, I get it*? Both were lies. She settled on, "You look gorgeous."

Kyla looked at Reese. "Told you. It's not that big a deal." She turned back to Esther. "He's always telling me I don't need any of this stuff. That's only because he never sees me without the stuff."

Reese laughed. "You're beautiful. With or without *stuff*." He said it like he was hoping it was the right answer.

Kyla rolled her eyes. "My go-to girl cut me off. She says I can't get anything injected for three months. I'd buy it off the black market and inject it myself if I could." She conveyed the closest thing to a smile Esther had seen yet. "Well, let's be honest. I'd let Reesey handle the black market part. But I wouldn't trust him near my face."

Reese's smile faltered ever so slightly. Interesting. Had Kyla hit a nerve mentioning the black market?

Kyla must have sensed it too, because she cleared her throat and changed the topic. "What do you think of this place, Esther? It's a touch overcrowded for me, but the food is outstanding."

Esther played along to keep the conversation going. "This is my first time here. They certainly know how to create an atmosphere," she said, looking around. "I think—" she paused when her eyes landed on a long row of booth tables. On every second table sat a metal candle holder, its base curling into the restaurant's initials: AR.

"Esther?" Kyla asked.

Esther snapped back to attention. "Sorry," she said, glancing at the tables one more time. "I was looking at those wrought-iron candle holders. Uma Holliday had similar ones at Faris's celebration of life, but with his initial."

Kyla looked at Reese with slightly widened eyes, clearly communicating something Esther wasn't aware of.

"You don't like them?" Esther asked.

Kyla lifted a shoulder. "They're beautiful. The real ones, that is."

"What do you mean?"

"Here we go," Reese said, shaking his head, smirking.

"She asked," Kyla told him. She refocused on Esther. "They've become all the rage in Yalfont over the last few years. Everyone has to have their custom wrought-iron candle holders, or it's like their event didn't happen. Naturally, there are tons of knockoffs out there. Aluminum, I think."

"I see," Esther said. "I guess it wouldn't matter if no one could tell the difference, though, right? To most people, they'd look pretty indistinguishable."

Kyla nodded. "They do look similar. But you can tell when you pick one up. The real ones are heavy." A few seconds later, perhaps realizing she might have accused the widow of being cheap, she added, "But I'm sure Uma's were real." With her face frozen in that blank expression, it was impossible to tell whether she'd meant it, or was being sarcastic.

The jazz band started up a new tune. The change in music made Esther feel like she'd been talking to the couple for too long. "I'll let you two get back to your dinner. Sorry to intrude. It was so nice meeting you, Kyla. And great to see you, Reese."

"You too," they replied at the same time.

Esther rushed back to her table. When she sat, she saw Kai was holding one of the candle holders from the booth tables, inspecting it the way cashiers checked large bills against fluorescent lighting. "What are you doing?" Esther asked. "Where did you get that?"

"Sheesh," Kai said, letting go of the candle holder as Bunny snatched it like a kindergartener desperate for her turn with the crayons. "Someone visited Uptight Island."

Esther hardly registered the comment, because the moment Bunny took the thing in her hands, she furrowed her brows. "That's weird."

"What?" Esther asked, already knowing what the problem was.

"Do you remember the candle holder at the Hollidays' house I couldn't stop gushing about?"

Esther nodded. "Let me guess. Much lighter than the one you're holding now?"

Bunny's jaw dropped. "Did you just read my mind?"

# CHAPTER 30

The next morning, Esther tucked two flower bouquets under her left arm as she opened the inn's front door. The paper wrapping crinkled in protest. "Oh, hush," she said.

She loved choosing flowers for the inn. This time, she'd gone with an arrangement of hot pink alstroemeria, red spray roses and pincushions, all wrapped in palm fronds. Molly had given her a month-long discount after the big Makers and Merchants order.

"You'll love it here," she assured the flowers. "And don't tell Molly I stuffed you under my arm. No one likes a snitch."

*Great, I'm talking to bouquets now*, she thought as she walked by the living room. She inhaled. Subtle, but she'd recognize the scent anywhere. Someone had spent an early morning on the lake.

A twin brother and sister sat side by side on the couch, both wearing thick-rimmed black glasses. Esther wondered if they coordinated on purpose.

They sipped Penny's coffees and passed two black cameras between them, studying the screens. Their faces were still flushed. Esther had heard they were planning an early photoshoot of the sunrise over Lake Ezra, and she couldn't wait to see the results before they checked out.

She tried to imagine the images, wondering how they'd compare to the real-life version she saw out her windows at home, a watercolor smear of hues welcoming the town to a new day.

Just past the staircase, a guest crossed her path, eyes down, fidgeting with a black tangle toy. It reminded Esther of the candle holder discrepancy, which she'd been thinking about all night.

Why would Uma, a woman who never left the house without a designer bag and her lipstick perfectly in place, display a knockoff? Especially knowing that to Yalfonters, costs and authenticity mattered. People noticed.

The only explanation would be if Uma knew she *wasn't* wealthy. At least, not anymore. Now that Esther thought about it, maybe hosting the event at home instead of renting out a space had been another cost-saving tactic. Maybe Uma had found out about Faris spending the trust fund money and lost her temper.

Or, maybe she figured getting rid of him, and pocketing what little money remained, was better than letting him waste it on some harebrained business idea.

Then there was Reese. He'd looked awfully uncomfortable when Kyla joked he'd be able to shop around on the black market. Why had she said that? Was it because she knew he had experience with other illegal activities?

Also, was it a coincidence Faris had been killed with the same substance presumably filling Kyla's face?

Maybe Reese had learned a thing or two about the substance from his wife, and got curious about if he could use it for more lethal purposes.

But how did that tie into Kai's Botox needle being found at the scene?

Kyla had gone on about how desperate she was for more.

What if Reese, knowing Faris was going to be inspecting a spa, asked him to secure some Botox under the pretense that it was for his wife?

It was conceivable that Reese knew where Faris would be that afternoon and what amount of Botox he'd have on him. Then, all Reese had to do was follow Faris and wait for him to be alone.

A flash of black darted past Esther's feet, pulling her back to the present. She was about to scold Sesame for being a tripping hazard when a familiar voice stopped her cold.

"Esther. Good morning."

Esther lowered the bouquets and was surprised to find herself standing face to face with Detective Ali in the middle of the lobby. Sabina was wearing her typical plaid blazer with a black turtleneck underneath.

Esther set the flowers down on the table. "Um, hi, Sabina. Was I…"

"Expecting me?" Sabina asked, finishing her question. She looked irritated.

"Yeah. Everything alright?"

Sabina leveled a stern look. "Actually, no. I got an interesting call yesterday. Someone complained about a woman, fitting your description, stopping people on the street, asking if they knew anything about the Faris Holliday case. Apparently, the woman was introducing herself as the manager of the Calliope Inn."

Esther drew back at the accusation. She hadn't done any of that. "Wait, what? What are you saying?"

Sabina didn't look impressed. "Let me rephrase it as a question. Esther, have you been stopping people on the street—"

Esther cut her off. "No! Of course not! Who called that in?"

Sabina shrugged. "It was an anonymous tip. I didn't recognize the voice, but it sounded like a grumpy older man. My guess? A tourist trying to enjoy their vacation without being questioned about an open case."

Esther tucked her hair behind her ear on the off chance she

hadn't heard correctly. "Honestly, Sabina, I don't know anything about that. Why would I want to call attention to a crime in our town? I work for a business that very much benefits from tourist traffic." She gestured toward the milling guests, lowering her voice. "Murder isn't exactly something I'd put in a brochure."

Sabina narrowed her eyes. "Okay, then. Maybe someone was playing a practical joke. It happens from time to time. Just in case, let me be very clear: let us handle this. Got it?"

Esther swallowed. Her acting skills were becoming more handy every day. "Loud and clear," she lied. "You're the expert here."

Sabina nodded.

Esther couldn't help it. She had to ask. "And as the expert..." she began, knowing she was pushing it.

Sabina rolled her eyes. "Don't."

"I'm asking as a concerned citizen." She searched Sabina's eyes for any sign of connection, any willingness to drop the wall of professionalism. "Sabina, I have to know. Is there a chance you'll release Kai's name to the public as a suspect? You know it would ruin her, right?"

Sabina looked at her squarely for a moment before averting her gaze. She lowered her voice. "We're doing everything we can to crack this thing. But the higher-ups are pushing for a progress update. If we don't find a more compelling suspect soon...the pressure to name someone will just increase."

"So you don't think it was Kai," Esther said, her voice betraying her hope.

Sabina met her eyes again. "What I *hope* to be true and what *is* true are two different things. I can't pick and choose when to administer justice based on my personal relationships. If the evidence points to Kai, I will act on that." The wall was rising again, brick by brick. "And unless you have pertinent information you'd like to share with me, I can't discuss it with you any further."

Esther considered what to tell her, if anything. The Oak's Rest Police Department obviously had resources and training Esther didn't. But if she told Sabina about her suspects, or the information she'd been digging up about Faris's past, Sabina would follow up on those leads.

If there was one person a killer wouldn't be willing to let their guard down around, it was the head detective on the case. Esther was in too deep to let her suspects get spooked and disappear.

Detective Ali put on a clinical smile, seeming to gather Esther had nothing more to say. She turned and started walking toward the entrance.

When Sabina was gone, Esther bent down to the bouquets, still innocently wrapped in paper on the lobby table. She took in a comforting whiff. Fresh, then a hint of caramel, just like Molly had said. "You're beautiful and all, but I'm mad at you for not warning me the detective was here. How about you crinkle a little louder next time?"

# CHAPTER 31

"Maybe it'll work this time," Esther said, holding the plug just in front of the outdoor outlet. Apparently, Esther hadn't been the only one rattled by Sabina's surprise visit that morning. The garden fountain seemed to be acting out too.

"Did it work the last seven times?" Mort asked, arms crossed. He was wearing a tan jacket over his green shirt, gloves dangling from one hand. He looked like a bouncer, ready to escort Esther off the premises if she suggested another YouTube tutorial.

"No…" Esther admitted. "But I wasn't asking nicely. I'll be more mindful of my tone this time." She blocked out Mort's skepticism and closed her eyes. "Miss Garden Fountain," she began.

"How do you know it's a 'Miss'?" he asked. "Why not a 'Mizz'?"

"I just know. Now shhh." Truthfully, she'd never been sure what the difference was. She wouldn't tell Mort that, though. "Miss Fountain, it's your loyal pal and manager, Esther."

Mort chuckled. "You sound like one of those companies that visits middle schools talking about the dangers of—"

"I'm sorry for kicking you earlier," Esther said loudly, talking over him. "If you could start flowing at full speed again, that'd be great."

Esther held her breath as she plugged the cord in, eyes still shut. "What's happening? Is it going?"

"Yeah," Mort said. "I could hose down the Empire State Building from street level with this kind of water pressure."

"Really?" Esther said, opening one eye. There was a pitiful splutter from the center of the fountain, giving way to a sad drip from the top petal to the second. The drip didn't even make it to the base. "Your career should have been in comedy, you know that?"

A gray bird with a white and peach underbelly perched on the edge of the fountain. It gave a few twitchy head turns like it was assessing their handiwork, then flew away, unimpressed.

Mort flipped the switch off. He removed the top layer of the fountain, turning the large stone petal upside down in one hand. With the other, he bunched up a pant leg before squatting to the ground. He let out a series of grunts that tempted Esther to offer help, but she knew he'd refuse.

Mort set the piece on the gravel beside him. He rooted around his work bag, without looking, for what felt like an eternity. When he finally pulled his hand out, he was holding a putty knife. He stood again, making more noises than he had on the way down.

Esther watched in silence. The fountain wasn't taking notes from her. Maybe it would respond to Mort.

He began scraping old sealant from the base of the fountain where the petal had been. "Gonna clean off all the old gunk and seal it back up with some fresh putty," he explained.

"And that will fix it?"

"I'd hold off on putting it in any beauty pageants," Mort said. "But should do the trick. I figure most of the water is escaping through the cracks before making it to the top. If not, could be a hose issue. Just a few bucks to replace."

"And if it's still not working after that?" Esther asked, bracing herself.

"Then we're talking about more than a few bucks."

Esther would have to make a tough call if the fountain needed a major repair. On the bright side, removing the fountain would free up some space in the electrical panel. Justice would be thrilled to plug in both the lamp and space heater at the same time in the basement office.

Esther didn't want to lose the fountain, though. It attracted colorful birds and butterflies and chipmunks. More than that, it gave their outdoor space a tranquility guests loved. The fountain wasn't *why* people stayed at Calliope Inn, but it was the little touches like it, all over the property, and worked into every aspect of the experience, that people remembered. That they gushed about to their neighbors, friends, and followers.

Plus, it would look great in all the Makers and Merchants Festival photos.

Where could she find money for repairs? Did Bunny really need three different types of cinnamon stocked at all times? Esther briefly imagined the earful she'd get just for suggesting a cut and thought better of it.

"I'll do my best, boss," Mort said, possibly sensing her worry. "No need to empty the bank account yet."

Esther smiled, perhaps too enthusiastically, trying to instill some optimism in the both of them. "If anyone can do it, it's you. Keep me posted."

The dining room was busy, and as soon as Esther inhaled, she knew why. Whatever the kitchen had made for lunch smelled heavenly. Guests sat around tables, eyes bright with anticipation. People always had better posture when they were expecting a great meal.

Through the window, Esther saw Mort tinkering with the fountain. Hopefully, the lunch rush had distracted everyone from watching her previously failed attempt.

She looked away, only to have her attention drawn back to the window by Mort's flailing arms seconds later. Esther spotted the red tophat first. The cardinal was back, and Mort had fallen right into its taunting trap, shooing and waving his arms like his sleeves were on fire.

Poor Mort had been recruited to clean more than a few dirtied side mirrors in the past few weeks. He was a champ, but Esther didn't want to keep asking him to do such an unpleasant job.

Esther was just about to plan for distracting guests from looking at the spectacle when kitchen staff emerged from the swinging doors, arms full of plates and bowls.

Esther felt someone tap her arm as she weaved through the tables. She turned toward a group of women who'd traveled to Lake Ezra to celebrate all retiring in the past year.

One of them, who'd had an impressively long list of room requests, leaned toward her in her seat. "I just wanted to thank you. I didn't believe you when you said I didn't need to double-stack my pillows. But you were right on the money. I haven't slept that well in years! I'll need to know what pillows you use, or I might have to move in." Her eyes sparkled with gratitude.

"We'll have you as long as you'll stay," Esther said. The hoops she'd jumped through were worth it to see the woman looking so refreshed.

Esther's stomach growled as she slipped behind the reception desk. She'd just logged in and pulled up her email when a bowl was lowered in front of her.

"For the manager and her very loud stomach," Bunny said, setting down a plate as well.

Esther rubbed her hands together, eyeing the meal. A bowl of rich orange soup topped with crushed nuts, and a sandwich on crusty bread with greens poking out. "It's delicious. I can already tell."

"Brie and cheddar beer soup," Bunny said, pointing to the

bowl. "And a curried chicken salad sammy. Extra green onions, like you like it."

Esther's mouth watered. "Only one question. To dip or not to dip?"

"Most people don't order these together, so you'll have to do your own experimenting. I brought you both because I know you like options," the chef said. "Speaking of investigation, any new ideas about who tipped off Sabina?"

Esther swallowed a spoonful of deliciously hot soup. "I can't think of any reasons someone would lie about me. Or why Sabina would have bought it in the first place. I mean, do I seem like the kind of person who would stop strangers on the street about a murder? Do I have a deranged look in my eyes or something?"

Bunny raised her eyebrows. "Only when you're eating my food. Maybe it was a joke, like Sabina suggested."

"I guess," Esther said between bites. "Weird joke."

Bunny snapped. "Oh yeah! I heard from Cindy, the real estate agent. She took a look at those business documents from Faris."

Esther put the sandwich down, eager to hear more. "Tell me."

Bunny went around to the front of the reception desk and leaned forward on her elbows. "Cindy doesn't buy the whole anonymous LLC theory. She says it's usually a celebrity thing to buy homes without attaching their names."

"So…?"

"She doesn't know what, but confirmed Faris was planning something big."

"Like what?" Esther asked. "Did you point out the note about Zoning and Compliance?"

Bunny nodded. "I did. That's what makes her think Faris had aspirations. A project so big the county zoning board needed to get involved."

"He must have been planning to buy up some real estate or land," Esther said, mulling it over. "Maybe he was trying to build a shopping mall in Yalfont or something. Try to make his invest-ment back quick enough to rebuild his trust fund nest egg."

"That's the thing," Bunny said. "Cindy told me it's next to impossible for a private company to do major development in Yalfont these days. Their residents are serious about maintaining their aesthetic. They'd never approve a big gaudy development project without layers of bureaucracy."

"Yalfonters pay for premium views, quiet streets, and low traffic. Prestige. And they want to keep it that way." Esther pictured how her parents and their neighbors would react if a mall went up in their neighborhood. She felt sorry for the town employees who would have to take those phone calls.

"Exactly. Which is why Cindy thinks the project was meant for Oak's Rest."

"Oak's Rest?" Esther asked. "What would he build here? A big mall doesn't exactly fit our community or tourist crowd either. People come here to get away from city life."

"That's all Cindy could tell me," Bunny said, shrugging. "Is it possible Reese didn't know anything about what Faris was doing? Maybe Faris had been planning to get in touch with him but never did."

"It's possible. I need to know whether Uma knew anything about it," Esther said, thinking out loud. "If Faris told her about spending the money, he likely would have tried to assure her he'd make it all back. Keep her happy."

"Probably," Bunny said. "How would you find out? *'Hey Uma, can you describe the real estate empire your husband was planning on ruining our town with?'* seems a little forward."

"I can be smoother than that! I just need to think about it. What I do know, though, is that I need to go back to the Holliday house. There might be evidence of what he was planning there. Maybe I'll go tomorrow morning."

"You're not weirded out? What if Uma is your stalker? She's still a suspect, right?" Bunny asked.

Esther was a little uneasy, but she wanted answers. "I'm not even sure she is the stalker. If she is, the sun hat I keep seeing will be there. All the more reason to go. And..." she said, giving Bunny her most charming smile, "I won't be alone."

Bunny smirked. "Looks like I'm having the guys make pancakes for breakfast tomorrow. I don't trust them to execute on the quiches without me."

"You're the best," Esther said, grateful to have a partner. "I'll have Justice and Luis cover breakfast service. Mort can run interference with Sveta if any guests have housekeeping questions."

"No biggie," Bunny said. "I'll go get started on the batter." Her smile faded suddenly. She turned toward the kitchen and cupped her ear. "Right after I talk some sense into Luis. This hooligan is using the serrated bread knife to chop celery again. I can hear it." She shouted, "Luis!" as she stormed off, ignoring the dining room full of guests.

Esther watched Bunny disappear into the back. "I can see it now. *Calliope Inn sued for wrongful termination after employee let go for using wrong knife.*" Thoughts of a lawsuit vanished when she saw how much of her lunch she had left to enjoy. "Hello, gorgeous," she said, picking the sandwich up. She could plan how to get information out of Uma later.

# CHAPTER 32

"I have zero information about any real estate company Faris was involved with," Uma said. "I wish I could help." She picked up the bowl of soup from the coffee table. She seemed much more at ease than at the celebration of life. "This is exquisite, by the way," she said, cupping the bowl. "I rarely eat in the living room, but this smelled so good I couldn't wait to try it."

"I'm glad you like it," Bunny said, looking at Esther with a question in her eyes.

It was hard to tell whether Uma was lying. If she wouldn't give up details about Faris, Esther would at least find out if the woman had been following her. With Uma busy savoring her soup, Esther kept eye contact with Bunny and pointed to her head, signaling they needed to find the hat.

*How?* Bunny mouthed. She motioned to Uma, indicating they couldn't get up and look around with her sitting right across from them.

Esther glanced around. She wasn't sure what she'd expected to see. Maybe binoculars or a wall of newspaper clippings connected by red string. Nothing screamed "stalker."

Then, she spotted a coat closet in the hallway off the foyer.

She hoped Uma kept her accessories in there rather than in her bedroom. She couldn't come up with a reason she'd need to go upstairs unaccompanied. "I'm so sorry to bug you, Uma," Esther said, pinching the bridge of her nose, trying to sound weary. "I've had this pesky headache all morning. Do you have anything I could take?"

"Absolutely," Uma said, setting down the soup. "I've got everything. Since Faris has been gone, I've been contending with migraines, restlessness, sleepwalking, you name it. I mix an upper with a downer to balance me out through the afternoon, then take something to turn the lights out closer to bedtime." She smoothed her shirt as nonchalantly as if she'd just explained how she washed produce. "What do you need?"

Esther eyed Bunny, who looked as out of her depth as she felt. "I was thinking more along the lines of an ibuprofen."

"Oh, sure," Uma said, looking somewhat startled, like she'd had to reach into the depths of her memory to recall what an ibuprofen was.

"Uma, sweetie," Bunny started, leaning in gently. "Is there anyone you have to…talk to? About everything you've been going through?"

Uma's description of her medication routine had been more than a little concerning. Even if she was a stalker.

Uma deflated against the sofa. "I'll be okay. I've just been dealing with a lot. I'd been managing to hold it together until a few days ago."

"What happened a few days ago?" Esther asked.

Uma turned her head to look out the window. "The police dropped off all of Faris's belongings. Phone, wallet, I'm not exactly sure what else. They didn't have a warrant yet to look through it all, so they returned it to me. I haven't had the heart to open the box."

Esther saw Bunny perk up at the same time she did. "That

does sound like a lot. And you've been holding onto his stuff? You haven't sorted through it at all?"

"I put it in the garage," Uma said, pointing to the door off the kitchen. "I don't know when I'll be ready to face it." She looked down at her lap, where she was picking at her nails.

Esther couldn't tell whether the sadness was real. Either way, they needed to get Uma out of the room so they could have a look around. Hoping not to seem insensitive, Esther rubbed her forehead as she said, "I'm so sorry about all that. I can't imagine."

Just as she'd hoped, Uma sat back up. "I'm being so rude," she said, standing. "Let me get you something for that headache." She walked through the living room toward the staircase. "It might take me a few minutes to find it," she called. "I haven't taken that stuff in a long time. Bad for your kidneys."

Bunny moved closer to Esther on the sofa. "Yeah, because a cocktail of uppers and downers is *great* for kidney health," she whispered. "You're not actually going to take anything she gives you, right?"

Esther made sure Uma was out of earshot before turning in her seat to face Bunny fully. The couch didn't make a peep. She didn't want to guess how much it had cost. She kept her voice low. "Of course not. I needed to get rid of her for a few minutes. We need to get our hands on that phone."

"Okay, but don't you also want to see if the hat is here?"

Esther thought quickly. "You go check the coat closet for the hat and I'll search the garage for Faris's stuff."

Bunny nodded once. "Let's do this." She stood. "Be in and out."

Esther crept to the door Uma had pointed to and put her hand on the knob. She tried to remember whether any type of alarm system had announced when Uma opened the front door for them. She didn't think so, but it'd be a gamble.

Holding her breath, she turned the knob.

Mercifully, no alarm. Better still, the garage was relatively empty. The floor was shiny, which made the garage feel like a car showroom. A luxury car, some gardening equipment, and a small marble chest of drawers.

And there, right on top, was a small box.

She walked over and lifted the lid, realizing she wouldn't be able to get into the phone without a passcode.

"You're kidding," she said, getting a look at the contents of the box. Sitting inside was a wallet, keys, and a flip phone. A wonderful, ancient flip phone.

She snapped it open. A red bubble caught her attention at the bottom of the screen. It looked like a text message inbox. It took Esther a few clicks to figure out how to navigate to the inbox, but it filled the screen once she got the hang of it.

Faris had three missed texts from a contact named *Incoming call*. Faris might have been a thorough health and safety inspector, but he was clearly not as skilled in the criminality department. Esther would have at least expected the paper trail of shady business conversations to use real-sounding fake names.

She opened the text thread and scrolled to the beginning. There were only a handful of messages in the exchange. He must have deleted the rest. *Now you're thinking, Faris.*

Then, she saw the date of the messages. They'd been sent the night Faris died.

Two messages from *Incoming call*:

**Incoming call:** Tell me when you're leaving Oak's Rest. Can't wait to see you, love.
**Incoming call:** Don't make me come to OR and find you!! Haha. Miss you xoxo

The final message:

**Faris:** Goimg to belate. See yov soon Butterfly.

Butterfly? Why did that sound familiar? Esther flipped

through the mental catalog of all the conversations she'd recently had.

Her breath hitched.

*Butterfly is a nickname my favorite person in the world gave me.*

It was Onyx. Faris had been texting Onyx the night he died.

Esther almost threw the phone when she heard someone walk into the garage. She put a hand on her chest when she saw it was Bunny. She waved for her to hurry over.

"What's wrong?" Bunny asked. "What did you find?"

Esther held up the phone for Bunny to read the messages. "Onyx told me that her 'favorite person' calls her Butterfly. She has a tattoo of it and everything. Seems like relationship status, no?"

Bunny's eyes widened as she read. "Well, if we had any doubt he was drunk, that's put to bed. But woah. Uma suspected he was having an affair, right?"

"Now we know who with," Esther said. "They had plans to meet that night."

Bunny covered her mouth. "Onyx told us Faris's coworker was the last person seen with him. Maybe that was a cover."

Suddenly, they heard Uma's voice call out from the living room. "Esther? Bunny?"

"Crap!" Esther hissed. She scrambled to put the phone back in the box and placed the lid on. Uma's footsteps were getting closer.

They hurried away from the corner of the garage and were approaching the car when Uma appeared in the doorway.

"What's going on?" she asked, holding a bottle of medication.

Bunny began whimpering. Esther looked over to see her best friend begin to cry.

Uma seemed worried.

Bunny sniffled. "We thought we heard the garage door shaking on its hinges. We came to check if the wind was blowing it off. When we walked in, I saw this," she said, motioning to the car.

"The Carrera?" Uma asked, looking uncertain.

Wherever Bunny was going, Esther hoped it would be convincing.

"Yes," Bunny confirmed, dabbing at the corners of her eyes with her fingers. "It's just...My abuelo drove this car. He saved up for years. He'd only gotten to drive it twice before he passed away." She sobbed harder, covering her face with both hands.

Esther rubbed her back, staying in character. "She can't see one of these things without it reminding her of him."

Uma looked like she was holding back tears too. "I'm sorry," she said. "Let's get out of here." She opened the door wide and took a step back. "I didn't have any ibuprofen, Esther, but I found something else that should take care of the pain. I'll get you some water." She turned toward the kitchen.

"Thank you so much," Esther said.

Bunny gave one last sniffle and dropped the act as soon as Uma was far enough ahead. "Do *not* take that medication," she whispered, eyes wide.

"I wasn't going to," Esther said, not sure why Bunny looked so concerned. "But why?"

Bunny glanced around the corner to make sure Uma hadn't turned back. "The coat closet. I saw a sun hat with a black ribbon."

Esther's stomach flip-flopped as Bunny searched her eyes.

"Uma Holliday has been following you."

# CHAPTER 33

"Turn it twenty degrees to the right."

"My right or your right?" Esther asked.

Justice lowered her phone and angled her head. "My right," she said, decisive. She raised the phone again and tapped the screen. The shutter sound was starting to grate.

Esther rotated the plate of glazed maple shortbread snaps, letting the afternoon sunlight trace the smooth, rounded edges of the icing. She crawled backwards on her hands and knees. "How many more shots do you need?" she asked, crouched behind the living room couch. "This glaze is going to turn into a drip if we keep working this close to the fireplace."

She glanced up at the books lining the shelves. Even they seemed to cast judgment about the cookie photoshoot, as if Esther wasn't aware how ridiculous she must have looked.

"Just a few more. I can feel it. We're close," Justice said with authority.

"You said that ten minutes ago. My legs are killing me. Wait—no," she shifted her weight. "They've lost all sensation." She was glad she'd worn pants.

"We would've had better lighting this morning. But *someone* was off interviewing suspects, trying to make our town a safer place or whatever. Besides, what's a little nerve damage for a great social media post?"

Esther was about to protest, but Justice beat her to the punch. "Now scooch back. Your foot is in my shot."

"I'm so glad we have a creative director with such vision." She was still early in her career. Maybe it wasn't too late for Esther to become one of those bosses who led from a cold distance. It wouldn't come naturally to her, but surely, those managers' workdays didn't include hiding behind furniture.

"And...got it!" Justice said, lowering the phone. "Come check it out."

Esther stood, stretched her legs, and watched as Justice swiped through the photos. She landed on the most recent. The plate of cookies was centered on the coffee table, each of them gleaming in the natural light. The fireplace, softly blurred in the background, made the whole scene look cozy enough for a nap. "Okay," she said, "you might have been onto something. Anyone who sees this is booking a trip."

Justice smiled. "Like you said, I have vision. And that vision includes lots of guests with deep pockets. Now, we need to convince Bunny to make these cookies for Makers and Merchants."

"I can't argue with that," Esther said. "Although I still don't get why I had to sit behind the couch. Couldn't I have just stood out of frame and walked over each time we needed to readjust?"

Justice busied herself looking at her phone. "That was for my own amusement."

"Hilarious," Esther said. "Just add a cute caption and you can post it to our socials."

Justice pretended to ponder as she left the room. "Please stay at our inn so I don't get fired for pranking my boss?"

"You have such a way with words."

Justice brushed past Kai in the doorway. Kai pointed over her shoulder with her thumb. "You know Sesame's running the reception desk, right?"

Esther waved a hand in dismissal. Justice was on her way back. She and Sesame could hash it out for the desk chair. "She's a smart cat. What's up?"

"What do you mean 'what's up'?" Kai demanded. "Spill it, Detective Esther! Bunny hit the highlights, but she's elbow-deep in a pot half her height right now."

"That sounds about right," Esther said. She grabbed two shortbread snaps and extended one to Kai as they sat on the couch. "I'm assuming she told you about the texts with Onyx?"

"She did. Three suspects now!"

"Maybe," Esther said. "It's not confirmed that Onyx was the one who sent the texts. It could be a complete coincidence."

"Sure," Kai said. "He could have a *second* secret girlfriend who he also nicknamed Butterfly."

That seemed unlikely. "When you put it like that…"

"My jaw hit the floor," Kai said. "Onyx seems like such a sweet girl. An affair with a married man is one thing, but murder too? Maybe that's why she's so into facials." Kai drew a circle around her face with her pointer finger. "Stress ages."

"I'm still thinking it through," Esther said, covering her mouth as she crunched on a cookie. "Assuming Onyx is Butterfly, we can confirm she knew where Faris was that night. So, what was the motive?"

Kai tapped her lips. "Maybe she knew about the trust fund. Thought she could get a slice of the pie. I'm sure he wouldn't have been the first rich man whose girlfriend was spinning the can-I-get-in-the-will wheel."

A guest did a double-take as she passed the living room, probably only catching that last bit of conversation. Esther smiled and waved, hoping to smooth it over.

She cringed internally. Wasn't she spinning the same wheel

with her parents? "Or maybe Onyx figured Faris was going to stand her up…or worse, would ditch her for someone else."

Kai nodded. "You lose 'em how you get 'em, right? She'd been to the spa plenty of times. I wouldn't be shocked if she knew where to look for the Botox."

Esther looked out the glass panes of the living room door. A squirrel sat up on its haunches like it was frozen mid-thought. A breeze stirred stray leaves and sent the little guy scurrying off. "And neither the police nor Uma have seen the text messages, which are the only obvious thing tying Onyx to Faris. She might not even be on the ORPD's radar."

Kai's eyes widened. "What if Uma and Onyx were working together somehow? The wife is conveniently out of town the night of the murder, and the lover knows she's safe as long as the police don't see the messages."

It was possible, but Uma didn't seem anxious at the thought of the police having Faris's phone. Her partner in crime getting caught would eventually lead back to her. Esther shuddered at the thought of Uma trailing her around Oak's Rest. For what? What did Uma want from her? "I wonder if Uma knows we're on to her."

"What do you mean?" Kai asked.

The more Esther thought about it, the more sense it made. "The only reason Uma would want to keep tabs on me is if she was guilty of something. Something she doesn't want me to uncover."

"Oh gosh," Kai said, looking worried. "Please don't put your-self in danger trying to get me out of hot water."

Esther managed a weak smile. Would Uma truly come after her for digging too deep? "I'm sure I'll be fine," she said. "We just need to get to the truth." Before the killer did more harm.

"So, the suspect list grows," Kai said, shaking her head. "Onyx, Uma, and Reese?"

Esther rubbed the back of her neck. "Every thread we pull

leads to a new suspect. But I think that's our only path forward, don't you?"

"I guess so," Kai said, inspecting what was left of her cookie. "Hey," she said, curiosity in her eyes. "You're gonna want to question Onyx, right?"

"Yes…" Esther said. "But the look on your face is scaring me."

Kai ignored her. "What if we talk to her at the spa? You know, invite her there for a treatment to thank her for all the 'help' she's given us." She used air quotes around "help."

"Okay, but why the spa? Why not meet her here at the inn? Or at the health department, on her own turf? Don't we want to make her feel at ease so she'll open up?"

"The opposite," Kai said. "We get her back to where the murder weapon was stolen and see if she gets squirmy."

"That's an interesting idea," Esther agreed. "Anyone who's not a professional actor would feel nervous about that. She'd have a tell."

"Yup. Little does she know, we'll be waiting for it."

# CHAPTER 34

The following evening, the sun was sinking quickly over Lake Ezra. Streaks of pink and tangerine melted into a deep violet, the rippling water catching every hue like a living, breathing canvas.

A few geese, not yet ready to migrate, lingered near the shore. The air smelled like woodsmoke and soil, and despite the chill, it was the kind of evening that invited Esther to stay a while longer.

She splayed her fingertips toward the crackling bonfire in Sugar and Guy Choo's yard.

Sugar, wrapped in a thick knit shawl, poked at the flame with a charred stick, sending a spray of orange sparks into the air. Guy leaned back in his weathered chair, placing an arm behind his head.

"Sure you don't want a s'more?" Sugar asked, raising an eyebrow as she pulled a jumbo marshmallow out of the bag. "You look like you could use a sweet pick-me-up."

Esther laughed. "Tempting, but I'll pass. My sister's due any minute. Best to go into family interactions on an empty stomach."

"I, for one, can't wait to see her," Guy said. "Do you look alike?"

Esther pressed her lips together, a lifetime of comparisons fighting to come up for air. "People have always said we do, but I don't see it. If we do look alike, our similarities pretty much end there."

"You're still upset about the fight, hmm?" Sugar asked.

Esther exhaled. "It's not just the fight. It's our whole lives. I've always been the odd one out in my family. It feels like...I don't know." She fumbled for the right words. How could she sum up a dynamic that shaped her whole childhood?

Sugar raised an eyebrow, waiting for her to go on.

"It feels like no matter what I accomplish—working my way from innkeeper to manager, supporting myself, building a wonderful life here in this amazing community—" she said, gesturing to Sugar and Guy, "nothing ever measures up to the Bennett standard."

Sugar listened quietly, turning a marshmallow over the flame. "Families have a way of making us feel like there are some invisible metrics we need to meet. But the only person you need to worry about impressing is you. What do *you* want?"

Esther considered the question. "Penny said something similar. She said I get to choose how I feel about my family." She'd tried to imagine her parents' perspective, how they *had* initiated spending more time together, even if their approach was more threatening than nurturing. "They are making an effort," she said softly. "I guess that counts for something."

"Are you?" Sugar asked. "Making an effort?"

"I don't know," Esther resolved. "There's so much baggage to unpack with my sister and my parents. I'm not sure I even know what making an effort looks like at this point in my life. Where would I start?"

"Find one thing you have in common," Sugar said. "Just one thing. And run with it."

The sound of tires crunching on gravel grabbed Esther's attention just before headlights peaked through the trees. Cameron's sleek black SUV was making its way up the driveway. "I better go," she said, growing nervous at seeing her sister's car. "On second thought, save me a s'more?"

Sugar smiled. "You got it. Go on, get out of here," she said, pointing to Esther's house with her stick.

Esther took a deep breath, stood, and started walking.

"And Esther?" Sugar called from behind her.

"Yeah?" Esther asked, turning around.

"You're already trying. I'm watching you do it right now."

Esther smiled. If Sugar thought she could do it, maybe she could.

Esther walked up to Cameron's car. Cameron cracked the door open with her foot, reaching across the seat for her bag. She met Esther's eyes for a brief second. "You have all the stuff?" she asked, looking away like she'd already moved on from the conversation. She was nervous too.

"I have it," Esther said. "Thanks for coming here this time." She heard how earnestly the sentence had come out, and instantly wished she could take it back. Why was it embarrassing? Was it so bad for her sister to hear her gratitude?

"Well, you texted me your address and said I didn't need to bring anything, so I didn't think I had much of a choice," Cameron said, pushing the door open and lowering her feet to the ground. She wore an expensive looking cream-colored barn jacket with brown detailing on the pockets.

Esther led the way, opening the side door to the house. She glanced back, expecting Cameron to be right behind her. Instead, her sister had drifted off to the grass beside the house.

Cameron stood still, her bag hanging loosely at her side, eyes fixed on the water.

Next door, Sugar held up a flaming marshmallow as she and

Guy shamelessly watched. Esther waved her arm to get their attention, trying to signal for them to stop staring.

Cameron gave a soft shake of her head as Esther walked up next to her.

"What's wrong?" Esther asked.

Cameron blinked a few times and swallowed, but didn't take her eyes off the lake. "You live here?"

"Guilty," Esther said, unsure how to respond. She couldn't tell what Cameron was thinking, but as she studied her sister's face, the way her eyes swept across the horizon and back again, she recognized the look. Cameron looked the way Esther had felt the first time she saw the lake. The way Esther knew she still looked at it every morning.

They stood silently side by side for a while, watching—for what, Esther didn't know. Down the lake, a single boat with a white sail glided along the water, in no hurry to get anywhere. The water shifted in the wind, glinting like hammered copper in the low sun.

Finally, Cameron cleared her throat and turned back toward the house. She didn't say anything more about it.

Inside, Esther had already pre-heated the oven and taken the cookie dough Bunny had prepared out of the fridge. She planned to make the cookie preparation as efficient as possible. All they had to do was flour the counter, roll the dough, shape the cookies, and bake.

They worked in silence except for a "thank you" here and a "can you pass me more flour?" there. It was like they'd made an unspoken agreement to avoid stepping on any landmines that could explode into a fight.

With the cookies loaded onto the baking sheet, Cameron washed her hands while Esther, still covered in flour, wiped down the workstation. Esther's phone started ringing at the edge of the counter.

She glanced at the screen. It was Kai. She debated letting it go to voicemail and calling her back later, but it was rare that Kai called instead of texted. It must have been important.

Esther looked around in search of something to wipe her hands on, but knew she wouldn't be able to pick up the call in time. "Do you mind getting that and putting it on speaker?" Esther asked hesitantly. She supposed Cameron could leave the room if she didn't want to hear the conversation.

Cameron swiped and a few taps later, the ringing stopped.

"Hey, Kai. You're on speaker. I'm baking with my sister."

"Oh. I—" Kai stuttered. "It's about...the boss. Want me to call you back?"

Esther moved closer to the phone at the mention of Reese. "No, it's fine. What is it?"

Cameron seemed intrigued by Esther's sudden interest. She watched but didn't move.

"I was getting dinner at the pub and Queenie and I got to talking. Apparently, Reese has an alibi for the night of the murder."

Cameron's eyes flew open and she mouthed, *murder?* reaching for her necklace.

Esther ignored her. "Spill," she said, leaning toward the phone. It's not like Cameron hung around Oak's Rest and was going to be gossiping about it.

"He was hosting a card game at his house that night. With all the other government fraudsters, if I had to guess. Anyway, there's a police report on record stating they went to his house that night for a noise complaint. Alibi verified."

"Wow," Esther said. "You're sure?"

"As sure as her professional insider can be," Kai replied.

Esther bit her lip in contemplation, which brought a not-so-pliable pair of lips to mind. "What about the wife, Kyla? She had enough cosmetic work done for the whole town."

Kai laughed. "She was the one who answered the door. Clumsily, from what I heard. Sounded like she and the other wives were in the next room over practicing their bartending recipes among each other."

Esther felt a combination of relief and disorientation at her suspect list being narrowed down so abruptly. "So that crosses Reese and Kyla off the list. I do wonder if he'll get caught for taking kickbacks for the inspection rates."

Cameron's brows were furrowed so tightly they almost became one. *Suspect? Kickback?* she mouthed, growing more animated.

Esther held up a finger.

"I'm sure it'll catch up with him," Kai said. "So, that leaves Uma and Onyx?"

"Just Uma and Onyx," Esther confirmed. "Hey, I'll see you tomorrow at the spa. I've got to make sure these cookies are burnt enough for my parents to think we made them from scratch, but not so burnt they're inedible."

"Bunny is a good friend," Kai said, before hanging up.

Esther slowly shifted her eyes from her phone to her sister, bracing herself for the barrage of questions she knew was coming.

Cameron stood with her arms crossed, eyebrows raised. "Talk," was all she said.

Esther gave her sister the most concise explanation of the situation she could. She had to stop every few sentences to answer questions or expand on certain details. Cameron was especially interested in the Butterfly reveal.

"You haven't seen anything about this in the news?" Esther asked when she was finished. They'd run some local stories on it, for sure, but Esther had avoided watching.

It took a few moments for Cameron to school her features back to normal. "No," she said. "Having kids is scary enough without constantly reminding myself of what could go wrong in the world. Plus, work keeps me so busy I rarely have time to watch the news."

"Well, now you know everything," Esther said. "There's no way I'm letting Kai be framed for a crime she didn't commit."

Cameron was quiet, looking at Esther like she was trying to puzzle something out.

"What?" Esther asked, growing uncomfortable with being stared at.

It seemed to snap Cameron out of her trance. "Nothing," she said, shaking her head. "It's just…" she looked away.

"Tell me," Esther said. "You can't start a sentence and not finish it." If Cameron was going to dangle the truth like a carrot, Esther would reach for it. Even if she wasn't sure she was ready to hear it.

Cameron shrugged. "You're willing to go through all this for your friend Kai. Dedicating your free time, potentially putting yourself in harm's way. You and I are sisters, and we've barely even spoken over the past few years."

Esther opened her mouth, but nothing came out. Cameron was right. Her friends were like family. But having it pointed out by her actual sister felt awkward. "I don't know what to say," she admitted, looking at Cameron.

Cameron maintained eye contact as she lifted a shoulder. "Nothing you need to say. You're just a good friend."

Esther broke first, looking down at her feet. She felt like the conversation was opening a door. She could either slam it shut or leave it propped open. She thought about what Sugar had said about trying, what Penny said about being in the driver's seat.

Esther had, technically, discovered one thing she and Cameron had in common. Was it weird that it was their interest in a murder case?

It didn't matter. It was something. *Run with it.*

"Remember that orchard and winery trip I was telling you about? When we made the banana pudding?" Esther asked, still looking downward.

"Yeah?" Cameron said, her voice unusually light. "It's on Monday, right? The day after dinner at Mom and Dad's?"

"Yeah," Esther confirmed, surprised she remembered the details. "I was wondering if you...I mean, I know I kind of mentioned it on a whim. I could cancel our spots if you can't go. It might be a hassle with the big group of guests, anyway." She felt herself rambling, but pushed through. "Or I could keep our spots? If you...did want to go?" She looked up to assess Cameron's reaction.

This time it was Cameron who looked away. "No—" she said, "Don't."

"Don't keep them?" Esther asked. "Or don't cancel them?"

"I want to go on the trip," Cameron said.

They met each other's eyes. "Okay," Esther said, feeling a smile tugging at the corners of her mouth. "We'll go."

"Okay," Cameron said, grinning.

# CHAPTER 35

"Ooo la la," Onyx said, reaching for the golden champagne. "Bubbly. Classy touch." She raised her glass in a toast. "You have *no freaking idea* how much I needed a spa trip. Thank you."

Lani smiled. "Our pleasure. And for you?" He asked, offering Esther the second glass.

She declined with a grateful smile. "I'll stick with water. Thanks, Lani." She wanted to stay sharp for questioning Onyx. She also had an inn to get back to. She had to admit, though, a glass of champagne followed by a spa treatment did sound like a perfect day.

Hopefully, Onyx would be relaxed enough to confess.

Esther adjusted her robe's belt. The fabric was so soft she wanted to hug herself in it, swaddle herself like a baby. She'd heard LouLou go on about Etana's Essence robes, but Esther hadn't ever gotten a treatment that required one until now.

It smelled good too, she noticed, pulling the lapel up to her nose. Actually, the entire spa had a pleasant aroma. Not overpowered by competing perfumes, but fresh, like an expensive face cream. *Well done, Kai.*

In matching white robes, Esther and Onyx could have passed for best friends on a girls' trip.

"Oops," Onyx said, bending to look at the floor. She'd spilled a splash of champagne as she set down the glass. Luckily, the plant on the table had gone unharmed. "Champagne can't be good for hardwood floors, right?" she asked, looking guiltily at Esther.

Esther glanced at the wide-plank wood floor. It gave the spa a homey feeling, which probably put people at ease before their more clinical procedures. "Doubt it. We can ask Lani for an extra towel."

Kai emerged from the treatment room, professional and calm. Even her movements were slow, her voice measured. Esther could see why people loved coming to her. "I'm ready whenever you are, ladies," she said, smiling.

Esther and Kai had agreed to book a couple's treatment room so they could talk to Onyx together. Esther was secretly excited to have some much needed R&R, even if it involved questioning a murder suspect.

After settling in, Esther lay face down on the table, her robe still on. Kai had assured her she could stay fully dressed until Onyx's eyes were covered.

A few feet away, Kai described that she was setting Onyx up with a facial steamer to open her pores and warm paraffin wax for her hands. She was about to place a heated towel over her eyes.

"Mmm. This feels great," Onyx said dreamily. "From now on, I'm warming my eye mask before bed."

Kai patted Esther on the shoulder to signal she was in the clear. Esther lifted her belly to untie the robe, then propped up on her forearms to slide her arms out each side.

Kai stood at the counter, her back to Esther, preparing hot stones and supplies like she could do it in her sleep. She made it look effortless.

Esther lay back down and peeled the robe off her back,

leaving her lower half covered. Kai had offered to get her a heated towel instead, but Esther wanted to be ready to dress fast if things went sideways. *I bet no one in the Oak's Rest Police Department has ever been this deep undercover.*

She hoped it paid off.

A moment later, Kai started setting the hot stones. She placed them along Esther's spine, in the palm of each hand, along the backs of her thighs, and finally, on the soles of her feet.

The world instantly started to melt away. Staying alert would take some determination.

Esther fought through the haze of pleasure. "So, Onyx," she said through the facial opening. "Do you think you'll keep sneaking off to see Kai once your regular esthetician comes back from maternity leave?" She wasn't sure how she was going to merge the conversation into a discussion about Faris, but she trusted herself to get there eventually.

After a few minutes, Esther knew more about Onyx's skincare routine than she ever thought possible. The girl could talk. Esther mumbled a few "wows" and "no ways" as Kai worked the stones into her skin.

Kai must have sensed that Esther was getting too relaxed, because she abruptly announced she was going to get started on Onyx's facial.

Esther objected, and they both laughed.

"Don't worry," Kai said above the nice, scritchy sound of her changing gloves. "I'll come back for you."

"You treat me too well," Esther said.

A phone started ringing somewhere in the room, which made Esther jump. She didn't recognize the ringtone.

Kai tsked. "Sounds like someone snuck her phone in."

"Sorry," Onyx said shyly. "I know I was supposed to leave it in the locker. I have a problem."

Kai laughed. "No big deal. Want me to silence it for you?

Given that your hands are covered in wax and you're kind of blindfolded at the moment?"

"Thanks," Onyx said, laughing. "It's in the right pocket of my robe."

Esther heard Kai's chair roll between the two beds. Silence stretched a beat too long. Then, Esther felt tapping on her shoulder.

She lifted her head to see Kai holding up Onyx's phone. Onyx was lying under the steam machine with the towel over her eyes, blissfully unaware. Esther squinted to get a better look without sending the paper on the bed into a loud, crinkly fit.

There was a colorful screensaver, some sort of collage. A pretty romantic one: a wedding ring with a big diamond, the back of a bride's dress made from sheer mesh with lace flowers, and two people holding hands on a beach with bright blue water.

Kai and Esther exchanged glances. They only had a few seconds to decide how to proceed. Kai switched the sound off and slid the phone back into Onyx's pocket. She cleared her throat, readying it to be professional again. "I'm going to uncover your eyes now so I can brush on your purifying green tea mask. You might feel some tingling. Totally normal." She motioned for Esther to lie down.

Esther complied. This was her in. She just needed to find a place in the conversation to jump in.

"That's a cute screensaver, by the way," Kai said offhandedly.

"Thanks," Onyx said. "It's sort of a vision board. I'm big on that."

"Oh," Kai said. "That's cool. By the looks of it, you have weddings on the brain?"

Esther took her shot. "Give us the details, already," she said, trying to sound more like a girlfriend than a bad undercover detective. "Are we going to be hearing wedding bells any time soon?"

Onyx gave a weary sigh. "I *was* seeing someone…it didn't work out in the end."

"In the end?" Esther asked. "What happened?"

Onyx was quiet for a few moments, then sniffled. Was she crying?

Esther couldn't resist looking. She lifted her head to see Onyx dabbing at her eyes with her robe sleeve. Her skin was coated in a light green mask. Kai rolled back in her chair, giving her space.

"Oh no," Esther said, trying to sound comforting. "Is it something I said?" *If I don't get the Oscar for this, I'm not tuning in to the award show.*

Onyx shook her head. "You didn't do anything." A tear fell, rinsing a thin line down the mask. "It's just…" The floodgates really opened then.

Kai took off her gloves and grabbed a tissue box from the counter. "What's wrong? You can tell us," she said, handing it over.

Onyx inhaled deeply and looked between Esther and Kai like she was debating how much to share. "There's something I haven't told you guys. It might come as a shock."

Esther and Kai exchanged perplexed looks like they couldn't imagine what she'd say next. "What is it?" Esther probed.

Onyx sniffed. "I was seeing someone. For a while. It was… Faris Holliday."

Kai gasped as Esther forced her eyes to go wide.

"You're kidding," Kai said, surprisingly believable.

"Did Uma know about you two?" Esther asked. Maybe that shouldn't have been her first question. She didn't want Onyx to feel judged and stop sharing.

Onyx pulled two tissues from the box. "Faris thought she'd been suspicious he was seeing someone. Always asking him about where he was going and who with. She didn't know it was me."

"Oh, honey," Esther said, before Onyx spoke again.

"He was going to leave her!" she said, her voice more confident. "At least, that's what he wanted me to think." Her chest deflated. "Obviously, it was all a lie."

Esther gave her a few moments to collect herself. She was all over the place. "What makes you think he was lying?"

Onyx held three balled up tissues in her lap. "He was always telling me we'd go somewhere tropical. Leave everything behind. But after a while, I started to lose my patience. And the more I pressed him about the timeline for our new life, the more he seemed to pull away. I think he was going to break up with me," she said, looking up at Esther and Kai.

Onyx had always seemed so confident. Now, though, she looked like a little girl who needed her mom. Esther felt a pang of sympathy for her. She didn't approve of affairs, but Onyx's naivety was written all over her face. She'd truly been clinging to the fantasy of starting a new life with Faris on some remote island. "Heartbreak sucks," she said gently. "I'm sorry you're hurting."

"I think he really did love me at some point," Onyx said, barely a whisper.

Kai looked at Esther as she gave Onyx a hug. "I'm sure he did, babe," she said, eyes widening in a *definitely not* fashion.

Esther needed to keep pressing. They were getting somewhere. With Onyx and Kai in an embrace, she quickly slipped her robe back on, tied it, and swung her legs over the side of the bed. "Sorry if this is hard," she started, "but can I ask how you've been since finding out about his death? I mean, it must have come as a shock when you heard the news."

Kai looked at Esther, seemingly impressed by the segue. Esther wiggled her eyebrows.

"You know, I actually had plans to see him that night. The night he died."

"Oh?" Esther asked. "But you didn't?"

Onyx hesitated, then a look of defiance crossed her face, like she'd decided to throw caution to the wind. "He was supposed to come over to my apartment after his dinner. I was texting him all night. But the later it got, the more drunk he seemed. Well, that's what I pieced together from his poorly spelled texts. I seriously considered going to find him. For all I knew, he was out with another woman." She was looking down at her hands again.

"That'd be unthinkable," Kai said, making eye contact with Esther.

Esther suppressed a smile.

"I know," Onyx said. "But I didn't want to be the stereotypical crazy, jealous girlfriend. I decided not to go."

"So, you didn't end up going out to find him?" Esther asked.

"No. I stayed home and ate ice cream," Onyx said. "Peanut butter cup heals all." She gave one final sniffle. The confession seemed to make her feel lighter. "Do you think you could get me some of those hot stones too?" she asked Kai. "Maybe for my shoulders?"

After the session, Esther changed and met Kai in the preparation room down the hall. She and Lani were speaking in hushed tones. Lani was holding a small piece of paper.

"So, what do you think?" Esther asked quietly, in case Onyx ventured out into the hallway. "I guess Onyx isn't our killer. She never drove to Oak's Rest that night."

"She's lying," Kai said.

"What?" Esther asked, wondering what she'd missed. "You were in there. You heard the part about the ice cream, right? What makes you think she was lying?"

Lani held up the paper. "Because I went through her purse while you two were back there."

Esther snatched it. It was a gas station receipt. "What is this?"

"Oh, nothing," Kai said, pretending to inspect her nails. "Just a receipt from an Oak's Rest gas station from the night Faris died."

Esther's jaw dropped. "Oh my goodness. So she *did* drive into town that night."

"She sure did," Lani said, looking proud of himself for making the discovery.

"And she got ketchup chips," Kai said, stabbing a finger at the receipt.

"So?"

"So, she can't be trusted!" Kai scream-whispered, as if it was obvious. "No one in their right mind eats those things. Nasty."

Lani nodded in agreement. "It's true," he said.

Kai crossed her arms. "She's been helping us this whole time. Maybe it was all to divert our attention."

Esther cleared all thoughts of what ketchup chips would taste like. She peered into the hall to make sure Onyx was nowhere in sight. "If she killed Faris, why would she confess to being in a relationship with him? Wouldn't she realize that would make her a suspect?"

"You know," Lani started, "I saw this crime show where they said killers only let victims see their faces when they're about to kill them. No sense in hiding their identities when the victim won't be able to tell anyone." He widened his eyes. "Which means you two better watch out."

"Don't be ridiculous," Kai said, swatting at the side of her nephew's head. "You're trying to scare us. Onyx is not going to kill us." She looked at Esther for a few moments, clearly thinking it over. "But just in case, Lani, you walk her out when she leaves."

# CHAPTER 36

The stairs creaked in welcome beneath the woman's tennis shoes. Esther followed, mentally checking off items as they went. From the living room came the gentle clink of teacups and the low murmur of guests swapping stories of their mornings on the lake tour boat. The soundtrack of everything running smoothly.

"This place is even lovelier than the photos," the woman said, hugging her purse to her chest. Her eyes swept over the inn with delight. "I can see myself curling up next to that fireplace with a good book. And that little kitty cat? Adorable."

Sesame was asleep on the living room couch, sprawled across the dip between two cushions. A couple sat shoulder-to-shoulder on the far end, unwilling to disturb Sesame's afternoon rest.

"She's a heartbreaker," Esther said, trying not to laugh at Sesame's command over her kingdom. She refocused on the guest. Watching first-timers fall for the inn never got old.

"Like I mentioned in my booking notes, I'll need some extra pillows," the woman said. She turned to face Esther as if underscoring the seriousness of the request.

"That's not a problem," Esther assured her. "Will two extra be enough?"

"Five. At least." The woman's eyes flicked side to side like she was doing mental math. "Make that seven. Seven should do it."

"Oh… sure," Esther said, already preparing for Sveta's wrath. She did not take kindly to frivolous linen use.

Just then, Esther heard a deep thumping coming from the Calliope Room down the hall, like tapping on a microphone.

Justice's voice came through like a grocery store employee announcing the store was closing in five minutes. "Testing, testing. Luke, I am your concierge."

Apparently, the festival sound check was underway. At least she knew the PA system they'd rented for Makers and Merchants worked, though in hindsight, Esther should have clarified Justice was supposed to test it outside. Mayor Early would be pleased she wouldn't have to shout through opening remarks.

Esther deflected by gently walking the woman a few steps further from the staircase. Was she planning on hosting a slumber party? "Sorry, just confirming it's only you on the reservation? I want to make sure we get our chef the right number of—"

"Just me," the woman said, cutting Esther off. "Seven extra pillows, please." With that, she put her purse on her shoulder and sauntered into the living room.

Esther admired a woman who said her piece and made her exit. Even if that exit was ten feet away. "Pillow fort it is," she said, heading for the lobby. She pulled out her phone and sent off an email to one of the housekeeping staff, hoping they could handle it before Sveta found out.

She was approaching reception when she spotted Bunny in the dining room, unmistakable in her pink chef's coat. She was deep in conversation with Luis, who stood beside the table holding a plate topped with a single scoop of vanilla ice cream with a green sprig of something decorative. Curious, Esther veered toward them for a closer look.

"Try again," Bunny instructed. "This time, angle the garnished side at five o'clock. It should be visible, but not facing the guest head-on. People won't want to remove the mint right away. They'll eat around it first, enjoying how pretty it looks. We want them to admire the vanilla bean flecks and texture of the scoop while they do."

Luis nodded, his eyebrows knitted in concentration, as if trying to memorize every word. Were his hands trembling?

"Hey, you," Esther said, taking a seat next to Bunny. "Planning to put Ben and Jerry out of jobs?"

Bunny brightened. "This," she said, pointing to the rapidly melting scoop, "is practice. No better way to train than against a clock." She turned to Luis and dismissed him with a, "We'll pick this up later."

Esther shared a look with Luis—equal parts sympathy and relief—before he excused himself.

Bunny unraveled the silverware set from its napkin, handed Esther a spoon, then dipped into the ice cream with a fork. "Tell me all about your spa trip this morning."

Esther filled Bunny in on the affair, Onyx's vision board, and her account of the night. She'd had to pause to say, "Hang on, there's more" a few times.

Bunny leaned back in her chair and whistled. "So, it's confirmed. Onyx and Faris. I did not see that coming. I mean, she's so…"

"I know," Esther said.

"And he was so…."

"I know."

"Does that take Uma and Onyx as a murderous duo off the table?"

"It seems like Uma was completely in the dark about Onyx's identity," Esther said, licking her spoon clean. "But they both had reasons for getting revenge on Faris. He'd wasted the trust fund Uma was counting on, and Onyx sensed he was going to dump her, possibly for another woman."

"They both have secrets too," Bunny said. "Onyx's gas station receipt, Uma lurking in the shadows…"

Esther picked at the mint. "I'm not sure what to think. Clearly, Onyx lied about where she was that night. Who's to say she didn't lie about other aspects of her story?"

"What was Uma's alibi again?" Bunny asked. "Where did she say she was that night?"

"Out of town," Esther said. "Visiting a friend in the city." Of course, there was a chance Uma had lied too. Suspects seemed to have a habit of that.

"Maybe verifying that is the next move," Bunny suggested. "Find out if there's any record of her trip."

"I'm not sure how I'd find it," Esther said, looking out the window. "I've already questioned her a few times, and I don't think I can come up with another reason to go to her house. She might get suspicious if I keep poking at her."

"What about Nolan?" Bunny asked. "He gave us information before. Maybe the police department has details we're missing."

"He told *Queenie* information," Esther corrected. "And with Sabina on my case about staying out of the investigation, I'm sure she wouldn't be too thrilled to find me bugging Nolan."

"Then have Queenie ask. You know, pillow talk."

Esther considered that. Queenie playing the curious girlfriend had way better potential than her barging in as a nosy sleuth. "You might be right. I'm sure the police talked to Uma early on and checked her alibi, but maybe they missed something. I'll call Queenie."

"Guess what?" Kai asked, striding into the dining room.

"You're going to offer me a complimentary hot stone massage too?" Bunny guessed.

"Even better," Kai said, sitting down. "My new inspection is next week. Ingram comes out on Wednesday."

Esther and Bunny clapped. "That's great!" Esther said. "I thought the health department was booked out for weeks."

"There was a cancellation or something. Who knows? The important thing is I'm prepared this time. There's no chance I'll fail again...right?" she asked, her confidence cracking.

"No way," Bunny said, rubbing her back. "Etana's Essence isn't going anywhere. You'll pass with flying colors."

"Absolutely," Esther said. "Without Faris, hopefully Ingram will be more reasonable. I haven't heard anyone wish for his death since he's taken over, so that's promising."

Kai eased out a breath. "Thanks. I'm still a little shaken up from the last inspection. I'm sure it'll be great. It has to be."

Esther was about to offer more words of encouragement when movement in the lobby caught her eye. Sveta was marching toward reception, holding her feather duster upright like a pitchfork. Apparently, Esther's promises of extra pillows had already come home to roost. "I have to go handle something," Esther said, standing up. "If I look back and blink three times, come save me."

# CHAPTER 37

"Here we are," Esther said, balancing the bag of donuts atop the coffee carrier. She carefully knelt on the blanket. "Penny wishes you all a happy Saturday."

"You're an angel," LouLou said, reaching for a coffee.

"Not so fast." Esther turned the carrier so LouLou's hand landed on the cup labeled with her name. "Penny has you on half decaf." She kicked off her ankle boots and sat down.

LouLou's smile faltered. "And she says nothing about *your* caffeine intake? Since when does she have a medical degree?"

"She doesn't," Bunny chimed in, "but I'm pretty sure your real doctor said *no* coffee. You should be thanking Penny."

LouLou took a sip and pouted. "I can taste the difference. It's the weekend. Can't I live a little?"

Sugar dug into the donut bag and placed a pink-frosted one on her lap. She reached in a second time, producing a chocolate donut, smiling like she'd hit the jackpot.

"You're really putting the 'sugar' in Sugar Choo, aren't you?" Bunny teased.

Sugar winked, already biting into the chocolate donut.

The beach was brimming with activity. The summer lake crowd had faded when fall rolled in, but with winter around the corner, no one was going to pass up a fair-weather day.

Dev Singh was playing frisbee with a group of three dogs, eagerly awaiting his every move. A wall of red and gold trees lined the far side of the lake, framing the dogs as they ran right up to the edge of the water, then back again. It could have been a TV commercial.

Mayor Early, walking by with a clipboard, narrowly avoided being toppled over by the biggest dog. "Leashes were invented for a reason, people!" she yelled, looking around, as though anyone were paying attention.

"You know," LouLou said, "aside from Bethany, I don't think I've ever seen anyone bring a clipboard to the beach."

"Our mayor is one of a kind," Bunny said, raising her coffee cup.

Esther and LouLou raised their cups to reciprocate the cheers, while Sugar kept busy with her donut. Esther removed the lid from her cup, the steam escaping along with that rich, soul-warming aroma she knew so well.

"Hey, Jim!" LouLou called, waving.

Esther followed her line of sight to the boathouse, where Jim White was helping a couple load a cooler and backpacks into a canoe.

"I see you got your boat back!" LouLou shouted.

Esther remembered overhearing Jim tell other shop owners about his missing boat the day she'd discovered Faris's body. What a chaotic morning that had been. She'd nearly forgotten about Jim's predicament.

"You bet!" Jim said, patting the side of the canoe. "Turned up half a mile down the lake. Tied up to the dock nice and neat. Probably a couple of love-struck teens, like I figured."

Sugar chuckled. "You know, when Mr. Choo and I started

dating, he was a hotel valet driver. One time, he borrowed one of the fancy cars to drive me to a date. Trying to impress me. Well, halfway through the ride, I took out my powder to touch up my makeup in the mirror..."

"Uh-oh," Esther said, sensing trouble. She loved hearing the stories from older women in her life, imagining how spunky they'd been in their youth. Luckily, she didn't have to lean too hard on her imagination, because they were still just as charismatic.

"I saw an actress do it in an old Hollywood movie!" Sugar said. "It felt so luxurious. Until Guy slammed on the brakes at a red light and powder went flying everywhere."

Esther laughed, plucking a blueberry donut from the bag. "Did Guy get in trouble at work?"

"His boss made him pay for the detailing himself. Couldn't afford to take me out for another six months."

"Ha! I've got you beat, honey," LouLou said, lifting the end of her long skirt to reveal a scar on the back of her calf. "Twenty years old. Boyfriend's motorcycle. Daisy Dukes."

"Ouch!" Esther said. "That must have hurt."

LouLou shrugged. "I'd do it again if I could get those legs back."

Esther sipped her coffee and leaned backward, resting one hand behind her. She looked over at Jim, every bit the proud captain of his little fleet of boats.

She tried to imagine how she'd handle it if teenagers stole from the inn. Would she be so easy going? She doubted it. Didn't they know small businesses didn't always bounce back from pranks like that? Sometimes, it could mean the end of everything.

Esther understood the urge to take. To see something so tangible, so vivid, that reaching out and grabbing it seemed like the only logical option. It was how she approached her goals. If other people could do it, so could she.

But that kind of determination could also lead someone astray. When applied to theft, for example. Or murder.

She hoped wherever those teenagers were, they'd eventually learn the difference between seizing an opportunity and taking what wasn't theirs.

# CHAPTER 38

"There's a smudge on this," Veronica Bennett said, inspecting her crystal water glass under the light of the chandelier. "Graham, there's a smudge on this."

Sunday nights seemed to come around faster every week. The Bennetts had settled into somewhat of a rhythm, with parents at the heads of the table and Esther and Cameron seated across from each other.

Esther's father leaned over his plate, shoveling food in his mouth with one hand, holding his phone with the other. They'd been served some type of poultry that Esther couldn't, or didn't want to, remember the name of. "Mhmm," he belatedly responded without looking up.

"Graham!" Veronica snapped. "Will you please, for the love of all that's good in the world, put that phone away? You know we don't do cellular devices at the table."

Esther eyed Cameron across the table. *Cellular devices?* she mouthed, holding back a smile.

Graham huffed. "Darling, you know I've been waiting on this deal to happen all month. We're in the final stages of firming it up, and I need to stay abreast of what's happening. Henry will have the whole thing tumbling down faster than a house of cards if I don't keep an eye on him."

Veronica rolled her eyes and sighed. "Great," she said, setting the glass down on the table. "I've got defective dinnerware and a husband who finds his email more engrossing than his wife."

"Lighten up, Mom," Cameron said, standing. "One of those problems is an easy fix." She swapped their mother's glass for their father's unspotted and untouched one. "See? Good as new."

"Yeah, Mom," Esther added, noticing her mother still wasn't pleased. "Plus, I don't think a smudged glass ever killed anyone. Unless it was smudged with arsenic."

"What?" Veronica asked, frowning.

"Arsenic. Deadly poison? Veronica-go-bye-bye?"

Esther's mother looked at her with an agitation that suggested jokes weren't on that night's menu.

"Forget it," Esther said. "Look it up on Dad's cellular device later."

Cameron snickered.

"Esther, please," Veronica said, rubbing her neck. "I'm in a state entirely too delicate to decipher one of your riddles."

"So, Mom," Cameron interjected, "how'd the charity event go?"

"Right," Esther said, remembering her mother's mention of it two dinners ago. "Did Betty and Sally manage to get decent flowers?" She shared a knowing glance with Cameron, who also found it funny how particular their mother's taste was.

Esther didn't want to know what her mother would think of the floral arrangements she displayed at the inn. No rhyme or reason, all play. Although, the tip about using non-perfumey flowers had actually been helpful. Esther wouldn't want to alienate guests with scent sensitivities.

Veronica stopped massaging the nonexistent tension from her neck. She looked at Esther, surprise etched on her face. "You remembered that?"

"I do listen when people talk, Mom," Esther said. "Occasional-ly." She was trying.

Her mother smiled. "Well, yes, by some miracle, they pulled off quite a decent centerpiece. Beautiful light pink and cream calla lilies from some who-knows-where hemisphere of the planet. I heard they even skipped customs. I was impressed."

"*Impressed*," Esther mimicked. "That's a glowing review coming from you."

"Oh, stop it," Veronica said, smoothing an invisible wrinkle on her blouse. "I'm impressed by plenty of things."

"No, really," Cameron said. "I don't think you told me you were impressed when I graduated from high school a year early. Or college. Or medical school, for that matter."

Esther's phone vibrated in her pocket amid the debate. She was supposed to leave it in her purse, but she loved the thrill of sneaking contraband to the dinner table. She tried to be sly as she slid the phone out under the table.

"Esther Bennett, I sincerely hope you are not looking at what I think you're looking at right now." Her mother was like a shark that could sniff out rule-breaking from a quarter mile away.

"I have to be reachable for emergencies at the inn. It's my job." It was technically true.

Veronica let loose. "For crying out loud. I have two people at my dinner table who are glued to their—" she turned toward the now empty chair at the head of the table. "When did he...? Graham?" she called out to no response.

"He got up like five minutes ago, Mom," Cameron explained.

"Utterly ridiculous," Veronica said, crossing her arms and glaring at Esther like she'd been the one to pull a silent exit. "Clearly, anarchy has touched down on our household. If you need to make a phone call, you may."

Esther was surprised. "Wow, thanks Mom. I didn't expect—"

"Outside," her mother cut in.

Esther laughed. "You're serious? You want me to leave the house?"

Veronica lifted her chin. "I'm as serious as whatever malignant health condition we threw the charity event for."

"Fine, Mom," Esther said, pushing back her chair. "Please excuse me for a minute so I can make sure nothing urgent needs my attention."

On her way out, she heard Cameron ask, "What disease was it?"

Veronica responded, "How would I know? Every condition we raise money for has more syllables than the last. It's a linguistic nightmare."

Esther unlocked her screen as she closed the front door behind her. She hunched her shoulders against the chill. At least she hadn't made the mistake of underdressing again. She wore a v-neck wrap sweater with lace and faux pearls along the chest. Pretty indoors, but currently not doing her any favors in the evening breeze.

She had a text from Queenie:

**Queenie:** N says Uma was in NYC that night. Gave over copies of train tix and everything. First-class aisle seat of course.

Esther read the message three times. Something was gnawing at her, like her brain was trying to tell her something. Then she remembered the story Uma had told her. *I remember the cold window feeling nice against the side of my head.* If she'd had an aisle seat, she wouldn't have been able to lean against the window.

She shot back a response:

**Esther:** Where was she staying in NYC?

Her heart pounded. If her suspicion was right, she was about to catch Uma Holliday in a major lie. Her phone vibrated.

**Queenie:** The Winthore.

There it was. The Winthore was one of Manhattan's swankiest hotels. Uma had lied about staying at her friend's place. Why?

Another thought nagged at Esther. Anyone could edit photos of train tickets or hotel booking confirmations. Had the police checked with the hotel for footage of her arrival and departure? Had they bought the tale Uma had spun?

Maybe it was good if they had. Let Uma think she was innocent long enough for Esther to find out what had really happened.

What if Uma had never left town the night her husband was killed?

# CHAPTER 39

"Watch your—" Esther called from the side lawn, wincing as Clint lurched forward, his foot catching the top step of the porch. Somehow, he kept hold of the dolly, which was convenient, since it was supporting an industrial-size stand mixer. A very expensive stand mixer. "—Step," she finished, a moment too late.

The stand mixer was a rental, but Bunny had been eyeing it for weeks. She said she needed serious horsepower to efficiently crank out food for the Makers and Merchants Festival. Normally, Esther would have asked her to make do with the extensive lineup of mixers already in the kitchen. But she also knew events usually lived or died by two things: fun and great food.

Clint recovered quickly, flashed a thumbs-up, and wheeled the mixer through the kitchen entrance.

Crisis averted, Esther jogged to the parking lot, where the group was gearing up for a morning at the orchard.

Justice passed out glossy trifolds to the guests, who all looked eager to get on the road. "Everyone should have a map," Justice said, projecting her voice. "But Marcus Hall knows the orchard like the back of his hand. If you get lost, don't worry, he'll find you in two to three business days, tops."

A few guests smiled, perhaps trying to figure out if Justice was joking. Others looked like they were estimating how long they could live off the land. Cameron, standing in front of Esther's car, was the only one who laughed.

Esther made a mental note to avoid putting Justice on greeting duty at the festival. "She's kidding," she said, stepping in. "I'll be joining you, and Marcus and his wife, Aggie, are dear friends. Let any of us know if you have questions once we get there. It's about a ten-minute trip. Drive safe, everyone!"

That seemed to do the trick. Smiles widened, and everyone turned toward their cars. Job done, Justice gave a small salute and headed back inside.

Esther heard voices coming from the kitchen. Moments later, Clint emerged, looking sheepish, a bread roll crammed in his mouth. Bunny steered him by the shoulders, leaving little room for argument. She dusted her hands like she'd taken out the trash as Clint trudged down the steps, empty-handed. *Hadn't he come with a dolly?*

The thought seemed to strike Clint at the same time. He paused, spun around, and took a cautious step up, only to be met by Bunny, stationed in the doorway like a one-woman security system, arms crossed, eyes unyielding. Clint slinked away.

At the front of the inn, Sesame was perched inside the living room window. No doubt she'd be watching the spectacle play out like a soap opera once Clint came into view.

Esther ducked into her car before Clint could spot her and file his complaints. For the rest of the morning, she'd be a tourist in her own town.

~

"If you can believe it," Marcus Hall said, motioning to the rows of trees on each side of the group, "these trees are the originals planted in 1964. These old ladies are still standing, generously giving us apples for cider and a few of our wines here at Hall Winery & Orchard."

Esther closed her eyes and breathed in. The sweet-tart aroma of fruit and fresh earth hung heavy in the air. Neatly lined rows of trees as far as she could see dangled bright red and yellow-green apples, bobbing at the ends of branches, threatening to drop.

Esther, Cameron, and seven guests formed a half-circle around Marcus. They each held an apple-picking tote bag decorated with red apples scattered around a full barrel. The phrase *Fresh Produce From Our Family to Yours* was written across the bottom.

One guest raised his hand and asked, "How do you know when the apples are ready to be picked?"

Marcus smiled and turned to face a tree. "What we have here are your Johnathan apples. These jewels should come right off the branch with a gentle twist." He demonstrated, reaching for an apple at his eye level. It came off easily in his hand.

"If you have to yank until the branch is about to snap, it's not ready. We treat the land with care, it rewards us in kind. Lucky for us, Lake Ezra acts like a natural thermostat. Keeps the temps more stable throughout the seasons. Means more time on the trees and even more delicious fruit."

Marcus tossed the apple to the guest who'd asked, an older man who caught the fruit with impressive agility. "If you want, you can give it a little polish using the inside of your jacket there. Brings the color out."

The man did as suggested, admiring the noticeably shinier fruit. He looked up at Marcus, a question on his face.

"Go right ahead!" Marcus encouraged.

The man took a big bite out of the apple. His eyes widened as he crunched. "Yum," he said, covering his mouth with his free hand. "Just the right amount of tart."

Marcus looked proud. He clasped his hands together. "Get picking, folks. We'll meet back inside the tasting room for a sampling of our adult beverages, made in-house. Your Calliope Inn cruise captain," he said, gesturing to Esther, "has made me promise to make sure no one leaves without their very own bottle of our signature wine."

The guests clapped with enthusiasm, looking from Marcus to Esther.

Cameron gave Esther's shoulder a nudge. "Aye aye, Captain," she said.

The group scattered, apple bags swinging at their sides. Esther and Cameron made a bet to see who could pick an apple with the most seeds. The loser had to buy the other person a gift shop T-shirt.

When they realized they'd tied, both their apples having six seeds, they decided to each buy shirts anyway. Esther loved picking up small mementos to commemorate places she'd visited, no matter how cheesy they were. It was like collecting memories and saving them for later.

Apple bags full, the group congregated back at the tasting room—though *room* hardly did it justice. It felt more like a deluxe ski lodge, with walls lined in light wood and rows of exposed beams stretching along the ceiling. Polished cherry tables and matching chairs gleamed in the sunlight streaming through the wide windows.

Through the open doorway beyond the tasting room, rows of oak barrels and shelves of wine bottles resting on their sides whispered the quiet promise of celebrations and memories yet made.

Aggie Hall walked into the tasting room to greet them.

"We have a wonderful selection lined up for you all today. We'll start with a crisp white, make our way to a deep red, and finish with our sweet, apple spice dessert wine. How does that sound?"

The guests buzzed with excitement.

Someone let out a "Whoop!"

Evidently, the trip was a crowd pleaser. Esther would be sure to post about it on social media. She'd tried to take as many photos as possible. Justice would be proud.

Aggie laughed. "We also have a selection of non-alcoholic wines for anyone interested."

"That would be us," Cameron said to Esther. Their gift shop souvenirs sat neatly folded on their table. Esther had picked a white tee printed with vintage-style rows of olive green trees. She could actually see herself wearing it regularly, maybe with jeans and sneakers.

"Thanks again for inviting me," Cameron said. "A field trip without kids is a rare occurrence for me these days. Especially on a weekday. Your job is pretty cool."

Esther laughed. "I love my job, but don't be fooled. It's also a lot of putting out fires. It's basically customer service, except the customers sleep over."

"When you put it like that," Cameron said, "it sounds a little less glamorous."

"It has its moments," Esther said. "What about you, Doctor Bennett? What would you normally be doing right now at work? Other than saving lives."

Cameron smiled. "Furiously typing chart notes and scarfing down protein bars between patients. Probably while on hold with an insurance company."

"Now *that's* glamor," Esther joked.

Employees arrived with the wine flights, setting them down on each of the few tables the guests were seated at.

Aggie came to Esther and Cameron's table last. "Hi, stranger," Aggie said, setting their flight down. It was a wooden paddle with five stemless glasses arranged along the perimeter. *Hall Winery &*

*Orchard* was engraved in elegant cursive lettering. "The last time we got a visit from you, I didn't have any gray hair."

Esther gave her a bemused look. Though Aggie Hall had to be at least two decades older than Esther, she didn't look it. "You don't have gray hair now, Ag."

"Movie magic," Aggie said, turning her attention to Cameron. "And this must be…?"

"I'm Cameron," Cameron said, extending her hand. "Esther's younger sister."

Aggie raised her eyebrows as she shook Cameron's hand. "What a treat. So, do I have two Bennetts to thank for the uptick in visitors the past few weeks?"

"We all have each other to thank," Esther said. "The Oak's Rest business community has taken social media in full stride this year. Especially in the last few months. We've all been doing a great job promoting our little town ahead of Makers and Merchants."

Cameron leaned closer to Aggie. "Yeah, because Esther told them to. But she's too humble to brag about herself."

"I am not," Esther retorted. "I'm talented at lots of things." She pointed to the flight. "Like drinking wine."

Aggie laughed. "Your specialty wines, as requested. I think you'll especially like the spiced cranberry and apple blush, as well as the tart Concord red."

"Thank you, Aggie," Esther said, excited to take a taste. "And thanks again to you and Marcus for volunteering to make apple cider for the festival. I'm sure Bunny is going to add some undisclosed ingredient to it, because she's Bunny, but know that everything you make here is beyond amazing."

"I'm sure whatever Bunny does will only make it better," Aggie said. "Enjoy, ladies. If you change your mind, and want to add a little 'adult' to your adult bevs, come find me." She winked and turned away.

Esther picked up a glass and swirled. The color was somewhere between pomegranate red and rose gold, with hints of amber when it caught the light just right. "Do you think we still have to stick our noses into the glass and pretend we know what we're doing for non-alcoholic wines?"

Cameron made a face. "Only around Mom and Dad and their friends." She picked up a glass and plunged her nose deep inside, giving an exaggerated inhale. Then, with pursed lips and perfect poise, she mimicked, "Cameron, darling, don't be uncouth. A lady samples, never snorts."

"Wow," Esther said, clapping on her wrist. "You really do a good Mom."

"Thank you," Cameron said, taking a fake bow. "Years of practice." She studied the glass. "I still can't believe Mom is serious about cutting us from the will. This is a whole new level of Veronica Bennett. Even for Veronica Bennett."

Esther took her first sip. It was bright and faintly tart at first, with the zing of cranberry leading the way. Eventually, it mellowed with the warmth of familiar baking spices—cinnamon, and maybe a hint of nutmeg. Fall in a glass. She set it down gently. "I'm still getting used to the idea of my mother controlling me with her purse strings. You two have always been pretty tight, though."

"We have a lot in common," Cameron said in between sips. "On paper."

Esther raised her eyebrows. "On paper? You ate lunch together every day while you were in school. You both have more letters after your names than I can count. You've created the perfect life, according to her."

She knew she was wading into vulnerable territory, but to her surprise, it felt okay. Even if the conversation got murky, she trusted they could find their way back to solid ground.

Cameron's smile faded. "Is that what you think?" she asked. "That I'm following some cookie-cutter life Mom laid out for me when I was little?" She didn't seem accusatory, just curious.

"Kind of," Esther answered honestly. "It is a beautiful plan."

Cameron looked at Esther inquisitively. "Why did you leave?"

Esther snorted. "How much time do you have?"

Cameron didn't laugh. She wanted an answer.

"Okay," Esther said, decidedly setting the glass down. "In a sentence, I had to get away."

"From the pressure, right?" Cameron asked. "The feeling that if you made one small misstep, you'd be committing treason against the family name?"

"Those are the headlines, yes."

Cameron waited.

Esther gave a half-smile, not getting what Cameron was hinting at.

One of the guests said, "Why haven't I ever had wine straight from a winery? Alan, why don't you buy me wine straight from the winery every week?"

The man next to her, presumably Alan, said, "Because we'd have to rob a bank to afford it, hun."

Cameron leaned forward. "Have you ever imagined that I might have felt that same pressure too? That I'm *still* feeling it?"

Esther blinked. "I guess not." Her voice sounded small.

"Well, I do," Cameron said. "Every single day. At least you got to break yourself out of that mold." Were those tears gathering at the corners of her eyes? "When you left, it felt like I had to achieve enough for both of us."

Esther swallowed, a lump forming at the base of her throat. "I'm sorry, Cameron. Really. I didn't know me moving away would affect you. I figured it would be easier for you to shine once I left."

Cameron snorted. "I know it must have taken bravery and smarts to start this new life, but you can be a little clueless."

"What do you mean?"

Cameron shook her head, smiling. "I've always looked up to you, you big dummy."

Esther felt the crease between her eyebrows deepen. "I'm sorry. I think my ears just stopped working."

Cameron rolled her eyes. "I think I could have used someone to talk to all those years. Someone who knew what it felt like."

Esther nodded slowly. All at once, she imagined her and Cameron gossiping over drinks, much like they were now, strategizing about how they'd make all their dreams come true. "I could have used that too."

Cameron smiled. "You're my big sis," she said, shrugging.

It was the simple, honest truth. Esther raised her glass. "Sisters."

Cameron clinked her glass against Esther's. "Sisters."

# CHAPTER 40

"You're not going to beat her," Esther said, watching the competition unfolding between Justice and Sesame.

Sesame crouched in position on the reception desk, waiting for her opponent to strike. Justice hovered both hands above the desk, unreadable. Suddenly, she lifted her right hand. Sesame swatted at it before she could pull away.

"Ow!" Justice inspected the back of her hand. "That was more claw than paw," she said with an accusing look.

Esther smirked. "Told you. Your self-proclaimed cat-like instincts are no match for an actual cat. Plus, I gave her an extra treat. She's carb-loaded and ready to pounce."

Justice sulked. "I bet you couldn't beat her either. Especially after glugging down wine all morning."

"I only drank non-alcoholic wine, thank you very much," Esther corrected. "And that was hours ago. I'm pretty sure I would have sobered up by now."

"I don't know," Justice said skeptically, "I had an ex who used to say fresh wine gets you more tipsy. He said the mass-produced stuff at the grocery store is mostly dyed water."

"Dyed water?" Esther asked, cocking an eyebrow. "Did your ex ever say anything scientifically sound?"

"Nope," Justice said, looking into the distance like she was reliving some fond memory. "But he always looked good sayin' it."

Esther waved a hand. "Alright, get out of here. I've had enough of you for today."

Justice stood and smoothed her skirt. "My favorite time of day—quitting time."

"I'll be sure to bring that up at your next performance review," Esther called after her as she walked away.

Sesame stared deeply into Esther's eyes. To the untrained, it was a picture of cuteness. But Esther knew that expression. "Don't give me that face," she warned. "I already snuck you that salmon earlier. Bunny's going to notice if I take any more."

The cat yawned, leapt down, and trotted off.

"Good to know what you value me for," Esther said. She startled as her phone rang. "Hey Kai, what's up?"

Kai sounded out of breath. "Something happened at the spa. Can you come over here? Like, now? I'm kind of freaked out."

Esther stood. "What happened? Are you okay?"

"I'm fine," Kai said. "Something's just off. Come as soon as you can."

"I'm on my way." Esther hung up and grabbed her things. She quickly logged out of the computer, grateful her past self had already confirmed there were no late check-ins.

As she jogged toward the front door, she passed Mort coming down the stairs. "Hey now!" he said, reaching out to steady her. "Where's the fire?"

"Sorry," Esther said, "I'm in a little bit of a rush. Shoot—" she remembered she hadn't done her end-of-day sweep. "Can you make sure all the staff-only areas are locked up before you go? Kitchen, Calliope Room, basement?"

"Can do, boss," Mort said. "Be safe."

Esther did her best to do just that, driving only a few miles over the speed limit. She hopped out of the car and rushed inside the spa to find Kai sitting in the waiting area, anxiously tapping her foot.

"What's going on?" she asked, looking around for signs of trouble. Everything appeared intact.

Kai stood, glancing from one side of the spa to the other. "I don't exactly know."

Esther paused, trying to piece it together. "You...don't know?"

"Things were out of place," Kai said. "When I got here. The back door was unlocked. The trash can in my office was moved."

"Okay," Esther said, pacing a few steps, peering around corners. Not that she knew what she'd do if she came face to face with a burglar. "And you're sure neither of those things could have been you? Was Lani here? Or maybe one of your assistants? Maybe they forgot to lock up?"

"It smells different," Kai said, biting her lip.

"It smells different," Esther repeated. She sniffed. It smelled the same to her. "I'm not following."

Kai heaved an impatient breath. "It smells different, Esther. Someone has been in here. Not Lani, not one of my assistants. We were closed today. I only came by to water the plants."

Esther was growing unsettled. "Sorry. I'm not doubting you. You know this place better than anyone." She lowered her voice. "Do you think someone broke in?"

"I don't know. Nothing is missing or broken..." Kai turned to Esther with a pleading look, like she was desperate for Esther to believe her. "I pick up on scents. It's my job. I use them to shape the mood of the space. I know I sound crazy."

"No," Esther said, wrapping an arm around Kai. "You don't sound crazy. Do you want me to call the police? Have them come check it out?"

Kai looked around like she was weighing her options. "I think

—" she broke off, her gaze landing somewhere down the hallway, near the prep room.

Esther tried to track her line of sight. "What, Kai?"

Kai wordlessly walked closer to what she was looking at, leering down at a spot on the floor. Esther followed her, eventually spotting the oddity. A floorboard at the end of the hall was lifted, just enough for someone to trip over if they weren't paying attention.

"This wasn't like this before," Kai said.

Esther didn't recall any problem with the floor when they'd brought Onyx in. She gently nudged the floorboard with her foot, testing it. It was looser than she'd expected. It flipped over and clattered to the side.

A white piece of paper with colorful marks was taped underneath. "What the—" Kai said, crouching down. She pulled the paper free and stood, eyes flicking rapidly as she speed-read.

"What is it?" Esther asked, unable to take the suspense. "Is it a note?"

Kai looked up, slowly, meeting Esther's eyes. "I'd say so," she said, handing the paper over.

Esther held Kai's stare for a few seconds. The fear in her expression was clear. Finally, she looked down to read it herself.

*You girls should stop digging into this case*
*Might find more trouble than you're ready for*

Esther's spine stiffened. The message was scrawled in bold, bright red.

"There's no chance they delivered this to the wrong person, right?" Kai asked, voice trembling. "Maybe they meant to break into another shop and threaten a different group of snooping friends?"

Esther swallowed. "I don't think so." The writing was creamy, almost crayon-like. She lightly swiped a letter, transferring some onto her finger without smearing it. "I think this is lipstick," she said, holding her finger up for Kai to see.

"It does look like lipstick," Kai agreed. "Or maybe lip liner. The letters are thin."

"Do you have makeup here?" Esther asked, looking around for any sign of the writing utensil.

"No," Kai said. "They must have used their own." She looked at Esther. "Do we know anyone that wears a red lip?"

Esther thought for a moment. Movies made it seem like women wore bold makeup looks all the time. In real life, though, the perfect red was impossible to maintain for more than an hour.

Then, it hit her. A flash of red lipstick left behind on a teacup.

"As a matter of fact, we do. Uma Holliday."

# CHAPTER 41

E sther was on her third coffee of the morning. She'd barely gotten any sleep, so directing the set-up for the festival was going to require all the caffeine she could get her hands on. Penny had capped her at two cups, but Esther snuck a third back at the inn.

"Almost got it!" Clint said, the ladder wobbling on the grass. "Just need to hook it through the eyelet."

Esther held her breath. She eyed the garden patio furniture, not too far from where Clint was setting up the tent on the lawn. She wondered how well a cushioned lounge chair would break a fall.

"What if we keep the tent as is?" Kai asked. "Is it worth Clint's life?"

"It's not a tent," Justice said, gesturing to the bare-bones structure. "It's a roof with legs."

"This is, what, his seventh try?" Bunny asked. "Makers and Merchants is in six days. At this rate, there won't be a refreshment tent."

"Have some confidence in the guy," Esther said. "He'll get it."

She wasn't sure if she believed her own words, but Clint had offered to help for a fraction of what a professional would have charged.

"Got it!" Clint yelled, sounding proud of his work. With one side of the tent wall secured, he climbed down. He carried the ladder to the next corner of the tent, where the other half of the wall laid on the ground.

"I can't watch," Kai said.

Clint grabbed the edge of the tent wall and began climbing back up the ladder. As he lifted the corner, the side he'd just hung collapsed to the ground. It was like watching a game of Whac-A-Mole.

"Okay. Justice, can you go find Mort, please?" Esther said, before turning away.

"Thanks again for finding a way to include me in Makers and Merchants," Kai said, holding a steaming mug of tea. "I think I'll have Lani set up the massage chairs, though. I need to preserve my strength for the big day."

"What's youth for if not hauling heavy stuff?" Esther asked.

"Anyone who experiences one of your shoulder massages firsthand is bound to become a spa regular," Bunny said. She snapped and turned toward Esther. "That reminds me! I decided on dark chocolate-dipped fruit kabobs."

"Simple yet tasty," Esther said. "Mayor Early can't object to that, can she?"

"She was serious about insisting the festival has a healthy food option?" Kai asked.

Bunny waved her hands. "Don't get me started. I know she's our mayor, but who's the professional chef here?"

"You let me handle Bethany if—" Esther started, before catching sight of two workers pushing the stakes for the event sign into the ground. "That goes on the front lawn!" she called. People needed to know they were in the right place when they arrived. Not to mention, a big sign blocking the view from inside the dining room wasn't exactly aesthetically pleasing.

"Someone's in boss mode," Bunny teased.

"Sorry," Esther said, turning back to Kai and Bunny. "Feeling a little on edge with the festival being so close. I think I'm still shaken up from the note too." She hadn't known what to make of the cryptic message. Clearly, it was pointed at both Kai and Esther, and possibly anyone else that had helped them along the way. What kind of "trouble" were they referring to?

"You really think it was Uma?" Bunny asked. "What if it was more of a warning from a concerned citizen?"

"A concerned citizen who broke into my spa and damaged my floor? Real neighborly," Kai muttered. "Why couldn't they have taped the note to the mirror or something? Why bring my hardwoods into it?" She pulled the folded paper from her back pocket.

"That could be a clue in itself," Bunny offered. "Whoever did it clearly loves drama."

"That would put *me* on the suspect list, if my mother had a say," Esther said, before refocusing on Kai. "Is carrying the note around with you the healthiest thing? Is it stressful to keep looking at it?"

Kai raised her hands, her palms facing the sky. "I don't know what's healthy anymore. Last night I drafted a statement for social media in case my name gets leaked as a murder suspect. There's not a whole lot of normal going on in my life right now."

Esther's stomach tightened at the thought of seeing that post. Kai's optimism must have been dwindling, and fast.

"Hear me out..." Bunny said. "Do you think you should give the note over to the police? What if you two are in real danger?"

Esther hated the thought of anything happening to her friends because of her stubbornness. But they'd come so far, and involving the police now would bring their investigation to a grinding halt.

She looked at Kai. Ultimately, it was about her. "If you think we should hand it over to Sabina, we can. But if we turn in this note, we'll have to explain the extent of the snooping we've done. I don't think we've done anything illegal, but…"

"But Sabina will be more than a little upset," Kai finished. "Plus, how would it look for me, a prime suspect, to hand in a lipstick-written note claiming it's from the real killer? As far as the police are concerned, I run a beauty parlor. It would make me look worse. Like I'm desperate to frame someone."

Esther nodded. Kai was right. Turning in the letter would probably raise some eyebrows. "Both Uma and Onyx lied about where they were that night. All we need to do is find out why and where they actually were."

She needed to think back to their early interactions. The things she'd first learned about the women.

"We knew early on the Hollidays had money problems looming on the horizon," Bunny said. "Maybe we retrace our steps down that path."

"That's not a bad idea," Esther said. "We've guessed that Uma knows about the trust fund being wiped out, given that she cut back on the budget for Faris's celebration of life. What else?"

Bunny gasped.

"What is it?" Esther asked. "Do you remember something?"

"No," Bunny said, looking at the kitchen entrance. "Those delivery guys are unloading boxes of purple grapes. I specifically ordered black seedless grapes. Excuse me," she said, trudging off.

Kai stopped walking. "What if we never prove what happened?" she asked, looking worried. "I could lose my business, Esther. I could lose everything. I could go to jail. We could be the next victims!" The anxiety in her voice was mounting with each sentence.

"Stop it," Esther said. "We are going to solve this. I'm worried too, I won't lie to you. But we can't give up. Remember that time we spent two hours transferring body lotion from the big bottles to travel size containers? Remember what Justice said?"

Kai cracked a smile. "She said our tenacity gave her a migraine."

"Exactly! We're tenacious women. We can do anything." Just then, Esther caught a glimpse of a floppy sun hat peeking around the corner of the inn. "And we're gonna show some tenacity right now," she said, pulling Kai by the arm.

# CHAPTER 42

"Hey! Stop!" Esther called as she and Kai broke into a run. The woman held onto her hat with one hand as she fled down the gravel path toward the parking lot.

"We know it's you, Uma!" Kai yelled, her voice choppy with footsteps as they pursued.

Hearing her name seemed to break Uma's momentum. Halfway across the lot, she risked a glance over her shoulder, slowed down, then came to a stop.

They caught up, chests heaving. Esther needed to renew her gym membership. "Start talking," she demanded.

"What do you mean?" Uma asked, cheeks flushed either with embarrassment or defiance.

Esther was too drained to bother with niceties. "Let's start with why you've been following me."

Uma looked away. She hesitated, like she was about to confess something. Maybe this was it, the moment they'd been working toward. "Fine. I was trying to figure out if…"

Esther gave an impatient nod. "If what?"

"I thought you might have been having an affair with Faris, okay? There, I said it." She crossed her arms.

Esther blinked. That was the last thing she'd been expecting to hear. Surely, Uma couldn't be serious. "You thought *what*?"

"Since we met, you've been asking questions about him nonstop. Frankly, there aren't many people who are upset about him not being around anymore. What was I supposed to think?"

Esther drew in a breath, measuring her response. "Uma, please understand that I have never, ever, *ever*—" she paused when Kai placed a gentle hand on her arm, likely signaling for her to ease up on whatever insult she had coming down the pipeline. "—Had anything resembling a romantic relationship with Faris." She paused for emphasis. "Even if I had, what do you get out of following me around now? I'm truly sorry about what happened, Uma. But he's gone."

"I don't know," Uma said, taking off her hat. Her voice dropped. "I guess I wanted to know more about you? Figure out what the other woman had that I didn't."

Esther clenched her jaw, fighting the urge to restate she wasn't the other woman.

Uma traced a line in the gravel with her toe. "I'm mad at my dead husband for cheating on me. Pathetic."

"Is that why you killed him?" Kai asked, leaning in.

"*Excuse me?*" Uma reeled back like she'd been slapped. "You think I killed Faris?"

This time, it was Esther who touched Kai's arm, prompting her to ease up. "Uma," she said as delicately as she could, "we know you weren't staying with your friend in Manhattan. You were at The Winthore. Why lie?"

Uma's shoulders slumped. She let out a sigh. "Faris and I had been having problems. For a while. I'd been talking to a couple's counselor. By myself. That night was our first in-person meeting." Her face was tight with pain, raw and unguarded. If she was faking, it was the performance of a lifetime.

"Why not tell the police the truth?" Esther asked. "You weren't afraid they'd find out you lied?"

Uma flapped her arms. "Because I was ashamed!" She shut her eyes, taking a moment to compose herself. "When your husband dies, you're supposed to be this distraught, adoring wife. People don't want to hear, 'Thanks for the sympathy, but we'd actually been driving each other nuts. Oh, and he had a girlfriend.'"

"I guess that explains the fake tears at the celebration of life," Kai said under her breath.

"And if I'd told the police about our marital problems," Uma added, "that would have shot me right to the top of the suspect list."

"Okay," Esther said. "That makes sense. But what about this?" She held her hand out for Kai to pass her the note, then held it up for Uma.

"What is this?" Uma reached for the paper.

"Someone broke into Kai's spa and left this threatening letter. Notice anything about the color?"

"Yeah," Uma said. "It's pretty. Almost like my favorite lippie."

"Exactly," Kai said. "So why'd you do it?"

Uma scrunched her nose. "I didn't write this."

"Do you have your lipstick on you now?" Esther asked, pointing at Uma's shoulder bag. She knew she was being pushy, but if there was ever a moment for truth, it was then.

"Sure," Uma said, rifling through her bag. She pulled out a tube and handed it to Esther along with the note.

Esther popped the lid off and twisted until the bright red lipstick surfaced. She lifted her knee and flattened the paper against it with the back of her hand, before swiping the lipstick across the top.

The colors were similar, but Uma's had more of a warm brown undertone compared to the blueish-red of the writing. The line Esther had swiped was also thicker.

She handed the lipstick back to Uma. "Not a match. And I think you were right, Kai. Looks like the message was written with lip liner. Not lipstick."

"Oh, I don't use lip liner," Uma said, shaking her head as she put the tube back in her purse. "I could have told you that. You can check my bag if you want to."

"Then how do you maintain such a perfect red lip?" Kai asked, sounding genuinely curious.

"It's all about the prep." Uma explained. "Exfoliate, prime with a little concealer. Lasts all day with a touch up or two."

"But you know about the trust fund money, right?" Esther asked. She didn't want to leave any stone unturned.

Uma looked surprised. "You know about that? Yes. Faris came clean about his gambling problem a while back. Ironic that his poker face was good enough to keep me in the dark for so long. Anyway, he assured me he'd figure out a way to build the funds back up. I haven't the foggiest what his plan was, but I suspect it had to do with the real estate documents you found. Whether he really envisioned a future with me, I couldn't tell you."

Esther and Kai exchanged looks. Faris hadn't told Uma about the real estate empire he'd been planning. Or the tropical getaway he'd promised Onyx.

Kai opened her mouth to speak, but Esther gave a quick shake of the head. No sense in upsetting the widow any further.

"What happens now?" Esther asked. "What's next for you?"

"Who knows?" Uma said. "I'll probably sell the house. I've always secretly dreamed of moving to the English countryside. Spending my days with the sheep in the fields. Maybe I'll finally get my chance."

"That sounds nice," Esther said, resting a hand on Uma's shoulder.

As they turned back toward the inn, Esther's mind was already busy. Another suspect had dropped from the list. Why didn't she feel relieved?

# CHAPTER 43

That afternoon, Esther made her way downstairs after meeting with Sveta. Housekeeping discovered a couple had packed their own blackout curtains and put them up in their suite. Esther left a complimentary pair of eye masks on the bed along with a note to collect their curtains from her before check-out.

Esther had given her staff a semi-in-service day, with short shifts staggered around event setup, meetings, and CPR training. Why not pack all the chaos into one day?

With the guests out at a complimentary lunch, Esther found Justice, Bunny, Kai, and Cameron gathered around the reception desk.

"These grossinis are delicious," Justice said, kicking her feet in delight. She held the snack up to admire as she chewed.

The toasted edges of the baguette were golden brown, and it was topped with a generous smear of whipped goat cheese, drizzled honey, sprigs of fresh thyme, and cracked black pepper.

"*Crostinis*," Bunny corrected. "Glad you like them. They should be easy enough for festival-goers to eat as they bop from booth to booth. The birds should handle the stray bread crumbs on the ground."

"Too bad they can't clean up in here," Esther said, eyeing the growing pile of crumbs under Justice's arm.

Justice set the crostini down. "I'm going to ask one more time."

"Brace yourselves," Kai said.

"If you're going to ask me about the soft pretzels again, don't," Bunny said, shaking her head. "We want Oak's Rest to be known for its charm and sophistication. Soft pretzels don't fit the menu I've curated."

"People love soft pretzels," Justice argued.

"Well, I think these are perfect," Cameron said, munching on her own crostini. "They almost make up for my unpaid labor."

"I like your sister, Esther," Bunny said. "We could have used her earlier. Clint claimed he sprained his ankle putting the tent up, but I saw him run full speed from a squirrel five minutes later."

Esther laughed. "Thanks again for coming in for the CPR lesson, Cameron. And for volunteering as our on-site medical professional for Sunday." There was never any telling what would happen when the whole town got together. Esther wanted to be prepared for every contingency.

"I still don't know what Clint managed to trip over at last year's festival," Kai said. "There was nothing in his path."

"Yet, he ended up in a cast from shoulder to finger. That man will always be a mystery to me," Justice said.

"Speaking of mysteries," Cameron said, turning to Esther. "How's your investigation going?"

Esther sighed. "Our two loose threads are Onyx's whereabouts the night Faris died, and Faris's secret business. If we can dig deeper into those, it should bring us closer to the truth." At least, she hoped so.

"You should show Cameron the business papers," Bunny suggested. "Fresh eyes."

"Okay," Esther said. "Can't hurt." She pulled up the images she'd taken of the paperwork and handed her phone to her sister.

Cameron used her fingers to zoom in, moving the image around on the screen as she read. "Kinghead Properties. A little egotistical, but whatever. Is this his lawyer's office?" She pointed to the address listed on the page. "Did you try calling?"

"No," Esther said. "We searched the address online, but no hits. If it was a legit business, something would have come up. Don't you think?"

Cameron took another look at the image, reciting the street name and number a few times, as if committing it to memory. Esther looked over her shoulder as she navigated to the internet. Cameron typed the address into the search bar, scrolled a few times, and clicked on a search result. "Looks like a private residence in Yalfont. Homelovers.com says the property belongs to a Lori Nelford."

Esther took the phone back and searched the name. "Nothing coming up in search results for a Lori Nelford."

"So, probably not an attorney or real estate agent," Kai said. "Maybe a friend who let Faris use their house as the business address?"

"I think we know by now Faris didn't have many friends," Justice mumbled.

"Could it be his parents' place?" Cameron asked.

"His parents weren't at the celebration of life. Do we even know his mom's name?" Esther looked around for confirmation. "Could Nelford be a maiden name?"

The women looked at one another. No one seemed to know.

"Well, whoever lives there might know something," Cameron said. "If I were you, I'd look into that."

"There *is* one way you could find out who lives there," Justice said, smirking.

"Dare I ask?" Esther said, preparing for an outlandish idea.

"Stakeout."

"A stakeout?" Esther repeated. "Like in a detective movie?"

Justice was full-on giddy. "How else will you get answers? I'm pretty sure Sabina's not going to high-five you for asking her to run a name through the database."

"What's the plan?" Esther asked, skeptical. "Knock on the door and say, 'Hi, can we interest you in a conversation about your shady business involvement?'"

Justice rolled her eyes. "I didn't say pretend to be a door-to-door salesperson. Scope the place out. Maybe Lori will be coming home from work wearing a uniform or something with a company logo. You'll need to dress in all black, obviously."

"Obviously," Esther deadpanned, like it was in any way a normal conversation. "I'm free tomorrow night. Would you like to join, Miss Stakeout Expert?"

"Can't, sorry. I have a nail appointment." Justice inspected her fingers, grimacing at the chipped polish. "Does that mean you're actually going to do it?"

It did sound a little ridiculous, but what if Justice had a point? Doing internet searches wouldn't get them much further. Maybe the best next move was getting closer to the action.

Cameron placed a hand on the desk. "As a medical professional, I feel obligated to tell you not to put yourself in a potentially unsafe situation..."

"But?" Esther asked, sensing there was more.

"But, as your sister, shopping for a pair of cute pink binoculars sounds kind of fun."

Bunny and Kai nodded in agreement.

"If I'm doing this, I'll need backup. Any takers?" Esther asked, looking around.

"Tamara has ballet tomorrow night," Cameron said.

"I have my health and safety inspection tomorrow," Kai said.

"I can go," Bunny volunteered. "I'll bring treats. It'll be fun!"

Esther puffed out her cheeks. "Alright, then. We're going on a stakeout."

# CHAPTER 44

E sther shifted in her seat for the tenth time, unable to find a position that didn't send pins and needles down her leg. Why was sitting still in a car so much worse than driving?

Overhead, the streetlamp clicked on as the sun dipped lower, washing the quiet street in an orange haze.

Bunny pulled her jacket tighter. "Can we please turn the car on? Just for a few minutes of heat?"

Esther surveyed their surroundings. No one was outside. If she started up the car, people would be able to hear it the next county over. "This is a stakeout. We can't afford to draw attention to ourselves."

They were parked diagonally across from the address listed on Faris's business papers, tucked neatly between two other cars along the curb. Maple leaves drifted lazily through the air, landing on windshields and hoods.

Esther hadn't expected this part of Yalfont to be so humble. The houses were small, bordering on plain. She'd assumed the entire town was made up of homes with multiple wings. Maybe the people here had kinder opinions of Oak's Rest.

The brick bungalow they were watching had a car in the driveway. The lights were on inside, but no movement.

"In the movies, they never talk about temperature control. It's false advertising," Bunny said.

"We just need Lori to come outside so we can lay eyes on her. It's dinner time. Maybe she'll take the trash out afterward." Esther dug in her pocket and extended a hand warmer to Bunny. "Here, take one."

"Thanks," Bunny said, curling her fingers around it. "I knew I was forgetting something."

"Justice made this seem like it would be all action," Esther said.

"She left out the part where you sit around forever and freeze to death," Bunny said through gritted teeth. "Remind me not to listen next time she recommends…anything."

Esther's stomach rumbled. She reached for the tin of caramel popcorn they'd been sharing, only for her fingers to hit the bottom of the pan. Empty. "Why didn't we eat first?"

Bunny must have sensed Esther's morale was plummeting, because she perked up and said, "Hey, wanna play Millionaire? Might pass the time faster."

Esther's instinct was to turn her down, but maybe the silly game would take her mind off the boredom and hunger. "Fine. You start. What's one thing you'd buy if you were a millionaire?"

Bunny tapped her chin. "Ooh! I know. I'd install an electric lift that would zip me all over the kitchen. No more sore feet. I say, 'stovetop,' and it whizzes me over. That sort of thing."

"If I could afford that setup, I'd never walk again," Esther said.

Bunny grinned. "What about you?"

Esther blew out a breath. What *would* she buy if she were wealthy? "I don't know. Maybe pay off my mortgage and take a trip somewhere? Is that boring?"

Bunny feigned a snore and closed her eyes, tilting back against the headrest.

"Ha ha," Esther said. "Your turn again."

While Bunny thought, Esther reached to the back seat for her second water bottle. She couldn't quite reach it, so she took off her seatbelt and twisted around. "I bet the detectives in Justice's movies would scold me for filling up my blad—"

"Car!" Bunny shrieked.

"What?" Esther said, still reaching into the back seat. "You'd buy a new car?"

"No!" Bunny yanked Esther's coat. "There's a car coming and your behind is about to get lit up by headlights. Get down!"

Esther swung around, her and Bunny nearly bumping heads as they both ducked toward the center console. Light flared through the windows, then dimmed. When the sound of the car seemed to pass, Esther risked a quick look. It was gone. "We're clear," she said.

Bunny lifted her head and peered over the dashboard before sitting up slowly. "You know, I'm starting to think this whole thing is pointless. We're not going to learn anything sitting here all night. Plus, it's going to be dark out soon. Should we go home? Grab a bite at Penny's?"

Esther took one last look at the house. No movement. No sign of anything happening. "I guess you're right," she said. "Let's head home. Kai's in her inspection now, but we can text her to meet us at Penny's when it's over."

"Hopefully, it'll be a celebration for all of us. Her passing, and us not starving."

"Hear, hear," Esther said as she started the engine. She was definitely going to ask Penny to add mac and cheese on her burger.

When they reached the end of the block, a chain of kids filed along the crosswalk, hand in hand. One boy dropped something from his bag and broke off from the group to pick it up. His breaking of the chain set the rest of the kids into a frenzy.

"Alright, you're cute and all, but keep it moving," Bunny said. "The grown-ups haven't had dinner."

Finally, the kids cleared the walkway. "Spot me. Are we good on both sides?" Esther asked, doing a visual sweep to make sure no more stragglers were going to pop out.

"Wait—what does that sign say?" Bunny asked.

Esther followed her line of sight to a sign planted at the corner of the playground. It had seen better days, paint chipping off and wood splintering. She squinted. "Home of the...is that a C? Or an L? Home of the Lings?"

"Nope," Bunny said, pointing further ahead.

Beyond the playground was a small field with a scoreboard mounted behind a metal fence. One side of the board read *Kings* and the other *Guest*. A lion baring its teeth stood in the middle.

"Kings," Esther whispered. She stared at the lion. Something about it...

Bunny gasped. "I get it! Kings. Their mascot is a lion. Like the king of the jungle. Very poetic for a kiddie field."

Then it clicked. Esther knew exactly where she'd seen that lion before. She grabbed her phone and quickly typed *Lori Nelford* into the search bar, along with the other name now blazing in her mind.

She tapped the first search result. It only took seconds to confirm what she'd been thinking. She handed the phone to Bunny.

Bunny scanned the first few lines of the obituary, her lips parting. "Richard Ellis is survived by his loving wife of thirty-five years, Lori, and their son, Ingram." She met Esther's eye. "Are you thinking...?"

Esther swallowed. "Kings? Like Kinghead Properties? Yeah."

"That wasn't Faris's mom's house," Bunny said.

"It was Ingram's."

# CHAPTER 45

"Kai's not picking up," Bunny said, stabbing at the screen. "She always answers her phone. We leave her alone *one time* with a guy who might have killed his business partner."

"Keep trying," Esther said, tightening her grip on the wheel. "We don't know Ingram was the killer. Just that he has some connection to Kinghead Properties." She didn't know who she was trying to convince more: herself or Bunny. She pressed her foot harder on the gas.

Bunny put the phone on speaker. Five rings, then Kai's voice, playful, asking the dialer to leave a message as long as they weren't calling to ruin her good mood.

"Stupid voicemail!" Bunny said.

"Okay, scratch that," Esther said. "We need to think."

"What's there to think about?" Bunny asked, her voice pitching higher. "Our friend is currently alone, in a secluded shop, with a potential killer." She sucked in a breath. "Oh my gosh, he's going to see we called and kill us too. Can't you go any faster?"

"Take it easy," Esther said, forcing her voice steady. "If I drive this car any faster, we'll be the ones needing rescuing. For now, all we can do is go over what we know."

"Okay," Bunny said, using her purse as a ventilation bag. "Let's think. Say Faris and Ingram were business partners. What would drive Ingram to kill him?"

Esther fell quiet, winding her way down back roads she knew were usually empty. Trees blurred past like falling dominoes as their tires kicked up loose gravel.

It would have been one thing if they'd been raking in millions of dollars, but Kinghead Properties hadn't even gotten past registration.

She thought back to what Reese had said. "There were rifts in their work relationship. Reese told me Faris had a habit of tearing down new employees with harsh peer reviews."

"Maybe Faris gave Ingram one of those bad reviews," Bunny offered. "Put his job in jeopardy."

"Maybe," Esther replied. "But is that enough to kill over?" She bit her lip, flipping through memories of each interaction she'd had with Ingram. A produce stand sign that read *Fresh Eggs & Milk* in faded letters flickered by in the window.

"What is it?" Bunny asked. "You've got your thinking face on."

Esther glanced at her, thoughts racing with every detail she hadn't been able to place. Questions were coming to the surface, filling her with equal parts urgency and dread. "The lifted floorboard," she said. "Ingram used to be a contractor. If anyone could break into a store and take a single floorboard out, wouldn't it be him?" She hated that the pieces were falling into place so logically, given that Kai was with him at that very moment. A new memory took shape. She sucked in a breath. "Sesame!"

Bunny looked around as though the cat was in the car. "What? Where?"

It nearly came out as one long word. "The day Faris and Ingram inspected the inn. Sesame was acting so strange. Vocalizing more than usual. Even you told me she was swiping at them. It wasn't because they were looking for a microchip. She was trying to tell me something...warn me about something." Esther should have paid more attention.

"I need air," Bunny said, cracking her window. She took a few deep inhales. "Alright. Let's go back to the night of the murder."

Esther had imagined how the night could have played out a hundred ways. "We know Ingram was at least *one* of the last people to see Faris the night he died. Aside from Onyx."

"Didn't Queenie say they were drinking all night?" Bunny asked. "Maybe Ingram was working up his nerve."

"Or maybe he wasn't drinking at all," Esther said, envisioning a new scenario. "Picture this: Faris gets sloppier as the night goes on. Ingram nurses a beer, but Faris doesn't notice, because of the state he's in. Ingram is glad because getting Faris drunk was his plan all along."

Bunny whistled. "Did Kai mention anything weird about the inspection? Anything off with Ingram? When did she even realize the Botox and needle were gone?"

Esther racked her brain. "Not until Sabina showed up at the inn. No missing inventory at the spa that morning at opening. Plus, she was so nervous about it going well, she followed Faris and Ingram around like a lost puppy. She would have seen them take something."

Esther replayed her conversation with Kai the day she got the news, walking through the timeline of the events. She remembered the look of disbelief and panic on her friend's face after finding out she'd failed. "Wait!" Esther said, jerking upright.

"What?"

"Kai told me Halley Jeffries tried to bring her dog into the spa during the inspection. Kai had to run over to usher them out."

"That pooch needs training," Bunny said. "Stole the hot dog right off Jim White's plate at the summer games. What's that got to do with Faris and Ingram, though?"

Esther slowed around a sharp bend. "Kai *did* leave Ingram

unattended, even if for a minute. If he knew where she kept the Botox, he could have quickly stepped away to swipe it."

Their eyes met. Esther picked up some speed, but she was driving as fast as she could without putting herself and Bunny in danger too. They weren't far from the town square.

"We need to hurry," Bunny whispered. "Or we might be too late."

# CHAPTER 46

The car skidded to a stop as Esther slammed the brakes. She threw it in park and jumped out, not bothering to pay the meter.

As they bounded toward the spa's entrance, Esther prepared herself for the worst. She didn't know what she'd find. Would Ingram be waving around another needle? Would Kai be hurt? Or worse?

Esther burst through the unlocked front door, a step ahead of Bunny.

She stopped as she took in the scene. "Onyx?"

Kai and Onyx sat side by side in the waiting area, just as Esther and Onyx had before their joint session. This time, though, Onyx was sobbing into Kai's shoulder, clutching a box on her lap. Kai rubbed slow circles on her back.

Kai looked at them, startled. "Esther? Bunny? What are you two doing here?" She looked them up and down. "And why are you breathing like you just ran a marathon?"

Esther looked at Bunny, both of them momentarily speechless. Where was Ingram? Why was Onyx there? Was she the actual killer? "Uh, we were wondering…is your inspection over?"

"Nope, Ingram cancelled at the last minute. Something about food poisoning. Which evidently worked out, because someone —" she pointed to Onyx, "is having a rough night."

Onyx lifted her head, sniffling. "Not a rough night. This is the first step in my healing journey."

Esther wasn't sure whether to stay put or step closer. If Onyx was the killer, would another sudden movement set her off? Better to play it cool. "What's in the box?"

Onyx rested a hand on the lid. "This is my Faris box."

"Your what-now?" Bunny said.

"What's a Faris box?" Esther asked, stalling so she could make sense of the situation. Was she about to confess?

Onyx wiped a tear from her cheek. "It's everything he gave me while we were dating. And some of my own things. Wedding invitation samples. Stuff like that. I didn't want to throw it all away, so I came by to give it to someone who understood what I was going through." She gave Kai a meaningful look.

"That's great," Kai said, shooting a wide-eyed glare at Esther and Bunny, indicating they should play along. "Such an important step toward closure. We're proud of you."

Esther couldn't tell whether Kai was afraid or if she felt sorry for the girl.

"Yeah...great," Bunny muttered. "Who doesn't love a box of dead guy gifts?"

Esther swatted at Bunny's arm and refocused on Kai and Onyx. "We just thought—"

Onyx scrunched her face, fully assessing Esther and Bunny for the first time. "You ladies do look terrible," she said. "You should let Kai give you facials. Stress is bad for the skin."

"We know you were in Oak's Rest that night," Bunny blurted.

"Subtle," Esther said without moving her lips. She needed friends with better timing.

Onyx shook her head. "What?"

Esther looked to Kai for reassurance it was alright to broach the topic of what they'd found in Onyx's bag.

Kai shrugged, a gesture for *cat's already out of the bag.*

"We know you stopped at an Oak's Rest gas station the night Faris died. You told us you were at home eating ice cream. What gives?"

Onyx's cheeks flushed.

Kai placed a gentle hand on her shoulder. "Just tell us what happened, Onyx. Tell us the truth."

Esther steeled herself for what she was about to hear.

Onyx exhaled and squeezed her eyes shut. "I did drive to Oak's Rest that night. I was going to check up on Faris. Make sure he wasn't with some other woman. But when I got here, I realized how pathetic it was, and I turned around to go home."

"You didn't realize how pathetic you felt until you got all the way here?" Esther asked. She was tired of being lied to. "I don't mean to sound harsh, but we've had a long day. Why should we believe you?"

"You don't need to believe me," Onyx said, pulling out her phone. "I filmed the whole drive."

"Why would you film a video of you driving?" Kai asked.

"For my YouTube channel," Onyx said, handing the phone to Esther. "Crying in the thumbnail photo gets clicks. But then I thought, you know what, I'll save this footage so I can batch content in the winter. Take some time off."

Esther dragged her finger across the bottom of the screen to speed through the footage. The video showed Onyx walking into the gas station, coming back out holding a bag of chips and a soda, and driving away. Esther kept her focus on the view outside the car window and recognized her town passing by.

By the end of the video, Onyx was walking into her apartment. Esther checked the timestamp from the camera roll. Based on the time of recording and how long the footage was, Onyx got home around ten-thirty, which is when the medical examiner had estimated Faris's death. She'd been in the car the whole time.

"Told you," Onyx said, reaching for her phone. "I'm not *that* pathetic. Only a little pathetic. Why do you care so much, anyway?" She looked around the group of women, waiting for a response. Understanding seemed to dawn on her face, then outrage. "Oh no. Did you think—"

"Kinda," Kai said.

"You're kidding! You thought I was a *murderer*?"

Esther tilted her head, feeling a little foolish. "You were a suspect, yes...but not anymore?" she added, hoping to soften the blow.

Onyx stood. "I'm gonna go. Clearly, I'm not welcome here." She walked toward the front door and turned back before opening it. "Kai, I'll be in touch about my next appointment."

"Sounds good!" Kai called out before the door closed.

Esther and Bunny collapsed onto chairs next to Kai.

"At least now we know it wasn't her," Bunny said, touching the table plant.

Esther sat upright again, remembering why they'd rushed back in the first place. "That for sure narrows it down to Ingram."

"Ingram?" Kai asked. "What am I missing here?"

Esther got Kai up to speed about what they'd discovered on the stakeout, and the details they'd put together on the drive over.

Kai put a hand over her mouth. "I was going to be alone with the guy! Thank goodness for food poisoning."

"What's our next move?" Bunny asked. "Do we take what we know to Sabina? Do we try to get him to confess?"

Esther's stomach made a noise that made both Bunny and Kai raise their eyebrows. "Should we plan over food? Bunny and I were thinking about hitting Penny's, Kai. Want to join?"

"Actually..." Bunny said, raising a finger. "I've got to be

honest. This wild night has my stomach in knots. I think I might head home. Can we scheme tomorrow?"

"Yeah, I'm pretty beat, especially after consoling Onyx all night," Kai said. "I think I'll head home too. Tell Penny we say hi."

Esther considered going to the diner alone, but imagined having to explain the events of the night to Penny or whoever else was there. That was the last thing she wanted to do. On the other hand, she knew her own kitchen would be empty. "Is your lasagna still in the fridge at the inn?"

Bunny smiled. "You bet. Three-fifty for ten minutes. Enjoy."

Esther smiled. "It's adorable you think I'm not using the microwave. But I could use some Sesame time right now, anyway, so it's settled. Tomorrow, we'll go over what we know and figure out how to end this thing once and for all. Tonight, we rest."

# CHAPTER 47

"Alright, I think you've had enough," Esther said, scratching between Sesame's eyes. "No more cheese. I'm not breaking into Bunny's stash again. And *you're* not getting a tummy ache on my watch."

Sesame protested with a raised paw as Esther lifted the napkin from the reception desk, just a dab of ricotta left behind.

Bunny's lasagna had been the exact comfort she'd needed. Satisfied, Esther padded back to the kitchen, tossed the napkin, and flipped off the lights.

When she returned to the lobby, Sesame twined herself around Esther's leg, tail flicking, body weaving back and forth. Perhaps Sesame could sense the intensity of the day on her.

Esther reached down in time to stroke the end of her tail. "Thanks for the love."

Sesame sat down in front of her, eyes locked, intense.

"What? The kitchen's closed," Esther said. "I can't help you, lady." Silly creature. Truthfully, Esther needed to stop spoiling the cat. Sesame's taste for human food was bordering on absurd.

Esther surveyed the empty lobby, dim and hushed. She loved the inn at night. Guests, worn out from a day of activity and exploration, were tucked away behind closed doors. The calm felt unanimous, like even the walls were in agreement it was time to settle into rest.

It was getting late, but Esther figured she'd check her email one last time before heading home. The Makers and Merchants Festival was just days away—prime time for last-minute vendor emergencies and panicked questions proving no one had read the info packet.

She decided against working from the front desk. Best to stay out of sight in case any night owls ventured downstairs looking for conversation, or someone to address the fact that their shower didn't reach the scalding hot temperatures they preferred.

Sesame followed her all the way to the basement door. "Sorry. Employees only," Esther apologized, pointing to the sign. If it was going to be a quick work session, she couldn't be lifting toe beans off her keyboard the whole time. As she eased the basement door shut, she nudged Sesame's paw with her foot, which poked through the narrowing crack down to the last sliver.

The basement smelled of old cardboard and window cleaner, though there were no windows down there. It was also in sore need of a cleanout. Boxes were stacked high in every corner, some half-crushed, others filled with things that should have been donated years ago. Retired armchairs and chipped side tables were scattered like forgotten memories.

Esther entered the office and hit the overhead switch. The fixture buzzed to life, washing the room in a harsh light that made her wince. Justice was right. The ambience was dismal. The only redeeming factor was the space heater, which would at least add some cozy warmth to the small space.

She found her mind wandering as she perused her inbox. Had Kai been in any danger tonight? What if Esther and Bunny had come to the wrong conclusion about Ingram being the killer, while the real one evaded them?

Would they strike again? What if Esther had put her loved ones in danger by getting them involved? How far would the killer go?

Her mind flashed back to all the conversations she'd had over the past few weeks. All the people she'd pulled into her amateur investigation. Even Cameron, who she'd barely seen in several years, knew the details about the murder. Would the killer threaten Esther's family? Or Kai's?

Esther shook off those thoughts, pulling her attention back to the screen. Thankfully, no major hiccups. LouLou had a concern about festival-goers in bare feet. Apparently, her garment pins had a habit of vanishing, only to reappear weeks later when she stepped on them.

Jim White wanted to confirm, for the fourth time, that there would be guaranteed space for a full canoe, not just the paddles he'd originally pitched.

Esther smiled. Even through email, their personalities came through.

She typed out her responses and scheduled them for delivery first thing in the morning. No need for anyone to give her grief for working late. Happy to have a lighter inbox, she switched off the computer.

As she walked around the back of her chair, she noticed a blue pencil eyeliner on the small table at the back corner of the office. It looked electric compared to the sad, darkened lamp it sat next to. She walked over and picked the eyeliner up, twirling it between her fingers. "No worries, Justice, I'll clean up after you. And this is *definitely* your shade," she said to herself, sarcastically.

"Thanks. I thought so too," a male voice said from behind her.

Esther froze.

She turned around slowly.

Ingram Ellis was standing in the doorway, watching her.

Her blood went cold.

# CHAPTER 48

I ngram leaned casually against the door frame, arms crossed.
"Ingram. What—" Esther stuttered.

He raised a finger to his lips, took a lazy step forward, and eased the door shut behind him, turning the handle so gently it hardly gave a click. "Do you like games?" he asked.

Esther was instantly aware of the position she was in. It wasn't until the back of her heel hit the wall that she realized she'd instinctively been stepping backwards.

She frantically scanned the room for something, anything, to defend herself with. She cursed silently for not spending more time in the basement. If she had, maybe she'd have built up an illicit collection of forks from the kitchen. Even some of Justice's hairspray would have helped.

There was a pen in the desk drawer, but Esther didn't want to weigh the odds of her making it to that pen before Ingram would reach her.

"Sure?" she managed, her voice traitorously small. "Games are fine."

"Good," Ingram said with lethal calmness, as if pleased by her answer. "I'll explain the rules." He stepped closer to the desk at the center of the room, now the only thing between them.

Esther had nowhere to run.

"Here's how this is going to go," he said. "I'll describe a few scenarios. You tell me if the person's behavior is wise or foolish. You get three tries."

Esther's heartbeat thundered in her ears. Her phone was on the reception desk in the lobby. She was two floors below anyone who'd be able to hear her yell. "Oh—okay," she sputtered, both palms gripping the wall behind her.

What was his goal? To terrify her? If so, he was succeeding.

"First," Ingram said, raising his thumb. "Let's say this wannabe Shirley Holmes is warned by the police after an anonymous tip. Concerned citizens complaining." Ingram looked like he was reciting folklore, clearly entertained by his own words. "But does she stop meddling?" He paused, looking intently at Esther.

He was obviously talking about her. She didn't know whether to stay quiet or to play along. She hoped she'd picked the option with the lowest odds of setting him off.

Esther swallowed. "No?"

"No," Ingram confirmed. "She continues to stick her nose into business that's not hers. Oh, and her friends too." A smirk was faint on his mouth. "Wise? Or foolish?"

What difference would her answer make? If she pleaded for forgiveness, would he let her go? Doubtful.

Before she could respond, Ingram nodded thoughtfully. "I thought you might be reluctant. Let's count that as incorrect. Two more tries. Ready?"

Esther could feel her glare harden. He was enjoying this.

She eyed the closed door behind Ingram, but knew in a race to run past him, she'd lose.

As if hearing her thoughts, Ingram followed her eyes, glanced behind him, then swiveled his head back, smiling. He didn't need to say anything. They both knew who had the upper hand.

He went on. "Next, this person's friend gets a warning at her business. A fairly unambiguous one, at that. But do they back off? No." He raised a finger. "In fact, they dig even deeper. Now, tell me: wise or foolish?"

"So that threat was you," Esther said, something inside her breaking open at the memory of the man threatening her friend. "You wrote it red in lip liner thinking we'd go off chasing Uma." She knew she should stop there, but couldn't help it. "You have a real talent for framing innocent people."

Ingram said nothing, only arched a smug eyebrow, impressed by himself.

Esther opened her mouth to speak again, but he cut her off.

"Careful. You're on your second try. Get this wrong, and you only have one more."

"What happens if I get it wrong the third time?" Esther asked, understanding she was walking on thin ice.

He laughed eerily and ran a hand over his beard.

It was then that Esther saw the glint of sharp metal jutting out under his sleeve. Her breath hitched, the threat of his presence confirmed.

He hadn't just come there to scare her. He was going to do something much, much worse.

"Let's cross that bridge when we get there," Ingram said.

Esther had to come up with a plan. She needed to think quickly. She needed more time.

"Maybe I could ask *you* a question or two," she heard herself say before thinking it through. Maybe she could keep him talking long enough to figure a way out.

Ingram turned his mouth down, amused. "What the heck," he said. "Try me."

Esther loosed a breath. The space heater's once-cozy warmth now felt suffocating. "What do you call someone who goes into business with the one health inspector no one, for miles, trusts? Wise or foolish?"

Ingram's face was still except for a slight twitch in his right eye. The tiniest crack in his confident demeanor. He hadn't liked that question.

"What kind of business was it?" Esther pressed, hoping to get him to open up. She needed him preoccupied. "Something morally gray, I presume? Something that required a little greasing from someone on the Zoning Board?"

"Shut up," Ingram snapped.

It was better than nothing. Esther was running out of ideas.

"You don't know what you're talking about. And you can't prove I had any association with Faris beyond our professional relationship as coworkers." Ingram had regained his arrogance. Like he was sure he'd get away with anything he wanted.

"No?" Esther asked. "Is that why the business address is your mommy's house?"

He lifted a foot, starting around the desk.

Esther side-stepped, feeling like a rabbit being stalked by a cheetah.

She saw it. The moment he slipped the vintage letter opener into his palm. A piece Dev might have sold at Used Books & More.

She was at a turning point. She either needed to get out of there, and fast, or accept the fact that she might never make it out at all.

What would happen if she didn't? Who would take over for her?

She hadn't been as diligent about writing down her passcodes and operating procedures as she should have been. She hadn't had the chance to give her employees the raises they deserved.

She'd never get to open her own inn.

She'd only just begun to have a relationship with Cameron. Sure, she still had a long way to go with her parents, but she finally had a sister. One she hoped to become friends with.

A faint scratching noise snagged her focus. Was it coming from upstairs? Was someone dragging furniture across the floor?

No. The scratching was too fast and sharp to be furniture. It was almost like...a cat's claws. Sesame. She must have still been at the basement door, trying to claw her way in.

Esther's attention was diverted back when she registered a jolt of pain. The side of her leg had knocked into the table where Justice's eyeliner had been sitting.

She stepped around the table to the perpendicular wall, then paused as an idea started to take shape.

She would not let Ingram get away with this. With taking out anyone who stood in his way. With threatening her or the people she loved.

Esther would make it out of the basement. She just needed to keep Ingram chatting.

"One more," she said, mustering all the fake confidence she could. "What about a guy who fails at one business, then doubles down with a new, shady one? And adding a murder to his resume before the paperwork is even finished? Sad. And not the most effective conflict resolution, by the way. Wise or foolish?"

Whatever calm Ingram had left evaporated. His face twisted with rage. He toyed with the letter opener in his hand.

"You know what?" he said through clenched teeth. "Game over. I've heard enough."

Esther really hoped her plan would work. There was no turning back now. She was out of options.

She remained statue-still as Ingram crept toward her, his steps slow and deliberate. He was so light on his feet, the only sounds in the room came from the overhead light and the space heater.

Esther held her breath as she let him advance two more steps. She took a mental snapshot of the layout of the room.

When he was behind the desk, a mere wingspan away, letter

opener pointed at her, Esther lunged for the lamp cord and jammed the plug into the wall.

The overhead light fizzled out. Blackness swallowed the room.

She'd never been so grateful for an electrical malfunction in her life.

"What?" Ingram muttered.

Esther bolted, heart pounding, praying not to trip. It was not the moment to fall on her face.

She found the door handle and flung it open, letting in light from the main floor of the basement. The last thing she saw as she closed the door was Ingram's face in the slice of light, stunned.

A split second later, a violent *thwack* hit the door. He'd thrown the letter opener right where her head had been moments before.

Esther yanked on the door handle as hard as she could. Like she'd hoped, it came clean off into her hand. She heard the handle on the inside of the door clatter to the office floor.

Ingram's fingers reached through the hole where the handle had been. He banged on the inside of the door with his fist, no way to free himself. "Hey! Get back here!" he roared.

Esther sprinted up the stairs and locked the basement door behind her with the key.

Sesame had jumped back when she threw the door open, but ran beside Esther as she raced through the lobby.

Thankfully, the first floor remained quiet. Ingram's fury was muted, a distant muffle.

Esther reached the reception desk. She picked up her phone and tapped feverishly at the screen.

The ringing lasted a lifetime. "Pick up, pick up, pick up," she said, tapping her foot.

A wave of relief washed over her when a groggy but familiar voice answered. "Esther?"

"Thank goodness. Sabina, you need to get to the inn right now. Get some officers here. Hurry!"

# CHAPTER 49

Kai draped a blanket over Esther's shoulders, careful not to let the ends catch beneath the dining room chair.

Bunny entered from the lobby, rubbing her hands together. "There. I'll have to make more lemon bars tomorrow, but the guests seem happy with their late-night snack."

A few had wandered downstairs, likely curious about the police vehicles parked outside. Nolan stood at the far side of the lobby, talking with another officer.

They'd already taken Esther's statement, and she was glad for it. She was still a little dazed. "Thanks for being here, you guys," she said.

"Are you kidding?" Bunny replied. "My best friend fights off a psycho killer and I'm not going to pause *Real Housewives* to haul it back here?"

"There's Sabina," Kai said, looking toward the front entrance.

Detective Ali walked past Nolan and the officer, exchanged a few words, and shook both their hands. She looked around the lobby, spotted Esther, and walked over.

"Well?" Bunny asked eagerly, before Sabina had the chance to sit. "Did he do it?"

Sabina sighed, running a hand through her short, low pony-tail. "He did," she said. "Ingram confessed to everything. Faris's murder, calling in the anonymous tip using a fake voice, placing the threatening note at Etana's Essence—" she paused, looking pointedly from Esther to Kai. "Which you should have told me about, by the way. But Mr. Ellis is in custody now."

Kai clapped. "See? Told you I was innocent. I'd never do something so heinous."

Sabina tempered her reaction, ever the professional. "My job is to keep the town safe. To be objective. Even if that means questioning my own assumptions about people I like."

Kai gave Esther's shoulders a light jostle. "You did it! You really did it."

Esther shook her head. "We did it." She squeezed Kai's hand and turned to Sabina. "Why did Ingram do it?"

Sabina folded her hands on the table. "Turns out Faris and Ingram were planning quite the entrepreneurial endeavor. Their scheme was simple: fail as many businesses on health and safety inspections as possible. Once they racked up enough violations, the owners would either face a mountain of bogus and expensive repairs, or be forced to sell."

"Let me guess," Esther said. "That's where Kinghead Properties comes in."

Sabina inclined her head. "Exactly. No one would have sold to Faris operating as himself, but maybe they'd have sold to a polished-sounding commercial real estate firm. They'd buy up everything they could and get rich exploding Oak's Rest's tourist scene. Faris saw it as his last chance to make real money."

"What was the deal with the trust fund?" Kai asked. "Didn't he gamble most of it away?"

Sabina tilted her head. "Spent, yes. Gambled, no. Although, that's what he told his wife. He'd lit a ton of cash on fire with risky stocks and bad long-distance investments. He knew he needed a business partner this time. Someone who understood commercial real estate. And construction."

"Ingram," Esther said.

"Yup. Who, as I'm sure you know, was a contractor. His hands-on skills plus Faris's regulatory knowledge? A real estate perfect match. They wanted to look legitimate. Started filling out the paperwork and everything. In fact, they were planning to file the next day."

"So, what happened?" Kai asked. "And how did the documents end up mixed in with my inspection paperwork?"

"Faris and Ingram had planned to split their profits fifty-fifty. But the deeper they got, Faris insisted he deserved more, since he was the one taking all the risk with inspections. So, Ingram said he'd help out. Train to be an inspector too. If he could get half the profits. Faris agreed at first, but got flakey. Ingram started seeing red. The idea hit him not long after he stepped into the spa." Sabina pursed her lips. "As for those documents in your paperwork? Just a rookie mistake."

"He *did* swipe the Botox when I wasn't looking," Kai muttered. "That darn poodle."

"How did you account for the phone GPS showing Ingram at his house at the time of the murder?" Esther asked. "Wasn't his story that he took a cab home after Faris refused to leave?"

Sabina raised an eyebrow, as if to ask, *And how, exactly, do you know that?*

"At least, that's what I figured he might say," Esther added quickly.

Sabina waved it off. "He did. His phone *was* at home. Just not with him. When the cab arrived at The Speckled Stein, Ingram made a big show of getting in and trying to coax Faris into the car too. Faris refused, and Ingram paid his neighbor the fare anyway. He'd slipped his phone under the seat."

"That weasel!" Bunny said.

Sabina nodded. "He'd scoped out the quiet area behind Paws

earlier. Convinced Faris he was going to show him a potential target for their scheme, so they walked over. After the murder, he stole Jim White's boat and paddled home down the lake. Probably slept like a baby, thinking he'd gotten away with the whole thing."

Esther pictured Ingram smugly walking through his front door. "He told me he grew up on the lake. Makes sense he knew how to tie up the boat neatly. What I don't get is why they used Ingram's mom's address for the business."

"They couldn't use their own," Sabina said, shrugging. "Ingram's mom's house was an easy option. Barely checks her mail or leaves the house. Would have been none the wiser."

"I'll say," Bunny muttered, perhaps thinking back to the unsuccessful stakeout.

Esther cringed at the word "wise."

She still had questions. "Why did Ingram stick around Oak's Rest for more inspections after killing Faris? Was he planning on going solo with Kinghead Properties?"

Sabina gave a wry smile. "He wanted to keep tabs on anyone sniffing around. You know, any amateur detectives." She issued them all another look. "Which is when he realized he might have had more loose ends to tie up."

"So, he had some pretty terrible intentions for me tonight," Esther said, feeling lucky to have escaped the basement.

"Me too," Kai said, voice trembling. "Why did he cancel my appointment, then?"

"He was watching the spa from afar," Sabina said. "He saw Onyx Opal go in and got spooked when he realized you wouldn't be alone. You can thank her for that."

Kai exhaled. "Remind me to give her a month of free treatments."

"Your sleuthing worked out this time," Sabina said. "And I thank you. But what you did was incredibly dangerous. I think you got to see that up close and personal tonight, so I'll spare you the lecture for now. Can you please leave it up to us to do our jobs in the future?"

"We can do that," Esther said. She had no intention of having any more face time with murderers. Besides, they'd definitely ruffled a few feathers along the way. "I think we put Uma and Onyx through the wringer trying to get answers."

"Wait!" Kai said. "What happened to Reese Williams, Faris's boss? His bribey side hustle had nothing to do with this?"

"Oh, yeah," Bunny said. "I mean, the guy might not have been a killer, but taking kickbacks can't be legal, can it?"

Sabina rolled her eyes. "How much interrogating—never mind. I don't want to know. Yes, we know about him. He's cooperating, but he's looking at probation and a hefty restitution plan. He won't be working in the public sector again."

"So, it's really all over," Esther said. "We can go back to our normal lives now. Oak's Rest is safe? Kai is safe?" She looked to Sabina.

Sabina gave a tired smile. "Safe and sound. Press release with Ingram's name will go out in the morning."

Esther could have cried with relief, or exhaustion, or both.

Nolan walked into the dining room. "Sorry to interrupt. Some guests are wondering if there are any lemon bars left. Oh, and Esther? A teen boy wanted me to ask the manager if there'd be more crimes next year when his family comes back. He says this place is awesome."

Esther laughed. "Let's hope not. But we *can* manage a few more treats. What do you think, Bun?"

Bunny grinned. "I'll whip up some cinnamon sugar toast sliders. Extra sugar."

"There's my award-winning chef," Esther said.

Nolan left, and Kai followed him out of the dining room.

Sabina rose to go, pausing to pat Esther's back. It was nice to be back on her good side.

Relief settled over Esther like sunlight after a rainstorm. She glanced around the lobby. Guests lingered, chatting in soft tones, filling what had been silence.

Kai nudged Nolan on the head, probably teasing him about his not-so-secret relationship with Queenie.

Sesame loafed on the reception desk, looking content that order was restored.

Esther slipped off the blanket and let it fall to the chair. She had all the warmth she needed.

# CHAPTER 50

"Mom! The cat purred when I petted it!" The little girl raced out of the living room, radiating excitement as she dashed onto the side porch.

"That's great, honey," her mother replied, shielding her eyes from the sun at the bottom of the stairs. "Did you grab Mom's purse like I asked?"

The girl formed an *O* with her mouth. "Be right back!" she said before disappearing into the inn.

The mother made a bemused, *what are you gonna do?* face.

Esther, coffee in one hand, handed her a map of the booth layout with the other. "Just in case you need another one."

The steam from her cup rose in a delightful white swirl in the fall air. It was the perfect day for the Makers and Merchants Festival. She was glad Sesame was soaking up all the attention she could. It was a big day for both of them.

Esther followed the gravel path to the front of the inn, where Sveta sat behind a table, greeting guests who approached from the parking lot and side street.

"Welcome to Calliope Inn Makers and Merchants," Sveta announced. "Please take map. Wipe feet if you must go inside."

She was smiling, but Esther knew her well enough to recognize the timbre of a mild threat. The visitors didn't seem to notice.

"All operations running smoothly?" Esther asked as she reached the table.

Sveta smiled. "Very smooth. One child sneezed into hand. I took care of it. Lots of compliments on sign."

Esther chose not to ask how she'd "taken care" of it. Instead, her attention shifted to the sign Sveta was pointing to. It was a showstopper.

Sugar and LouLou had outdone themselves. The large canvas was stretched between two reclaimed wood posts, and Sugar had hand-painted "Makers and Merchants" in a bold, sweeping script. Around the canvas, illustrations representing Oak's Rest local businesses danced: books, a sewing machine, oars, and more.

Two trees bordered the left and right edges of the canvas, their branches arching toward one another at the top. Where they met, a calliope hummingbird was embroidered with intricate magenta feathers, ready to take flight.

The event sign, against the real-life backdrop of the trees surrounding the inn, leaves falling around them, felt like a storybook come to life. Esther's heart swelled at the thought of hanging the sign inside, a lasting snapshot of the day.

She continued through the backyard, where the festival was in full swing. The peaceful lawn had been transformed into a sea of booths, each showcasing the talents of Oak's Rest's finest.

Residents and tourists weaved through the displays, bursts of laughter punctuating the hum of conversation. Esther heard a round of clapping and followed the sound, spotting Guy Choo gesturing wildly while Sugar sat off to the side, face in her hands. Whatever corny jokes Guy was telling, the crowd was eating them up, though they were clearly mortifying Sugar.

Esther ducked into LouLou's tent, which the seamstress had paid extra for. Shirts and pants hung precariously from the ceiling. A sign propped against the table read, *Sew good, I could do it blindfolded.* Esther had to give her points for showmanship. The business had been in LouLou's family for so many generations, it wasn't inconceivable.

A small crowd had gathered to watch, drawn in by LouLou's antics.

"I think she's gonna do it," someone whispered ahead of Esther.

Behind the table, LouLou was wearing a pink heart-patterned blindfold, her lips pursed as she focused intently on a navy blue corduroy jacket. Her hands moved with precision as she threaded a needle through a buttonhole, cut the thread, and tied it off.

She pulled off her blindfold and held the jacket up triumphantly.

"I'll be darned," Esther said, clapping along with the crowd. "She really can repair anything blindfolded."

"That'll be twenty-five dollars, please," LouLou said, extending her hand toward the man who'd presumably given her his jacket for repair.

For mended clothes and live entertainment? A steal, in Esther's mind.

Esther felt herself smiling as she left the tent. Dev Singh occupied the next display, deep in conversation with a festival-goer, both of them pointing to various pages as they flipped through an old book.

A pack of visitors walked by holding small plates, and the scent of baked goods lingered, carried by the breeze. Others sat, happily munching in the garden, content to enjoy a snack break. A child splashed his sister from the garden fountain, now bubbling with full pressure, sending her running off in a fit of giggles.

A centerpiece took root in the middle of the garden, courtesy of Molly Murphy. A large letter M, no longer bare metal, stood nearly as tall as Esther, anchored deep in the gravel. It was wrapped in moss and dried grapevine, giving it a fairytale-like earthiness. Bunches of golden chrysanthemums, orange zinnias, and bold red dahlias were tucked into its nooks and curves. Vines of bittersweet twisted halfway up the M, dotted with gumdrop-like orange berries.

The squashes that guests had decorated in Sugar Kim's workshop made for a colorful bed around the display. Esther's handmade squash Sesame sat proudly next to an oddly shaped baseball.

The display was breathtaking. Even the squirrels seemed to appreciate it, using the base of the letter as their personal jungle gym.

Beside the garden, Clint and Mort's tent was the ideal spot for the food spread. Visitors loaded up on fancy crostinis, maple shortbread snaps shaped like letter Ms, and fresh fruit kabobs, more dark chocolate than kabob.

What truly seemed to draw people in, though, was a spinning display of soft pretzels dotted with coarse salt. Justice was off to the side, dipping her pretzel in cheese sauce, looking as content as Esther had ever seen her.

Penny was busy at the drinks station, filling people's cups to the top with hot, fragrant coffee or rich apple cider. The smell of cinnamon wafted in every direction.

"Try this," Bunny said, appearing at Esther's side with a creamy brown drink.

"What is it?" Esther asked, eyebrows raised.

"Caramel apple latte."

Esther held up her half-empty coffee cup. "I'm already on my second. If I drink any more caffeine, Penny's gonna suspend me from the diner."

"Just try it," Bunny insisted, swapping the cups with a quick motion.

Esther took a sip. It was delicious. The bitterness of the strong coffee was cut by the sweet apple flavor and cream. "Okay, this is dangerously good. What's in this thing?"

Bunny looked smug, like she'd known Esther would love it. "I started with Marcus and Aggie's cider base, added caramel and a few top-secret spices. Combined with coffee and cream, and boom," she gestured to the cup. "Now that I have your approval, I'll make a big batch back at the tent."

Esther took another sip. "Freestyling the menu on the day of the event. Did you ever see that coming?"

Bunny gave a soft laugh. "Flexibility. The one ingredient I've always been short on." She put her hands in her chef's coat pockets and looked around. "I think this might be the best Makers and Merchants turnout ever. Should we host it here again next year?"

Esther smiled, taking in the scene around her. "I wouldn't write it off completely. I think coordinating it took about three years off my life, but this is pretty great."

"Couldn't have been worse than what Jim is putting those poor kids through right now," Bunny said, pointing a few displays down. Jim White was lecturing a group of kids sitting in the canoe with life vests on, using his pointer finger to emphasize what he was saying.

Esther chuckled. "Safety first." She scanned the crowd. "Speaking of, where's Doctor Bennett? I haven't seen her in a while."

Bunny pointed toward the edge of the inn, where Cameron was seated in an upright massage chair, her posture slack with relaxation as Kai worked on her shoulders. "I think she's fitting in just fine here."

"Oh, good. I wouldn't want her staying alert for any medical emergencies," Esther quipped, taking another drink of the caramel apple latte.

As they shared a moment of silence, Esther felt Bunny's eyes on her. "Yes?" she asked, turning toward her.

Bunny's lips curled into a smile. "You're a lot like her, you know."

"Cameron?" Esther asked. "You think so?"

Bunny tilted her head slightly. "You both show up for the people who matter to you."

"I bribed her with a mountain of food options," Esther said. "But point taken."

"And," Bunny added, "you both know what you want and do exactly that. No more, no less."

Esther looked over at her sister, who, without lifting her head, swatted Clint away as he tapped her shoulder, looking eager for his turn in the chair. Cameron didn't seem ready to give up her moment.

A month ago, Esther thought she'd had her little sister all figured out. She wouldn't have believed they'd be spending time together without obligation, much less have fun doing it. She was glad to be wrong. "You might be right," she said. "Maybe we are alike. Stranger things have happened."

Bunny grinned. "You mean, like becoming a super kick-butt sleuth?"

"I don't know about kick-butt," Esther said, laughing. It did have a nice ring to it, though. Esther Bennett, Kick-Butt Sleuth. She wondered if she could have business cards made up, just as a light-hearted reminder of everything they'd been through.

The sudden high-pitched screech of microphone feedback pulled her from her thoughts.

"Yikes," Bunny said, looking in the direction of the sound.

Next to the food tent, Mayor Early was standing on a makeshift platform of stacked crates. She waited for the crowd's attention before speaking. "Welcome to—" the microphone emitted another screech, making everyone wince.

Clint rushed over from the sidelines. He lowered the stand, adjusted something on the side of the microphone, and gave Mayor Early a nod, signaling the go-ahead.

Bethany cleared her throat and began again. "Welcome to our annual Makers and Merchants Festival, everyone. As mayor of Oak's Rest, I would like to thank you all for coming out today. And a special thank you to the Calliope Inn team, and manager Esther Bennett, for hosting such a wonderful day for us all."

The crowd cheered and clapped. Bunny lightly scratched Esther's back. Esther smiled and mouthed a quiet *thank you* to the few people nearby who'd turned toward her, giving her thumbs-ups and smiles.

Bethany continued. "As some of you may know, Oak's Rest has contended with unprecedented circumstances over the past few weeks. But I'm proud to say that we are stronger than ever. We know the integrity of our residents, and we support each other."

Esther caught sight of Kai across the festival. Even from a distance, Kai already looked more at ease than she had in a long time. Lani wrapped his arm around her shoulder. Kai softly patted her heart when she met Esther's eyes, a silent gesture that made Esther's smile widen.

Mayor Early's speech faded into the background as Esther's attention drifted, her gaze sweeping over the audience. She took in the faces—both familiar and new—the people who made Oak's Rest home. Her people. Her community. Her friends. Neighbors who each added something special to the tapestry of their little town.

There was nowhere she'd rather be.

The sound of applause snapped Esther back to the moment, and she saw Mayor Early's speech was winding down.

Bethany reveled in the spotlight. "And as an additional gesture of gratitude," she said, "please enjoy twenty percent off your General Store checkout total for the next twenty-four hours. One discount per customer. I remember faces. Thank you!"

As the crowd cheered again, she lowered the microphone by her side and turned to walk off the platform, only to hurry back. "One more thing," she said, her voice now quieter and more pointed. "Esther Bennett, please come see me for a private conversation regarding a parking lot matter."

Bunny leaned in, her voice low but teasing. "You never did manage to scare that cardinal away, did you?"

Esther shook her head. "Nope. I've been thinking. Maybe we should name him. Clearly, he's here to stay."

"Any ideas?" Bunny asked, sounding amused.

Esther hesitated, trying not to betray that she'd already picked out the perfect moniker. "Sir Remington Red."

"Noble," Bunny said.

Esther smiled. "So you like it? Think it suits him?"

"Oh, sure," Bunny said. "Now, tell that to Bethany. She's headed straight for you."

Esther ducked low. "Go!" she whispered. "I need to try dipping some of those crostinis in the cheese sauce before it's all gone."

Bunny didn't hesitate. She extended an arm as she escorted Esther through the crowd with the seriousness of a celebrity security detail.

Esther followed behind, popping her head up every few steps to track Bethany as if she were running from a pigeon on the attack.

She didn't want to think about the bird, or the parking lot, or the mayor's rules. Today, she just wanted to savor the moment. And maybe a treat or two.

# AUTHOR'S NOTE

Dear Reader,

If you've made it this far, I hope you loved reading about Esther and her community as much as I loved writing them. Let's meet back in Oak's Rest soon. Until then, give a shout wherever you review books, and let's stay in touch!

*Yours in clues,*
*R*

**Sign up for my newsletter:** RuthieEast.com/contact
Be the first to know about the next installment, get sneak peeks into the writing process, and more.
**Website:** RuthieEast.com
**Instagram:** ruthie_east
**TikTok:** @ruthie_east

# ABOUT THE AUTHOR

Ruthie East was born and raised in Pennsylvania, where the high-rises and cobblestone streets of the City of Brotherly Love were a stone's throw away, but cows and pastures were never out of the question.

After starting a career in healthcare, she turned to writing as a place to explore seemingly ordinary characters who discover the extraordinary within.

When she's not writing, she's probably staring woefully at all the unread books on her TBR, or scheming up ways to trick her cat into drinking more water. You can find her at RuthieEast.com.